D0065462

Praise for
# FALSE FLAG

"Spy fiction has a new superstar, F. W. Rustmann Jr., a retired twenty-four-year veteran of the CIA's Clandestine Service who it turns out has a terrific talent for fiction. I loved *False Flag* and you will too. One wishes Rustmann were running the CIA in his spare time, when he isn't writing!"
   **—Stephen Coonts,** bestselling author

"With *False Flag*, Fred Rustmann presents another case for convincing James Bond wannabes to keep their day jobs. CIA work isn't all high-balls and exotic climes. It's dangerous, dirty, tedious, and requires nerves of tungsten. Rustmann learned it the hard way—twenty-four years in the field—so that readers can experience it in a comfortable chair. Rustmann exposes the Agency's underbelly and its ripped six-pack. *False Flag* is a damn good yarn—or is it from his personal history? We'll never know."
   **—Phillip Jennings,** author of *Nam-A-Rama* and *Goodbye Mexico*
   (with a bit of combat time and Agency experience of his own)

"Warning! You'll lose sleep with this one. Former CIA clandestine ops officer Rustmann states up front the book is fiction, but the plot and fast-paced action brims with the latest tradecraft and knowledge of real-world intelligence operations, which makes for late-night page-turning to see how it all turns out, and wondering, 'Did this really pass CIA censors?'"
   **—Gene Poteat,** President Emeritus, Association of Former
   Intelligence Officers

# FALSE FLAG

# FALSE FLAG

## F.W. RUSTMANN JR.

REGNERY FICTION

The CIA's Publications Review Board has reviewed the manuscript for this book to assist the author in eliminating classified information, and poses no security objection to its publication. This review, however, should not be construed as an official release of information, confirmation of its accuracy, or an endorsement of the author's views.

Regnery Fiction™ is a trademark of Salem Communications Holding Corporation; Regnery® is a registered trademark of Salem Communications Holding Corporation

Cataloging-in-Publication Data on file with the Library of Congress

ISBN 978-1-62157-738-6
e-book ISBN 978-1-62157-752-2

Published in the United States by
Regnery Fiction
An imprint of Regnery Publishing
A Division of Salem Media Group
300 New Jersey Ave NW
Washington, DC 20001
www.RegneryFiction.com

Manufactured in the United States of America

10 9 8 7 6 5 4 3 2 1

Books are available in quantity for promotional or premium use. For information on discounts and terms, please visit our website: www.Regnery.com.

## Also by F. W. Rustmann Jr.

*The Case Officer*
*Plausible Denial*

*For Carolyn*
*With Gratitude*

*"Used to be...dignity and courage
were the measure of a man..."*

—From the song *Used to Be* by Charlene and Stevie Wonder

# PROLOGUE

I t happened every time she returned to Beirut; that sense of trepidation, fear, excitement, risk. The part of her job she loved and feared the most. Like a receiver standing alone in the end zone during the opening kickoff of a football game.

The ferry from Limassol slowed and settled down into the water as it neared its berth. The sun sank low on the horizon, falling below the distant mountains of Lebanon and casting a red glow over the waters of the Mediterranean. Red at night; sailors' delight. If the old adage were correct, it would be a beautiful day tomorrow.

She was among the first to disembark, hurrying through the cursory customs check, pulling her luggage straight toward the taxi queue outside the terminal. The ride along the corniche to her *pied-à-terre* apartment took a little over thirty minutes. She felt safer when she entered her apartment and latched the door behind her.

Tomorrow would be a big day.

She awakened early the next morning and dressed casually in faded, torn jeans, a long-sleeved blouse, and tennis shoes. She brewed a pot of coffee and ate a cup of yogurt from her nearly empty fridge as she began preparing herself mentally for the operational task that would follow.

The brush pass was scheduled for exactly 11:43 a.m. on the third-floor, center aisle of the Galleries Lafayette department store on Hamra Street. Prior to the meeting, she would need at least three hours to run her surveillance detection route—a morning of shopping designed to lull any possible surveillance team to sleep. Her contact, a female case officer assigned under official cover to the United States Embassy, would be doing the same thing. Each would be carrying an identical white envelope containing a passport and other identity papers—pocket litter. The photos and descriptions on both sets of documents were of the same woman.

■ ■ ■

At exactly 11:42 a.m., she turned the corner into the center aisle and examined a selection of pots and pans. Out of the corner of her eye, she spotted her contact entering the aisle from the other end. She began walking slowly up the aisle, examining the housewares on her way. Her contact did the same. When she was abreast of the other woman, they switched envelopes and continued on their way toward opposite ends of the corridor.

She could breathe easier now.

She continued to shop leisurely along Hamra Street until a little past one o'clock in the afternoon. Confident she was not under surveillance and that the brush pass had gone unnoticed, she realized how hungry she was. She stepped into a café and ordered a quiche and an iced tea for lunch.

While devouring her lunch she removed the envelope's contents—a Jordanian passport, driver's license, two credit cards, and various club membership cards—and placed them carefully into a red leather billfold. The billfold then went back into her purse.

She paid the bill and continued her stroll toward her apartment. She was done for the day. Mission accomplished.

Two blocks from the corniche, she stopped at a busy intersection. While she was waiting by the curb for the light to change, a dark van turned in front of her. The van's door slid open and two men jumped out, startling pedestrians waiting to cross the street. The men surrounded the woman, grabbed her from both sides and pushed her into the van.

The van sped off leaving the pedestrians gawking.

# CHAPTER 1

The drive from Belmopan to the central prison of Belize in Hattieville, affectionately known as the "Hattieville Ramada," took almost two hours, mostly on narrow, dusty jungle roads. The seventeen prisoners, each one handcuffed to his seat, bounced along in an old, gray school bus with dead shocks and springs.

Culler Santos was in a foul mood. The prisoner sitting across the aisle from him, a heavily tattooed young man of mixed race named Aduan, would not stop glaring at him. Santos had heard about Aduan in the Belmopan jail. He had a reputation for being a psychopath, the worst of the worst.

Although he was only a few months past his nineteenth birthday, Aduan had admitted to killing six people, including one of his uncles. The latter murder, the killing of a close relative, had elevated him in the ranks of the Crips. Each of the murders, with the exception of the last one, which landed him in prison, was recorded on his chest in a row of tattooed, half-inch circles.

The Crips and their archrival gang, the Bloods, were strong in Belize, having immigrated there from Los Angeles in the mid-eighties. And nowhere were they stronger, or more heavily represented, than in the Belizean prison system.

Santos decided it was best to ignore the kid, so he concentrated on looking out the window at the passing jungle scenery. But each time he looked over, he caught the kid staring at him.

He didn't need this. On top of everything else, he was still wearing the jeans, tennis shoes, and sweat-stained, white polo shirt he had been wearing when he was taken into custody. He had not had a proper shower or shaved in the four days since his arrest. He knew he reeked because the stench of the other prisoners reminded him of a horse barn.

The kid was dressed in rags like most of the other prisoners. He wore stained, khaki cutoffs, a pair of worn out flip-flops and an Army camouflage tee shirt. The sleeves of the tee shirt were cut off to better display his powerful, tattoo-covered arms. He sported a head full of long, filthy dreadlocks, a stringy Fu Manchu mustache, and a braided goatee.

They reached Hattieville at the two-mile marker of Burrell Boom Road. A guard walked down the aisle unlocking handcuffs. The prisoners were led out the door in single file, through the main gate of the prison and into the prison yard. It was surrounded by stained, two-story, white-cement-block buildings, which housed the cells. A chain-link fence topped with hoops of concertina razor wire surrounded the entire 225-acre plot of land. Guards armed with AK-47 automatic weapons patrolled along the roofs of the buildings and stood in towers in each corner. The entire facility stank like a barnyard.

After a short "welcome" speech from the warden, who laid out the usual warnings about the consequences of escape attempts, the group was split into smaller groups and led to their cells in the "Remand Section" of the prison. There they waited for trial. Some of them had been there for more than five years. The judicial system in Belize was in no hurry.

Santos was led to a cell on the ground floor along with four other prisoners from the bus, but not before each one surrendered his belt. All other pocket litter had been confiscated at the Belmopan jail. He assumed the belts would be added to those other belongings. After the surrender, some of the men had to walk with one hand holding up their drooping pants. Santos reflected on the "low pants" tradition that was common among young blacks in American ghettos. This is where it all began—in prisons. Why those kids wanted to emulate prison inmates was totally beyond him.

One of the prisoners in his group was Aduan. Santos cussed his luck and immediately began to think about how he would neutralize this obvious threat. Aduan was hugged and high-fived by several other inmates when he entered the cell. This macho display added to Santos's dismay.

The filthy, twenty-by-twenty-foot cell was already filled with more than a dozen inmates. Santos counted the double bunks that lined two of the walls—there were four. That meant eight beds for about sixteen smelly men. *This is going to be cozy*, Santos thought.

All of the bunks were occupied, so he looked for a place on the concrete floor where he could stake out a space. Grabbing one of the bunks was out of the question. It would have meant an immediate confrontation, and he was not ready for that. Not yet.

In one corner of the room, he noticed a plastic milk carton cut in half and realized it was being used as a toilet. *Better stay as far away from that as possible*, he thought. He found a spot near the corner on the other side of the room, plopped himself down between two other inmates and put his head on his knees.

*Hurry up, Mac. Get me out of here. Please hurry…*

The crowded cell was a cacophony of smells and noises. A few of the prisoners, like Santos, sat quietly with their eyes closed and arms folded around their knees, trying to block out their surroundings, submerging themselves in their thoughts.

It did not take Aduan long to saunter over to Santos's side of the cell and stop in front of him. He stood there, swaying back and forth, glaring down at the American. The cell suddenly became quiet. Three other heavily tattooed prisoners, all with long dreadlocks, moved across the room and converged alongside of Aduan.

Santos sensed the arrival of Aduan and his fellow Crips and watched them from the corners of his eyes. He sat there quietly for a few moments and then looked up and locked onto Aduan's threatening stare. He knew now that confrontation was unavoidable, but he was not afraid.

His thoughts centered on how best to neutralize the four thugs. With one attacker, it would be simple: take him to the ground and dislocate his arm with an arm bar. That was the quickest and easiest way to neutralize an opponent. But in this case, there were too many of them. He needed to remain on his feet while sending them all to the ground. Tactics spun through his mind. He knew he could beat them. It was just a matter of how.

His head rose slowly and he quietly asked, "Do you want my spot?" Aduan threw his head back and laughed heartily. He looked around at his friends and then began to reply.

As soon as Aduan's mouth opened, Santos unleashed a sweeping kick with his right leg that knocked Aduan's legs out from under him and dropped him hard on his tailbone. There was an audible thud as he hit the concrete floor, forcing the air from his lungs in a gasp.

Santos spun to his feet in one motion and caught the tall Crip to Aduan's left with a roundhouse, backhand punch to the side of the head, dropping the thug like a stone.

He turned to his right and confronted the wide-eyed, fat Crip who was swinging a lame roundhouse at his head. Santos blocked the punch with his left forearm, stepped in close, looped his right arm under his attacker's right arm and, with two hands grasping the wrist, snapped the arm down. An audible pop and a scream told him the elbow was dislocated. He followed up with a sharp right elbow to the temple and the Crip went down in a heap, unconscious and with his arm jutting out at an awkward angle.

Aduan jumped to his feet and attacked. Santos stepped back with his left leg to dodge a right hook, crossed his right leg over his left and launched it screaming toward Aduan's head. Santos's foot connected at the ear with a sickening thud. Aduan careened across the room, into the wall and down in a heap.

In a blur Santos spun around and delivered a side kick directly to the knee of the forth thug. The force of the kick snapped the Crip's knee backwards, dislocating it and sending the thug to the ground screaming in pain. He was no longer a threat.

Santos dodged a kick to the head from the only standing Crip and delivered two sharp blows to the solar plexus, knocking the wind from the thug's lungs and sending him to his knees. He went down into a fetal position.

Santos stood, panting. He surveyed the carnage. Two of the Crips were permanently out of commission with dislocated limbs. Aduan was unconscious and the other Crip was moaning and gasping for breath in a heap.

He stepped over to Aduan who was lying face down on the floor. He stood over him, brought his leg up high and stomped down on Aduan's right shoulder with the heel of his shoe. He heard the shoulder crunch, rendering the arm useless.

He turned to the remaining Crip, moaning and lying on his side. He brought his leg up again and brought it down hard on the femur, snapping the bone and eliciting a scream from the thug.

Satisfied, Santos surveyed the carnage he had inflicted. Now all four of the Crips would be taken to the hospital with broken or dislocated limbs, which was Santos's plan in the first place. They would be removed from the cell and no longer a threat.

Santos walked to the center of the cell, looked around at the inmates surrounding him and addressed the motionless, gawking group. "I had nothing to do with this, get it? These guys got into a fight and beat the crap out of each other. Understand? That's your story when the guards get here." He glared around the room, locking eyes with each one of them in turn.

The shocked inmates nodded in agreement, some muttering in approval and awe of what had just occurred. Santos then walked over to the nearest lower bunk, pushed aside two inmates standing in front of it, and plopped himself down.

Lying on the bunk with his legs crossed and his hands behind his head, he said, "And this is where I will spend the rest of my time here, right on this bunk. Does anyone have any objections to that?"

There were none.

# CHAPTER 2

S ometimes things don't go exactly as planned. Other times nothing goes as planned. This was one of those times.

MacMurphy was known as a meticulous planner of operations. It was one of his strengths and was well documented during his almost fifteen years with the CIA. He had the uncanny ability to see all possible outcomes for his operational moves and adapt accordingly to ensure operational success.

In this case, Murphy's Law was written all over the operation.

His colleague, Culler Santos, had been arrested and was being held in a steamy prison in the jungle on the outskirts of Belmopan, Belize. At first glance, though, the operation had been promising.

The child's Belizean mother, a tall, thin, pale woman with stringy, waist-length brown hair named Elmira Minita, had abducted the six-year-old girl and taken the child to live with her parents in Belize. She had secured a job as an administrative assistant for the Belizean Tourism Authority.

The father, an American citizen living in St. Augustine, Florida, had legal custody of the child. The girl was a United States citizen by birth and the mother, a cocaine addict and convicted felon, was deemed unfit by the United States courts. The father had exhausted all legal efforts to get the child returned to him. Belize, despite being a signatory of the Hague Convention—which was established to ensure that the best interests of the child were paramount in international abduction cases—refused to order Elmira to return the child to her American father.

So he turned to Global Strategic Reporting, a business intelligence and investigation firm located just down the Florida coast in Fort Lauderdale. The firm had a reputation for "getting things done" in all manner of unusual cases. The father wanted GSR to help him re-abduct the child and return her safely to the United States. And, at first, the operation went smoothly.

Santos set up his cover as a point man for a large United States developer exploring tourism opportunities in Belize. That justified his request to meet with the head of the Belizean tourism director in the government office building where the mother worked. Santos bluffed his way into the American embassy to discuss his Belizean development plans with the embassy's economic officer. The economic officer was helpful and offered to call the Belizean tourism director to set up a meeting for Santos.

The following day Santos drove his rental car to his meeting with the director. Santos was ushered into the director's office by his assistant, Elmira, who occupied a desk outside of the director's office. When his meeting was over, Santos stopped at Elmira's desk, exchanged some pleasantries, and engaged the woman in conversation, asking what she liked to do for entertainment in Belmopan, what the best restaurants were and what hotel she would recommend. His questions about her marital status and whether she had children were deftly evaded.

Elmira was polite but did not pick up on any of his veiled efforts to get her to show him around town. Finally, Santos just came out and asked her to have dinner with him. She politely refused, saying that she was seeing someone who worked in the building and that he would not take too kindly to her having dinner with another man.

Disappointed and wishing he possessed the good looks and easy charm of his partner, MacMurphy, Santos returned to his hotel to mull things over and eat dinner alone. His goal had been to learn more about Elmira Minita—where she lived, what her personal circumstances were, how the child was doing and what the kid's daily routine was—but he had failed miserably.

MacMurphy shouldn't have chosen him for this task. He wasn't the cool, suave type who could easily pick up women. Just the opposite actually. He was direct and forceful and sometimes women were put off by his looks. Santos was built like a tree trunk, with a face scarred by many battles.

He needed to gather enough information about the mother's lifestyle to figure out how the child and father could meet with enough privacy and time for the exfiltration team to spirit them out of the country and back to the United States. The exfiltration route had been outlined, but the plan lacked very important details about how they would get the child away from the mother and safely into the arms of the father and the exfiltration team.

Santos concluded that if he couldn't gather the information he needed the easy way, through direct contact with the mother, he would have to get it the hard way, through surveillance.

That's where things started to unravel.

The one thing that Santos was not aware of—and that Elmira had not revealed during their conversation—was that the mother's current paramour, the one who occupied the other corner office just down the hall, was the country's solicitor general.

He also was unaware that as soon as he left Elmira's office, she walked down the hall to the office of Shankar Gandhi, the solicitor general of Belize, and told him all about the rugged American with the Kennedyesque-Bostonian accent who had tried to pick her up and had asked too many questions about her and her daughter.

She was aware that her husband wanted the child back in America and thought there was a connection.

As she was relating the story to Gandhi, they walked over to the office windows overlooking the parking lot and watched Santos walk across the lot, get into his black Chevy rental car and drive away.

Gandhi was one of the many Indian functionaries who remained behind when, in 1981, British Honduras obtained its independence from the United Kingdom and was renamed Belize. Now in his sixties, the bespectacled little man had reached the pinnacle of his career and felt all-powerful. Moreover, he carried a strong grudge against those colonial powers that had once lorded over him.

He had also fallen in love with the tall, willowy, fair-skinned drug addict and had vowed to protect her and her child. So, when Culler Santos showed up late the following afternoon in his black rental car and took up a surveillance position in a shaded corner of the parking lot, Gandhi called the police.

Elmira and Gandhi watched from his office window as the police arrived, checked Santos's identification papers, cuffed him and took him away in a patrol car. On Gandhi's instructions, the police charged Santos with conspiracy to commit kidnapping—specifically, Elmira Minita's six-year-old daughter.

# CHAPTER 3

The gang at GSR had not heard from Santos for three days and was becoming increasingly concerned. Calls to his cell phone and hotel room went unanswered. The staff at the small El Rey Hotel where he was staying said they had not seen him since the day after he had checked in.

This was not like Santos. He usually called MacMurphy every evening to discuss progress.

When a call finally came, it was collect from the jail in downtown Belmopan. "It looks like we've been blindsided, Mac. Our client never told us he brought his sailboat down here a couple of months ago and tried to grab the kid. He was caught in the act and thrown in the slammer. They let him go after paying a big fine and kicked him out of the country. They've been on high alert ever since then. Mom's boyfriend, who just happens to be the solicitor general of this godforsaken country, handled everything for her."

"Good god! Now what? What are they planning for you? What are the charges?"

"Conspiracy to commit kidnapping. It carries a fifteen-year sentence and a $250,000 fine. I'm being transferred tomorrow to the central prison in Hattieville. It's a nasty place from what I hear. I'm in deep kimchi, Mac."

"We'll get you out of there. I'll get you a good lawyer. Do they have any evidence to back up this conspiracy charge?"

"No, but from what I understand they don't need any. Their law is based on old English law. They can lock me up while they conduct an investigation to gather the evidence they need. Not like the good ole U.S. of A. at all."

MacMurphy grimaced. "Okay, okay, we'll get working on it. Call me again tomorrow evening, same time. Hang in there. If we can't bail you out, we'll bust you out…"

■ ■ ■

Maggie Moore was the "mother hen" of the GSR and was used to handling senior case officers during her thirty-plus years at the agency. She had quickly risen through its ranks, starting as a GS-5 secretary to the senior intelligence service and retiring with flag rank. She was now the de facto manager of GSR, although MacMurphy retained full ownership of the company.

She sat at the foot of the conference table in the GSR conference room while MacMurphy finished his call with Santos. "How could this happen, Mac?" she asked, glaring at him over her rimless granny glasses.

MacMurphy ran fingers through his prematurely gray hair and shook his head. "We weren't given the full story. That's what happened. They were waiting for us. Now we just have to deal with the hand we've been dealt and get on with it."

He was in no mood for recriminations. He wanted to get his friend back as soon as possible. Then he would think about what went wrong and who would pay for it.

Maggie pulled a yellow pencil out of her graying, red, washwoman bun and began ticking off a list of lawyers she had found in Belize. She briefly described them to MacMurphy before recommending a firm headed by a recently retired Supreme Court justice named Dean Lindo. It was likely he would have the best chance of influencing the court in Santos's favor.

"Okay, call him back, engage his firm and wire him a retainer. Send him whatever he wants. Just get him on it immediately. I don't want Culler sitting in that hellhole for any longer than necessary. And I'm sure that Gandhi bastard is going to play hardball with us."

# CHAPTER 4

The next few days were hard on Maggie and MacMurphy and the rest of the GSR team. They worked tirelessly contacting congressmen and other influential government officials to pressure the United States ambassador to make a démarche to the Belizean government to release Santos. Unfortunately, the United States Embassy refused to take any action on Santos's behalf. The petty ambassador was angry that Santos had manipulated the embassy with a phony "tourist development" cover story.

More bad news came when Dean Lindo reported that Gandhi was indeed digging his heals in and refused to budge regarding Santos's release. He was dragging out the court process to punish Santos as much as possible.

Finally, a full month after Santos's arrest, Gandhi could delay the bail hearing no longer. That was the good news. The bad news was that he had set the usual $5,000 bail at $50,000. During the bail hearing, Dean Lindo argued forcefully that the lack of evidence did not justify the treatment Santos was receiving by the court. But Gandhi stood firm, stating that there was plenty of evidence for the conspiracy out there and that he simply needed more time to gather it for the trial.

This is how things work in third-world countries like Belize; a person can be held indefinitely while evidence is gathered for conviction. So much for due process.

Thus, bail was set at $50,000, which was paid immediately by Lindo per MacMurphy's instructions. Santos was forbidden to leave the country pending trial and his passport was confiscated.

Santos returned to the El Rey Hotel where he showered, put on clean clothes, ate an enormous steak dinner, got totally smashed, and passed out on a real bed for the first time in over a month.

The next morning he collected his car from the police impound lot, purchased a new pre-paid cell phone and called MacMurphy to plan his exfiltration. There was no way he was going to hang around Belize for a rigged trial that would almost certainly convict him.

MacMurphy and Santos agreed on a simple plan to get Santos safely out of Belize and set a date for the exfiltration one week later. That would allow Santos time to give any hostile surveillance the feeling that he was settling in to await trial.

He prepaid his hotel for another month, took several trips to Belize City to visit his attorneys, drove around the country sightseeing and generally played his role to a T. It wasn't difficult. The court had his passport and he couldn't leave the country without that travel document.

Exactly seven days after his phone conversation with MacMurphy, Santos put the "Do Not Disturb" sign on his door and left the hotel unnoticed in the early morning hours. He carried all his belongings in a small suitcase and a backpack.

Santos drove west on the two-lane George Price Highway toward the Guatemala border and pulled off to the side of the road at a secluded spot about ten miles out of Belmopan. There he cached his suitcase and backpack in the underbrush, took one more look around to memorize the spot and then headed back to his car. It would not look good if someone spotted him getting into MacMurphy's car with bags in his hands. Not after receiving a court order forbidding him to leave town.

After driving back to Belmopan, he parked his car in a lot near the center of town and paid for a full day. Stomach rumbling and in need of caffeine, he walked to a nearby café where he indulged in a large breakfast of ham, eggs, pancakes, and several cups of strong, black coffee. He spent about an hour and a half there, sitting on the restaurant porch, eating while leisurely reading a newspaper.

He had noticed no surveillance since leaving his hotel in the morning and felt confident he was clean. But just to make sure, he left the restaurant and took a long, slow stroll through the center of town, visiting shops along the way and checking for surveillance at various spots along the route. After conducting this final surveillance detection route, he was certain he was alone.

He timed his arrival at the town square at exactly 10:15 a.m. The air was heavy with humidity and the sun bore down like a space heater. He was already sweating through his shirt when a white Ford Mustang with Guatemala tags approached. A grinning MacMurphy leaned his gray head out of the window and called, "Need a lift?"

■ ■ ■

The white Mustang circled the town square's center fountain and headed west toward the George Price Highway and the Guatemalan border. They stopped long enough to retrieve Santos's bags at the roadside cache and continued toward the border. Santos was happy to see Belize disappear in his rearview mirror.

Four hours later, they reached the sleepy border town of Melchor de Mencos. On the southern edge of the town was a two-lane bridge over the Mopan River that divided Guatemala and Belize. The Guatemalan customs and immigration office—little more than a one-man border-crossing checkpoint—was located on the Guatemalan side of the river.

MacMurphy pulled the Mustang off the road onto the gravel on the Belize side of the bridge. The two men got out of the car and walked the short distance to the riverbank. They surveyed the area and Santos, looking down at the river in disbelief, said, "Holy crap, Mac. You don't expect me to swim across that, do you?"

The river was about one hundred meters wide, not a bad swim, but the muddy water was gushing under the bridge in a torrent. "Maybe it's better a little further upstream," said MacMurphy. "You can handle it."

"I sink like a rock in the water. You know that."

Although it was clear MacMurphy was worried, he said, "It's those big bones of yours. Don't worry. We'll find a spot upstream where the current will help carry you across. And we'll buy you one of those little kiddy tubes you can hang on to during your crossing. How's that?"

Santos rolled his eyes. "Sheesh…"

They drove about a half-mile upstream until they reached a small dirt road that ran into the riverbank. They parked at the end of the road, which was nothing more than a trail at that point, and once again surveyed the river. It was wider and the current was not quite as swift, but it would still be a risky swim.

MacMurphy turned to Santos. "Whaddaya think?"

Serious now, Santos walked down the bank until he reached the water's edge and surveyed the rushing water. "If I enter here and swim hard with the current, I should hit the other side about there. Just before the river bends to the left." He indicated a grassy spot on the bank about two hundred meters downstream. "How deep do you think the damn thing is?"

"Probably pretty deep in the middle judging from the current. At least there aren't any rapids. I'd hate to see you careening downstream, bouncing from rock to rock."

"Sure you would. Okay, that's the plan. You drop me off here and pick me up over there on the other side after you go through the checkpoint. Let's go get some dinner and wait till it gets dark."

■ ■ ■

They found a small, family-run Italian restaurant near the center of town overlooking the Mopan River and settled into a booth with a river view. Santos couldn't take his eyes off the swiftly flowing current. The engineer with two advanced degrees from MIT was calculating speed and distance. The river was wider and deeper here, so it was a bit slower than where the river narrowed near the bridge downstream.

MacMurphy asked, "Do you want to look for another crossing place further upstream?"

"No, I think we're okay. You're going to have to trek back through the jungle on the other side to reach the pickup spot. That's not going to be fun or easy. Let's keep it as close to the bridge as we can or we'll be out here all night long."

"Hmmmm. What's with all of the sudden concern? Now you're making me feel bad about making you swim across this bitch."

Santos laughed. "Just be there when I get there."

"Aren't I always there for you when you get yourself in a jam?"

"What do you mean? You owe me big time, bud. Just think back to that time I saved your sorry ass in that hotel in Chiang Rai."

Now it was time for MacMurphy to laugh. "Okay, okay, you win…"

Santos ate very little and drank no alcohol while MacMurphy feasted on pasta, salad, and a half-bottle of Chianti. MacMurphy looked up from his plate. "You're going to waste away to nothing. You must have lost thirty pounds in that slammer, and now you're refusing to eat."

"Twenty-eight pounds actually. I'm down to 180. Lean and mean. I don't want a belly load of pasta and wine dragging me to the bottom of that bloody river. I'll take a doggie bag and eat when we're safely on the other side and cruising down the highway toward Guatemala City."

# CHAPTER 5

It was a little after nine in the evening when they reached the crossing point. The weather was hot and muggy. The sky was alight with stars, but only a quarter-moon illuminated the muddy river. They stood on the riverbank for a few moments reviewing their plan. Finally, MacMurphy said, "Okay, give me your clothes and shoes and I'll get moving."

"What do you mean give you my clothes and shoes?"

"Well you're sure as hell not going to swim across this river in them, are you?"

Santos looked down at the river and across at the landing spot on the other side and then back to MacMurphy. Nodding his head he said, "Always think of everything, don't you?"

"That's my job."

Santos rolled his eyes but stripped down to his boxer shorts and handed the bundle to MacMurphy. Starlight danced on the muddy river but the other bank was a dark blur.

"Okay, Mac, let's do it."

MacMurphy glanced down at his watch. "Right. Give me an hour to get into position. I'll signal with three short blinks from my flashlight. I'll start blinking at exactly ten fifteen, so just guide on my light."

"You got it. See you in an hour."

They shook hands and MacMurphy made his way up the bank and back to his car. Santos sat on a flat rock at the river's edge and calculated his swim.

MacMurphy drove to the bridge and crossed through the checkpoint. The guard on duty barely glanced at his passport before raising the barrier and waving him through.

It was very dark. This side of the crossing was mostly uninhabited, although he could see the hazy lights of the town a couple of miles to the north. The thick underbrush ran up to the side of the road. MacMurphy began to worry that he might not find a place to park the car and enter the jungle. He drove slowly along the dark road looking for a suitable spot.

Finally, about a quarter-mile down the road he found a good spot and pulled over. It was 9:40 p.m. He had thirty-five minutes to get to the rendezvous point, which he estimated was a quarter-mile away. He pushed through the thick underbrush as quickly as possible but was worried he wouldn't make it in time.

He was almost there when he heard voices. He stopped, turned off his flashlight and listened, targeting all of his senses on the noises. He concluded the sounds were men's voices and laughter and estimated the men were fifty meters in front of him—near or at the rendezvous spot.

He quickened his pace without his flashlight, stumbled, and fell noisily. He listened intently again as the voices grew louder. The blood pounded in his ears. This was bad, very bad. Who were these people? What the hell were they doing at the river's edge at this hour?

Then he saw lights dancing up ahead. The men had flashlights. He moved closer until he could make out three men in the grassy opening they had chosen as their rendezvous. They were aiming their lights out over the water. What in God's name were they doing? His mind raced. Could they be police? Fishermen?

The only thing he knew for certain was that he had to divert Santos from swimming toward that spot. He retraced his steps for about another fifty meters and headed down to the river's edge. It wasn't an ideal spot because there were rocks and trees in the water near the bank, but it would have to do.

He got down on his belly and scanned the top of the water to spot Santos. Too dark. He began blinking his flashlight across the river. Dot-dot-dot. Dot-dot-dot. Over and over again.

Santos sat on the rock watching the river current whip by, ticking off the minutes until he would enter the water. About thirty minutes into his wait, he noticed lights moving through the darkness on the other side of the river.

Could this be MacMurphy? There appeared to be more than one light. Strange. The lights moved through the underbrush to the river's edge and stayed there, flickering and dancing on the water at the exact spot they had chosen for their rendezvous.

He checked his watch. Ten past ten. Five minutes before he was supposed to start swimming. What the bloody hell was going on?

He waited an extra five minutes and then spotted three short blips from MacMurphy's flashlight. The blips continued from an area further downstream from their original rendezvous point. That would give him more time to get across the river, but there was no beach there at all. Santos concluded that MacMurphy had to move away from the interlopers, whomever they were.

He stepped off the bank into the warm, muddy water of the Mopan River and was almost immediately knocked off his feet by the swift current. He could feel it grab him as he swam as hard as he could for the other side. By the time he reached the middle of the river, he was fatigued. The current had whisked him downstream faster than he had expected. At this rate, he would pass MacMurphy before reaching the other side. He switched to a breaststroke and continued to pull toward the blink, blink, blink of MacMurphy's flashlight.

He was now directly in front of their original rendezvous spot, and he could make out the three men scanning the water with their flashlights. Suddenly a shot rang out and he dove beneath the surface, still pulling for the shore. He rolled over on his side and slowly poked his head out of the water to stifle any splashing.

Were they shooting at him? He could see the men on the shore looking in his direction and scanning the water with their flashlights. He continued to swim cautiously downstream in a sidestroke, trying his best not to splash or to raise his head too far out of the water.

His adrenaline pounded and he forgot about being tired. He was making steady but slow progress toward the shore when he realized he was going to overshoot MacMurphy's location. Santos was about ten meters from the shore when he slipped past MacMurphy. He could see MacMurphy and his flashlight on the bank but was too afraid to call out or signal. Hopefully, MacMurphy would see him. If not, he would find him later. His main concern now was reaching the shore.

He was almost there when he spotted a partially submerged log in the water directly in front of him. Unable to stop, he crashed into it with a thud and held on for dear life. The current pressed him against the log, trying to push him under it, scraping skin from his ribs, and forcing the breath out of him. He clawed his way along the length of the log, to the shore and onto the riverbank. There he lay, exhausted and breathing heavily.

The next thing he saw was MacMurphy standing over him. "You made it!"

Culler Santos moaned, "If it hadn't been for that fucking log, I'd be in Guatemala City by now."

Santos dried himself off with his shirt and blotted the blood as best he could. As he painfully got dressed, he guessed he had bruised a couple of ribs but didn't think anything was broken. They walked quietly back to the car, being careful not to alert the three men upstream.

Santos whispered, "Who the hell were those guys?"

MacMurphy shook his head. "Well, I didn't see any fishing poles. And they didn't look like cops. I think they were hunters."

"Hunters?" Santos blurted, "What the hell would they be hunting out here on the riverbank at night?"

"Crocodiles, probably."

"There are crocodiles in these waters?"

"That's what I've heard."

"Why didn't you tell me?"

"Didn't want to scare you."

Santos grabbed MacMurphy's arm and looked him directly in the eyes. "Then they *did* take a shot at me. They thought I was a fucking crocodile."

"Yep, that's probably it." MacMurphy smiled and patted Santos on the side of the face. "I'm glad you're okay. I was real worried for a bit there."

"Holy shit…"

They walked the rest of the way back to the car in a silent single file. The two men arrived in Guatemala City in the early morning hours and stopped for breakfast at an all-night café on the outskirts of the city. Feeling well fed yet tired, they followed the signs to the La Aurora International Airport and checked into the nearby Hilton Garden Inn.

Santos crashed in his room while MacMurphy called the United States Embassy to make an appointment with the consular section to pick up a replacement passport for Santos's "lost" one. He also reserved two seats for them on a flight returning to Miami later that evening.

Getting a replacement passport for Santos was easy, but the fact that there was no record of his arrival in Guatemala was problematic. When they passed through customs at the airport later that afternoon, MacMurphy quickly surveyed the four customs booths and selected the one manned by a not-too-unattractive young woman. He presented his passport to her and flashed a flirtatious smile. They exchanged pleasantries while she chopped and returned his passport. He thanked her with a broad smile and hovered at the end of the booth while Santos presented his passport to her.

Santos admitted that he had lost his original passport and that the United States Embassy had provided a new one earlier that day. That explained why there was no entry chop in the passport, but it didn't explain why there was no record of his entry in her system. When she questioned him about this, he shrugged and said he had entered the country at the exact same time as his friend MacMurphy.

MacMurphy joined Santos at the window, flashed a wide grin filled with perfect white teeth, and confirmed Santos's story. That was enough to convince her that there had just been an error or a delay in the database's most recent update. After all, the new passport was clearly authentic. How could it have been issued without the embassy verifying some prior record of an entry chop? She chopped it, sending both men on their way with a big smile.

# CHAPTER 6

ack at the Fort Lauderdale offices of Global Strategic Reporting, Maggie Moore was briefing Santos, MacMurphy, and other staff members on the events of the past week. The meeting attendees included GSR's secretary and receptionist, Christy Wright; the editor of the firm's weekly *CounterThreat* publication, Wilber Millstone; and the company's head researcher and Millstone's assistant, Jake Bartlett. The group sat around an expensive marble and walnut table in an eighth-floor conference room, which overlooked the Intracoastal Waterway and the Atlantic Ocean beyond.

Maggie looked especially disheveled today, having lost sleep last week worrying about "her boys" down in Belize. Her graying, auburn hair framed her face in dangling wisps. Bloodshot, pale blue eyes peered over her ever-present, rimless granny glasses. She looked older today than her sixty-one years.

Maggie Moore was a fiercely loyal former CIA officer. At the time of her retirement, she was the highest-ranking female officer in the Clandestine Service. Early in her career, she married a fellow CIA officer who, shortly after their wedding, was killed in a helicopter crash in Laos. Her grief contributed to a miscarriage, which heightened her depression. She compensated for her loss by throwing herself into her work.

Early in her career, she also caught the eye of Edwin Rothmann, who was then a rising star in the CIA. Rothmann mentored her and brought her along in the slipstream of his own career into the senior ranks. There she did a fair amount of mentoring of her own. One of her favorite mentees was a young former Marine named Harry MacMurphy. She recognized his talents from the outset and protected him from his many detractors, most of whom were simply jealous of the tireless work ethic that helped him rise swiftly through the ranks.

It didn't hurt that Edwin Rothmann, who by that time had assumed the rank of DDO, the head of the Clandestine Service, was also one of MacMurphy's biggest supporters.

Maggie reported that GSR revenues were up slightly due in most part to the *CounterThreat* publication, which was now being distributed to almost ten thousand subscribers worldwide. The popular weekly newsletter kept its subscribers up to date on the status of security, politics, and economics in various hotspots of the world.

But the company had taken a heavy financial hit due to the snafu down in Belize.

GSR had a lot on its plate at the moment. She ticked off the jobs they were working on one by one from her project list: an international due diligence on a company in Saudi Arabia targeted for acquisition by a United States company; two background investigations on potential hires for a Fortune 100 pharmaceutical firm in Dallas, Texas; an internal fraud investigation for a large construction company in Miami, Florida, that suspected its CFO of embezzling funds; locating a deadbeat dad in Minnesota; investigation of a suspected advance-fee schemer in New York; and, of course, the disastrous child recovery operation in Belize.

She moved on to potential cases that were in the discussion phase but not yet contracted. When she mentioned another possible child recovery operation, this one on Roatán, an island off the coast of Honduras, she elicited groans from Santos and MacMurphy.

Santos raised his thick, muscular arms in a gesture of surrender. "Hey, when you count everything up—my bail, the cost of sending Mac down to get me, the fact that the client won't pay another dime because we failed to get his kid back—we lost about seventy grand on the job. It was a total failure. Blame is everywhere. There are simply too many variables with these types of operations. Sure, our hearts go out to the parents who want their kids back, and we're on the right side of the law—U.S. law, at least—but they're just too risky. I vote we get out of the child recovery business entirely."

MacMurphy turned his chair from Santos to Maggie. "I agree with Culler. We're all ready to risk life and limb for our country but not for corporate America or for individual clients. It's hard to say no to some of these people, but these kinds of operations are simply too full of heartache and danger. I say we reserve the heroics for when it's really needed."

Maggie said, "Okay, can't say I don't agree with you. But let's just keep an open mind and look at each one individually as they come in. We can't take another hit like this. That's for certain."

When they finished discussing the current and potential cases and some general housekeeping matters, Maggie adjourned the meeting and asked Santos and MacMurphy to remain behind. When the door closed and the three of them were alone, she looked up and said in a low voice, "Edwin Rothmann called. He needs us."

# CHAPTER 7

When MacMurphy was released (okay, fired) by the CIA a little over two years ago, Edwin Rothmann suggested he set up a front company to cover occasional, "off the books" activities for the DDO. He explained, "We're going to do the things that need to be done: covert action and a whole range of things this great outfit used to do but won't do anymore. No more timidity. We'll be bold. Just like in the old days."

So, MacMurphy set up GSR in Fort Lauderdale with money from the operation that had gotten him booted from the Agency. Santos, who had been an audio tech with the CIA's Office of Technical Services, joined him after flipping his badge at the director and quitting in protest over MacMurphy's firing. Maggie had just retired and joined them a few weeks later.

It wasn't long before Rothmann jokingly dubbed the firm "CIA, Inc." The only people who were aware of the deeply embedded "CIA, Inc." were Rothmann, Maggie, Santos, and MacMurphy. They worked in the shadows, financed by millions of dollars from an alias bank account in Switzerland. GSR's only true client, the only real reason for its existence, was the DDO.

■ ■ ■

Even though they were alone in the room, MacMurphy, Santos, and Maggie gathered at one end of the conference table and spoke in hushed tones. Maggie said, "While you two were off on your little jaunt in the jungle, Edwin called and invited me to dinner. You know what that means. I flew up to D.C. and met him at that little Turkish restaurant in Vienna off Route 123 he likes so much. He was quite agitated. I think the job is finally getting to him..."

"It's the political correctness of the place these days. I know it's driving him crazy. They can't get anything accomplished," said MacMurphy.

"I can't imagine why he keeps hanging on," said Santos.

"Because he cares too much, and he loves sticking his finger in the director's eye. Plus, they can't get rid of him. He knows where all the skeletons are buried," said MacMurphy.

Maggie stopped them. "Let's get on with it. He's got a hostage problem and he needs our help."

"Hostage!" Santos said.

"Yes, hostage, and a bad one." She looked from one man to the other. "One of ours."

"Oh shit," MacMurphy muttered.

"Yes, and she's an NOC."

"She?" Santos said.

"Yes, she's a she..."

"Who's got her?" said MacMurphy. "You said she's under non-official cover?"

"If you guys will stop interrupting me, I'll give you the whole story."

They settled into their chairs and waited for her to continue.

"Okay. Where was I? Yes, she's a female and one of our most promising young officers. She went through the career training program about five or six years ago and is now on her second tour. She's currently assigned to Cyprus as a counterterrorism officer attached to the counterterrorism center, a CTC officer. She speaks fluent Farsi and Arabic and has a master's degree in nuclear engineering from Yale. She is—or should I say was—deeply involved in our collection efforts against the Iranian nuclear program. In fact, the human source information she collected made up a good part of what we now know about Iran's less than honorable conduct."

"Where did all this happen?" asked MacMurphy.

"I was getting to that." Maggie brushed a wisp of errant, graying, auburn hair back from her face and fiddled with her pencil. "As I said, she's assigned to Cyprus but travels frequently to the Middle East, mostly on an alias Jordanian passport. She does this by leaving Cyprus on her U.S. passport and going to Beirut where she meets with one of our inside officers and switches passports for onward travel to Iran, Syria, Libya, or wherever."

"That's one ballsy woman!" exclaimed Santos.

"You bet she is. She's one of our most sensitive and effective NOCs, and now someone's got her. Rothmann is pulling his hair out. They're deep into the damage assessment and still have no idea how her cover got blown or whether whoever's got her even knows whom they have."

MacMurphy put his hands together in front of his face and massaged his nose with his fingers, thinking. "When did all of this go down? Who do they think has her?"

Maggie said, "There's so much we don't know. But we do know she was grabbed off the street in Central Beirut about an hour after she made a midday brush pass with one of our officers to switch passports. It happened three days ago. We think our inside case officer was under surveillance and led the kidnappers to our NOC."

"So, whoever has her may believe they have a Jordanian woman. They may not even be aware she's an American," said MacMurphy.

"Maybe…probably," Maggie nodded. "But we just don't know. Her Arabic might be accented."

Santos asked, "I imagine the Agency is pulling out all the stops to locate her and get her back, so what does Rothmann want us to do?"

"The Agency is doing what it can, but it's limited in what it can do due to the sensitivity of the operation and of her in particular. Very few people even know of her existence. Her activities are highly compartmented and the bigot list is very short. They think it was Hezbollah. That would make sense. They've got us under almost constant surveillance in Beirut. But all we really know is that she was grabbed by a couple of Arab-looking men and forced into a black van with local plates. Eyewitnesses told us that. Or rather, they told the police who then told us. Abductions take place all the time in Beirut. Mostly they just want ransom."

"But no one has contacted anyone for ransom," said MacMurphy.

"They probably wouldn't know who to contact if they were common criminals. She wasn't a resident of Lebanon."

"What a mess," said Santos, shaking his big head.

"What's her name?" MacMurphy asked.

"The name on her Jordanian passport is Abida Hammami. Her true name is Yasmin Ghorbani. She's thirty-three years old with waist-length black hair, green eyes, and a slender build. You'd like her, Mac. Beautiful. Just your type."

"Your reputation is catching up with you, Mac," chided Santos.

"Maggie knows everything."

She pushed back in her chair. "What's the plan?"

"Damned if I know," said MacMurphy. "But if we assume she's being held by Hezbollah and that Hezbollah knows they have someone important, like a Jordanian agent of the CIA…"

"Or worse…" said Santos.

"Yes, or worse. They could know they have a CIA case officer. An NOC. In that case, they—I mean Hezbollah—would probably be forced to give her up to Iran. The Ayatollahs in Iran call most of the shots as far as Hezbollah goes. We'd never get her out if they did that. Not with this mealy-mouthed administration. There are four other American hostages who have been languishing in Iranian prisons for years." MacMurphy turned and looked directly at Maggie. "In any event, why does the DDO think we can do this when the Agency can't?"

"I asked him that. He said you were the best case officer he had ever worked with. He said that you could move faster than the CIA bureaucracy could and that you were a great recruiter. But don't let any of that go to your already over-inflated head."

"Recruitment?" MacMurphy shook his head. "He wants a source inside Hezbollah. But none of those fanatics would ever work for Americans."

Maggie said, "Rothmann said you'd figure something out."

"Sounds pretty complicated to me. Where do we even start?" asked Santos. "We'd at least need an access agent to get things rolling, wouldn't we?"

Maggie started scratching her head with her pencil. After a moment she said, "I know this fellow in Cyprus…"

# CHAPTER 8

The CIA's Nicosia station is the focus of all of the Agency's worldwide counterterrorism operations. It's CTC turf. Located in the eastern Mediterranean about midway between Turkey to the north and Lebanon to the southeast, Cyprus serves as a transit spot and communications hub for Middle Eastern terrorists in Europe and the Middle East. The island nation is divided roughly in half with the northern part occupied and controlled by the Turkish population and the southern half by the Greeks. A United Nations "Green Line" divides the two parts and keeps them from going after each other's throats. It has been this way for more than forty years. Greeks and Turks are like oil and water.

The United States Embassy is located in Nicosia on the Greek side of the island.

■  ■  ■

MacMurphy's plane touched down a little before noon on the southern coast of Cyprus at Larnaca Airport. He stopped at the Avis counter, rented a car, and took the highway north to Nicosia, arriving a little over an hour later.

He was no stranger to Cyprus. During his active career with the CIA, he had visited it many times on temporary duty. His travels there taught him that almost every Middle Eastern terrorist case had a Cyprus connection.

He pulled into the Hilton Hotel on Archbishop Makarios III Avenue and parked his car. There were newer and better hotels in Nicosia these days, but this one was located near the center of town and was familiar to him. MacMurphy was funny that way; he liked returning to familiar places even when he had better options. It made him feel comfortable. Perhaps this familiarity offset the danger he frequently faced during his Agency career and occasionally struggled with after.

His meeting was not until eight o'clock that evening, so he checked into his room, worked out in the gym and walked to the pool to cool off and lay out in the sun for a while. He returned to his room at 6:02 p.m. for a shower and a twenty-minute power nap—whenever he slept, he had the ability to bring himself down to a relaxed state almost akin to hibernation. Then, refreshed, he dressed casually in tan slacks and a blue polo shirt and headed down to the Hiltonia Bar for a well-needed vodka tonic while awaiting the arrival of his contact.

Hadi Kashmiri walked into the Hiltonia Bar at exactly eight o'clock. The short, balding, plump millionaire was known for his punctuality. He sported a well-trimmed moustache and goatee and a grey, three-piece, pin-striped suit. Regardless of the oppressive Cyprus heat, the suit was his uniform. He survived by ducking from one air-conditioned place to another. He paused for a moment at the bar's entrance, scanned the occupants within and settled on the athletic man with salt and pepper hair—mostly salt—wearing a pale blue polo shirt.

MacMurphy immediately recognized Kashmiri from Maggie's description and slid off his barstool to greet him. He grabbed his half-finished drink from the bar and guided his contact to a booth near the back of the paneled room. A waitress took their drink orders—another vodka tonic for MacMurphy and a Dewar's on the rocks for Kashmiri—and they settled in.

Kashmiri had had a long career as a contact for the CIA. He was never officially an agent because he was never paid, which meant he was never under any kind of control. He offered his services for strictly ideo-logical reasons—he hated the fanatical Ayatollahs and their murderous ways—and presumably because he enjoyed the excitement of working with the Agency. His family was part of the aristocracy in Iran before the revolution. After the Ayatollah Khomeini deposed the Shah in 1979, he remained in political favor due to his family's indispensable business connections around the globe. Kashmiri was permitted to run his fam-ily's international business investments relatively unhindered by the usual restraints placed upon Iranian citizens. He maintained residences in Tehran, London, and Cyprus and traveled freely on Iranian and British passports, whichever served his purpose.

They were halfway through their drinks when MacMurphy asked, "You were such a valued friend of the Agency for so long. Why did you break off the contact?"

Kashmiri smiled, "It wasn't me. It was you guys. I never knew the reason, but I think I figured it out. For years I did the bidding of the Ministry of Intelligence under Mohammad Reyshahri, you know, the new SAVAK. Reporting directly to him on what I saw and heard during my travels, which was nothing much. Nothing of any great importance, but he hung on every word because they lived in such a vacuum. They had no idea what went on outside their borders. Then they started asking me to do little things for them. Things like renting apartments—they were probably for safe houses—and arranging furniture shipments to their embassies abroad. They had no idea how to get things done abroad. Even simple things like buying drapes. They're morons."

He swished the ice in his glass before continuing. "Where was I? Oh yes, and during these meetings we would talk about other things. Mohammad was very chatty, especially after a good meal, and we always had dinner during our meetings. He had no money so I always bought. He liked visiting fine restaurants. He would tell me about this and that. Complain about his job. Gripe about the pressure the Ayatollahs were putting on him. Those kinds of things. And of course, I would tell you people everything he said and about the things he asked me to do for him. Then, one day, he asked me to give him the name of the CIA station chief in Cyprus. I said I didn't know it. He told me to find out for him and to let him know as soon as I had it. It appeared that this was very important to him."

"Did you give it to him?" asked MacMurphy.

"Never. I never knew it. I knew the guy I was meeting in Nicosia couldn't be the chief. He was too young. And he was probably using an alias with me anyway. How was I going to find out something like that?"

"So what did you do?"

"Of course, I reported it all to my CIA contact and asked him what I should do. He told me to try to use my contacts to figure it out like I normally would and asked me to report back to him before saying anything to Mohammad."

"Did you get the right name?" MacMurphy was uncomfortable.

"Yes, I got three different names from my sources in the Cypriot government and police. All three of them were on the U.S. Embassy diplomatic list."

"What did you do then?"

"Well, the young officer read the names and handed the list back to me without giving me any indication of whether I had the right name or not. Then he told me to go ahead and give my report to Mohammad like he had asked."

"And?"

"I went back to Tehran and gave Mohammad the list and told him the source of each name. That's it…except…"

"Except what?"

"I returned to Cyprus three weeks later and signaled for a meeting, but the young officer never showed up. I tried repeatedly, but no one ever came to meet me. Not until now."

"That's very strange. Very odd…"

"Oh yes, this may be important. I checked around later and learned that one of the guys on the list had gone back to Washington on short notice. I drove by his house and it was empty with a 'For Rent' sign in the front yard."

MacMurphy knew right away what had happened. Langley had yanked their officer out of there as soon as they learned he was being targeted by the Iranians, and then they had broken off contact with Kashmiri. That's not what he would have done, but it was symptomatic of the way things were at headquarters in those days. They would toss away an excellent contact on the off chance that the Iranians might figure out he was the source of the information that caused the departure of the station chief. This overabundance of caution was ruining the CIA.

They were halfway through another round of drinks and had ordered dinner and wine. MacMurphy felt Kashmiri was relaxed enough to move the meeting on to more substantive issues. He was satisfied that Kashmiri was trustworthy and could be helpful. MacMurphy began, "I have something very important to discuss with you, something very sensitive."

"I figured. If I can help, I will."

MacMurphy looked him directly in the eyes. "We have a very big problem."

He explained what had happened and asked Kashmiri to gather as much information as possible about the welfare and location of Abida Hammami. But he withheld the fact that the woman was actually an American citizen of Persian decent named Yasmin Ghorbani. For the time being, it was important to stick to the cover story: a Jordanian woman of interest to the United States was abducted off the streets of Beirut, and the United States wanted her back.

"What do you want me to do?" Kashmiri asked. He was quite serious now and leaned in as he spoke.

"First, make inquiries among your contacts. We want to know who abducted her and why. That's very important. Do they think she's an American agent, or do they simply want a ransom? We have reason to believe Hezbollah is behind the kidnapping, but we really don't know for sure."

Kashmiri studied MacMurphy. "So, she's a CIA agent." It was a statement, not a question.

"Yes."

"Then it's Hezbollah. That's a big problem."

"Do you know someone who would know whether Hezbollah grabbed her and why?"

"Not directly. Has anything been reported in the press?"

"Not so far."

"Then where do I start?"

"Good question." MacMurphy looked down at his meal, arranged his fork and knife on the side of his plate, and picked up his glass of wine. His mind was spinning with thoughts, none of which gave him any answers. How would Kashmiri broach the subject of the woman's abduction if no one was supposed to know anything about it? The only people who knew about the incident were in the CIA station in Beirut, a few people in Langley, the eyewitnesses, and presumably the police. He finally broke the silence. "Do you know any journalists in Beirut?"

Kashmiri thought for a moment. "Yes, I know several."

"Any with Hezbollah connections?"

"Sympathies maybe, but I don't know about connections. I see where you're headed, though." Kashmiri's eyes brightened. He felt himself being pulled into the conspiracy with MacMurphy. "What if I made some inquiries for you? I assume you can give me all the details of the abduction, like the exact location, the vehicle, and descriptions of the men and the woman."

"Yes, I can give you all of that. You can attribute your knowledge of the incident to hearsay from one of the eyewitnesses. Great idea." Mac-Murphy's admiration for Kashmiri took a big leap forward.

Kashmiri grinned, "It was your idea. You just planted it in my head."

"No, not at all. Like they say, great minds think alike."

They continued eating their dinner, content that they at least had a clear direction in which to proceed. At the end of the meal, MacMurphy gave Kashmiri his throwaway phone number and instructed him to purchase a similar pre-paid phone so they could maintain contact with a fair degree of security. MacMurphy also forced Kashmiri to take an envelope containing $10,000 "for expenses."

At first, Kashmiri resisted because he had never taken money from the CIA before. But MacMurphy eventually wore him down. It was important to maintain a degree of operational control over an asset. That was the difference between a "contact" and an "asset." Control. MacMurphy also wanted Kashmiri to feel like part of the operation, and the money proved MacMurphy had confidence in him.

Kashmiri didn't know it, but he had just been recruited.

# CHAPTER 9

MacMurphy returned to Fort Lauderdale the following day. Three days later, Kashmiri had a meeting in Beirut with a journalist friend who worked for the French language daily newspaper in Lebanon, *L'Orient-Le Jour.*

Kashmiri told the journalist what he had heard about the kidnapping and asked whether Hezbollah was back in the kidnapping business. The journalist immediately picked up the phone and queried one of his Hezbollah contacts. The contact feigned ignorance at first but said he would do some checking and get back to him. The journalist got the impression his contact knew something but did not know how to answer.

Satisfied that the meeting had run its course, Kashmiri left the offices of *L'Orient-Le Jour* and walked down to the Paris corniche that ran along the bank of the Mediterranean. It was a beautiful afternoon and a great day for a walk. He certainly needed the exercise, so he headed north in the direction of his flat.

He passed the spot where the old American embassy used to stand and couldn't help but remember the bombing that occurred there almost thirty years ago. So much had happened in the world of terrorism since then. Beirut had been transformed from the Paris of the Orient to a bombed-out ruin. Yes, there were construction cranes all over, and the city was trying to dig itself out of the ashes and rebuild. But it would never be the same.

At least it was still beautiful along the corniche. A light breeze wafted across the sea and enveloped him as the sun slowly drifted downward, reflecting off the sparkling waters of the Mediterranean.

He thought about his relationship with his new CIA contact. Mac-Murphy was different from the rest. More self-assured, yet his dark eyes exuded an air of compassion that made him feel comfortable. Still, Kashmiri knew not to be careless. He understood the dangers of working with the CIA. After all, he was playing both sides. He traveled frequently to his home country of Iran and kept a small *pied-à-terre* in Tehran. If someone discovered his duplicity…well, it would not be pretty.

He longed for the way things were. When Beirut was a beautiful and gay city and Iran was a strong nation of free people. Of course, the Shah had been a bit of a despot and ruled with an iron fist, but there had been freedom and the country had been a great place to live and work. How had things taken such a horrible turn? It all happened so fast.

When America abandoned the Shah and agreed to bring back the Ayatollah Khomeini, everything went downhill. Millions were killed in the war with Iraq, which was such an egregious foreign policy error. It was true that when America sneezes, the whole world catches cold.

Well, he would help make things right again. He would work with MacMurphy to do whatever he could to help his country and the world.

He reached his flat and went up to shower, change clothes and get ready for dinner with friends. At least there were still some very fine restaurants in Beirut.

After dinner, Kashmiri received a call from his journalist friend. The journalist confirmed that Hezbollah had "an American spy" in custody but was unable to give any further details. When he returned home, he called MacMurphy on his throwaway phone and brought him up to speed.

"You were right, Mac. They've got one of ours—I mean yours."

"You were right the first time. She is ours. We're in this together. It's our fight. Did you get any more details?"

"None, but my contact confirmed the spy is a she."

"Good, then we're probably talking about the same person." Mac-Murphy smiled. Kashmiri was quick on the uptake. "It's important we find out just how much they know about her. Do you think you can get anything more?"

"I'll try. I've got more than one source in this city."

"We need to know how to play this. Our actions will depend upon what they know. Please do your best."

"You can count on me. I'll phone you as soon as I have something to report."

# CHAPTER 10

Yasmin Ghorbani was frightened. Two weeks had passed since her brutal abduction. She could not help but think about the last time this had happened to a CIA officer. His name was Bill Buckley, the Beirut station chief. Buckley was tortured and killed, and his body was placed in a plastic garbage bag and dumped on the side of a dark road near the Beirut airport. That was back in 1991. Hezbollah had been the culprit. She was quite certain Hezbollah was behind her abduction too.

The *modus operandi* was the same, but she couldn't figure out why they had chosen her. Her cover was airtight, or at least she thought it was. So far, her captors had only referred to her as madam or miss. That added to her discomfort.

Surely, they must know her real identity. Why else would they have abducted her? At least there had been no interrogations. They hadn't even asked her name. It was all very disquieting. She was quite sure ransom was not the motive. And that plagued her.

She had been moved twice since her capture, another similarity to Hezbollah's *modus operandi*. Each time she had been blindfolded and covered from head to toe in a full-body, black burqa. She had been placed in the back seat of a car and transported through the city to a location within a half-hour's drive of her previous spot. But there were a lot of twists and turns during the drive, so the distances between safe houses could have been shorter.

Her escort was a large, older man referred to as Abu Salah. It seemed Abu Salah never left her side or at least was never far away from her. He spoke very little and appeared to be very professional in her handling. He had an assistant, a woman covered in a black burqa, who also spoke very little and whose main role seemed to be escorting Yasmin to the bathroom and back.

She was currently being held in a modest, upper-floor apartment somewhere in Beirut. It had two rooms that were basically the same. Her room had one window, which was barred and blocked, a small bed, a dresser and a sink. There was a bathroom down the hall. She could hear street noises, airplanes overhead, and occasional chatter from inside the apartment and adjacent apartments. The nearby apartments probably belonged to Hezbollah supporters who would ask no questions.

Her meals were brought to her by either the woman or Abu Salah. They were always from local takeout restaurants. Falafels, all sorts of local dishes, and even the occasional McDonald's burger were the standard fare. But there were gaps in the meals. Some days, she was only given one or two. She dreaded the day when food would stop coming altogether. And her constant hunger fed this paranoia. It rankled her that their tactics were already getting to her.

She never saw the face of the burqa-clad woman, but she had plenty of opportunities to scrutinize Abu Salah. He was a large, dour, menacing, older man, with yellowing teeth and thick hands, who smelled of stale cigarettes. He was always dressed in a traditional *dishdasha* robe, a man-dress.

What she did not know about Abu Salah was that he was a trusted Hezbollah operative who gained his experience handling captives from Sheikh Fadlallah and Imad Mughniyah back in the 1980s when the murderous pair controlled the now famous ninety-six foreign hostages. But she did know that Hezbollah had strong connections to the Islamic Republic of Iran, and that back then hostages were used to extract concessions from the United States and the West, concessions that successfully advanced Iranian foreign policy interests. She worried that this was the purpose of her own abduction. If they knew her true identity, she would be as valuable to them today as Bill Buckley was back then.

Her training had taught her to make every effort to escape and that escape was less and less possible the longer captivity continued. But Abu Salah kept her handcuffed to the bed when she was alone in her room. And he made it quite clear that any attempt to escape during the times she was not cuffed and in his custody would be futile and lead to great bodily harm.

She was confident she could not overpower the monster, so she needed to think of another way. Intellect and persuasion were her only tools. She had always been able to use her charm and good looks to manipulate people, but this was different. It was as if her sexy figure and beauty were turnoffs to her captors.

She was a shade over five feet tall, slender with ample breasts and a natural, sexy swing to her hips. Flawless olive skin, soft green eyes, and silky black, waist-length hair rounded out the package.

But now she didn't feel very attractive. Since her capture, she had only been permitted to use the sink and a washcloth to bathe. Her once shiny hair was now matted, oily, and dirty. And her full figure was starting to wane.

She still wore the same clothes and lingerie she had been wearing when she was taken. All were soiled and her body odor was apparent even to her. She felt degraded and knew that was the purpose of her neglected hygiene. She suspected the interrogations would begin soon.

# CHAPTER 11

Kashmiri's call jolted MacMurphy awake in his Fort Lauderdale home. It was three o'clock in the morning in Florida. MacMurphy scrambled to find the source of the ringing on his night table and knocked his water bottle to the floor in his haste.

"Hello," he grunted into the phone.

"I'm so sorry. I just realized it's the middle of the night where you are. Shall I call you back later?"

MacMurphy sat up and tried to shake the sleep from his brain. He recognized the voice on the other end of the line. The woman beside him moaned, pulled the sheet up over her head, and turned away. "No, it's okay. What's up?"

"You'd better get out here. I've got information for you."

"You're in Cyprus?"

"Yes, I returned yesterday."

"Okay, I'll get out there a quick as I can and call you when I get to the hotel."

"Thanks. I'll wait for your call. Good night. And again, I apologize for waking you."

"That's not a problem. Thanks for the call. See you soon."

The woman snuggled up to him when he ended the call. "Who was that calling you in the middle of the night?" she asked sleepily.

"Nothing, go back to sleep." He wanted to add her name to the statement, but he couldn't recall it. Lola? No, Lorna. Maybe, but he couldn't be sure.

She snuggled closer. "You were wonderful," she purred.

"You were the wonderful one," he lied. "Now go back to sleep. The morning will be here before you know it."

She tried to arouse him with her hand but he gently pushed it aside and turned away, feigning sleep. Finally, she gave up. Her breathing became heavier and he knew she had fallen back to sleep. But his mind was still active, and it was not concerned with Kashmiri.

What the hell was her name? Was he experiencing memory problems? She had introduced herself at the Taboo Bar in Palm Beach earlier that evening, but he couldn't recall what she had said. These one-night stands had to stop. He was drinking too much and constantly drifting from one bimbo to the next. Was he becoming addicted to alcohol and sex? Should he be worried about it? Clearly, he was.

Santos had warned him about his behavior. Even Maggie had looked askance at him and commented about how wretched he looked in the mornings after too much booze and sex and not enough sleep. What was he trying to prove?

Nothing seemed to be going right in his personal life since the death of Wei-wei Ryan. God, how he missed her. She had been his anchor for so many years during his CIA career. She always seemed to be there for him. Then, after years of off-and-on romance in all the corners of the world, they had finally come together in Paris and decided they would never be separated again.

Paris, the end and the beginning for Harry Stephan MacMurphy. The end of his CIA career. Wei-wei's murder. His own vengeful rampage. He shuddered at the memories.

After his rebirth in Fort Lauderdale with GSR, everything came crashing down around him again in Thailand when he almost got the beautiful Charly Blackburn, a fine young case officer, killed. A very close call. They had survived, barely, but the emotional toll on him was great.

*Suck it up, MacMurphy! Stop whining and get on with it.* He rolled over and pressed his body against what's-her-name's back. He grasped her breast, caressed her nipple, and heard her moan in her sleep. Then he released it, rolled away, and tried to sleep for another couple of hours before the new day began.

# CHAPTER 12

MacMurphy was up early and went for his regular morning jog along the Intracoastal Waterway. When he returned, what's-her-name had already showered, dressed, and made coffee for them.

He felt sorry for her, so he went through the usual motions of caring for a stranger he just had a wild night of uninhibited sex with. But he got her out of there as soon as he could do so gracefully and then prepared himself for the day ahead.

It was three o'clock in the afternoon when he arrived at the airport for his American Airlines 5:47 p.m. flight to Athens. He planned to spend his three-hour layover in Athens in the Admiral's Club lounge before the short hop down to Larnaca, Cyprus. During his layover, he called Kashmiri and scheduled an eight o'clock dinner appointment at the intimate Chez Nicole restaurant on Aphrodite Street in the center of Nicosia.

MacMurphy arrived ten minutes early to find the restaurant almost empty. He remembered that Cypriot hours were like Greek hours, which contributed to the lack of productivity of both countries. For the most part, the working population would rise early in the morning, begin the day at around seven in the morning and work until about one in the afternoon. Then they would go home for lunch and a four-hour nap. This was not a "kick off your shoes and stretch out on the couch" type of nap. It was a "put on your pajamas and get under the covers" type of nap. Most shops closed during the afternoon hours.

After the nap they were supposed to go back to work for another three hours or so, but many of them did not. So, when they finally got around to eating dinner, it was late, about ten o'clock in the evening. But they were well rested when they awoke; they had already had four hours of sleep. So, when they fell into bed in the early morning hours, they only had to sleep another four hours to get their required eight hours of rest.

Unfortunately, not everyone, especially not Americans, functioned well on this schedule. But not even the advent of air-conditioning, which allowed people to work indoors during the hottest part of the day, could change these deep-set habits of the Greeks and Cypriots.

MacMurphy was jolted out of his musings by the touch of Kashmiri's hand on his shoulder. "Hi, Mac, good to see you."

"Good to see you, Hadi." MacMurphy stood and shook his hand warmly.

MacMurphy ordered them a slightly chilled bottle of Chateauneuf-du-Pape wine from the Rhone region of France and they perused their menus. When the waiter had left, MacMurphy said, "I can't stand it any longer. What did you learn?"

Kashmiri frowned, "I learned a lot, but it's not good."

"I suspected as much. They know who they have…"

"Exactly. And, it's definitely Hezbollah. The kidnap order came directly from Tehran."

"What do they call her?"

Kashmiri flinched. "What do you mean? Don't you know her name?"

MacMurphy hesitated before answering. How much should he tell this agent? He decided to go all in. "She has two names."

Kashmiri sat back in his chair and eyed MacMurphy. "Ah, I understand. She's operating under cover and using an alias."

"Yes, like the leaves of an onion. We need to know how many layers they have stripped off so far, how much they know."

Kashmiri nodded. "Whether she's sticking to her cover story…"

"Right."

"You told me her name was Abida Hammami, a Jordanian woman. That's who they think they have. That's her alias, isn't it?"

MacMurphy considered. How far should he go with this? He trusted
Kashmiri and knew that full disclosure would work to his advantage,
but the other side of the coin was security. If he knew too much and was
captured...

"Trust goes both ways. I want to level with you, but I also need to
protect you. I'm sure you have heard about the need-to-know principle.
It's pervasive in the intelligence business, and for good reason."

Kashmiri replied, "I do understand, and I've got no problem with it."

"Okay then, I can tell you this much, Abida Hammami is not her
true name and she is not Jordanian. Hammami is an operational alias.
Her cover story allows her to travel unrestricted throughout the Middle
East as a Jordanian businesswoman. The business is backstopped with
a telephone number and an address in Beirut, but it's not airtight."

"So, she's actually an American citizen and a CIA employee." It was
not a question.

MacMurphy answered, "Yes and yes."

"Then you really do have a huge problem," said Kashmiri with great
concern.

"Tell me about it..."

A waiter walked up to take their orders. On MacMurphy's recom-
mendation, they both chose the house specialty, *caneton á l'oignon*, and
then continued their conversation.

MacMurphy said, "Now it's your turn. Please begin at the beginning
and walk me through your efforts since our last meeting."

Kashmiri took a sip of wine, regarded his glass for a moment, and
set it down in front of him. "I may have stirred things up a bit with
my questioning. I got the impression that they, Hezbollah I mean, were
not prepared to release any details about the abduction as soon as they
did. My journalist friend, the guy from *L'Orient-Le Jour*, will release
the story in the morning. Essentially, it will report that Hezbollah has
announced the capture of a Jordanian businesswoman who was spying
on Iran for America. That's about all the article will say other than
she was captured in Beirut, and it won't be a headline, just a block on
page four."

"And other papers will pick it up."

"Yes, everyone is out digging for details now. But that's all that is known in Beirut at the moment." Kashmiri paused to let that sink in. "This duck is delicious," he said.

"Indeed it is, but don't keep me hanging. What other information outside of Beirut are you talking about?"

Kashmiri smiled broadly. "I called one of the guys I used to work for in Tehran, you know, in the new SAVAK. He gave me the number of his former boss, the guy who used to run the Ministry of Intelligence, Mohammad Reyshahri. Reyshahri is retired now, but when I called he remembered me right away. He's still well connected but bored with his new life of leisure. He's not permitted to travel outside of the country, but he invited me to visit him the next time I'm in Tehran."

"Wow! Great work."

"Thanks. He'll make an excellent source for us. He's very chatty. During our conversation, I mentioned what I had heard about the American spy captured in Beirut, and he said he knew all about it. I could hardly control myself. I just let him talk after that. He said she was spying for the Americans and that Hezbollah picked her up off the streets under direct orders from his old outfit, the Ministry of Intelligence. How about that? Direct orders."

MacMurphy was visibly excited. "What else did he say?"

Kashmiri grinned broadly. "I'm getting there. Someone got suspicious about her and reported her to the ministry. Apparently, she'd been asking too many questions about Iran's nuclear program. That's a very sensitive subject these days, especially in light of the recent Iran nuclear agreement with the U.S. So, they told Hezbollah to pick her up for interrogation."

MacMurphy shook his head. "They're going to let Hezbollah interrogate her about Iranian nuclear matters? I don't think they would ever do that."

"Maybe not. Maybe they'll send one of their own interrogators. We didn't get into that."

"Okay, good. Where are they holding her?"

"In a Hezbollah safe house in Beirut under the control of the same guy who used to oversee security for Imad Mughniyeh, the bastard who was responsible for the 1983 Marine barracks bombing. More than two hundred Americans died in that attack. The subsequent U.S. Embassy bombing killed another sixty-plus Americans."

"I remember Imad Mughniyeh very well. He did a lot of damage before he died. Did Reyshahri tell you anything more about the security guy?"

"He didn't have to. I know the guy who ran security for Mughniyeh." Kashmiri paused to let it sink in.

"You know him?"

"Well, we've never actually met, but I know all about him. He goes by the name Abu Salah. I don't know his family name. He must be in his late sixties or early seventies by now. He's a big brute of a man. Never smiles. One of Mughniyeh's most trusted lieutenants. Fearless. Except for one thing…"

"What's that?"

"He doesn't drive. The story is, he was involved in a serious automobile accident when he was a teenager or maybe in his early twenties. Almost killed him. Crushed some ribs. Broke both his legs. And a couple of young passengers died in the wreck. He was the driver. He never got over it."

"So how does he get around?"

Kashmiri shrugged, "He won't get back behind the wheel himself, so he has a full-time driver. Always has."

"Can you find out for me who his current driver is?" MacMurphy asked.

Kashmiri looked puzzled and hesitated to answer. After a moment, the light came on in his eyes. "Yes, perhaps I can."

■ ■ ■

MacMurphy dispatched Kashmiri back to Beirut and gave him another $10,000 to cover his expenses. Kashmiri did not hesitate to take the money this time. He was totally on board with his new case officer and excited to be back in the game. The money didn't hurt either. Even the wealthy can use a little extra cash.

Kashmiri was given only one requirement: learn the name of Abu Salah's driver. MacMurphy viewed the driver as a prime recruitment target due to his access to Abu Salah and the places Abu Salah visited, such as the safe house where Yasmin Ghorbani was being held.

MacMurphy decided to remain in Cyprus until Kashmiri returned. He was excited about this potential lead. It was the kind of thing case officers lived for.

# CHAPTER 13

The interrogations began two weeks after Yasmin Ghorbani's abduction. It took the Ayatollahs in Tehran that long to decide on an interrogator, agree upon a course of action, and negotiate an agreement with Hezbollah.

The interrogator they chose was a forty-seven-year-old woman named Pouri Hoseini. She was attractive, smart, and a niece of former leader of the Islamic Revolution Ayatollah Ali Hoseini Khamenei.

Pouri had a reputation of being a tough—some said ruthless—and skilled interrogator. She had initially risen swiftly through the ranks of the Ministry of Intelligence. But despite her high-level connections, she was denied advancement beyond the senior working level to management because of her gender. She accepted this as an unpleasant fact of life in the Islamic Republic of Iran but did not like it one bit.

Her entire upbringing was one of privilege in a society where privilege was frowned upon. Her family played the game of supporting the revolution and the Ayatollahs and Sharia law. But behind the closed doors of their family mansion, they watched bootleg American movies, listened to Western music, and eschewed all trappings of a strict Muslim culture. And they were not alone.

She married a like-minded man who held a relatively high position in the Ministry of Foreign Affairs. They had two grown children, a boy and a girl, ages twenty and twenty-five. Overseas assignments in London,

Brussels, and Paris with her family taught her what life was like outside of Iran.

Although she was happy enough with her life, she frequently thought about what it would be like to live in a free Iran, the way things were before the Ayatollahs ruled the nation.

A deferential Abu Salah led Pouri into the safe house. He unlocked the door to Yasmin Ghorbani's room, ushered Pouri inside, and backed out, locking the door behind him. He gave little thought to the possibility that his prisoner might try to escape or attack Pouri. But just to be on the safe side, he propped a chair against the outside of the door and sat down to wait.

The small bedroom consisted of a rumpled, steel cot in one corner, an old card table in the middle of the room, and two wooden chairs. The only window had been blacked out with aluminum foil and barred from the inside. The bars appeared to be a recent installation. Street noises, traffic, beeping horns, and airline traffic ebbed and flowed into the room through the window.

Yasmin sat in one of the wooden chairs, facing the door, head down. Pouri regarded her from just inside the doorway. The prisoner wore filthy, faded blue jeans with fashionable tears in the knees and thighs and a sweat-stained, long-sleeved blouse with its buttons askew. Her hands were handcuffed in her lap. Her stare was unblinking and vacant.

Pouri walked slowly to the opposite chair and sat down. Yasmin looked up briefly and then let her eyes fall again toward her lap.

After a while, Pouri spoke softly in English, "Hello, my name is Pouri. What is yours?"

Yasmin looked up, puzzled. "Don't you know my name? Why are you speaking English?"

Still very softly, Pouri replied, "Yes, I know your name. I know a lot about you. We have a very thick dossier on you. We have known about you for quite some time. And to answer your other question, I am using English because you are most comfortable in that language. You are American after all. And your Arabic is, shall we say, not perfect."

Yasmin raised her head and carefully regarded her interrogator for the first time. Who was she? How much did she know? Yasmin resisted the urge to respond and remained silent. She retained a vague, puzzled look on her face as she surveyed the woman sitting in front of her.

Pouri was wearing a fashionable, maroon, flowered *hijab* headscarf, but aside from that, the rest of her clothes could have been purchased at K-Mart or The Gap. She wore tight-fitting blue jeans, black pumps, and a black sequined T-shirt with the word "Paris" and an Eiffel Tower emblazoned across the front in gold sequins.

She was actually quite attractive, which surprised Yasmin for some reason. Pouri was blessed with a nice, full-bosomed figure, slender hips, and long athletic legs. Her English was perfect and she spoke with a slight British accent.

Pouri broke the silence, "Come on, I'm not going to bite you. Actually, I am here to help you. You look like you could use a good bath and have your clothes laundered. Would you like that? What else do you need? A toothbrush? Hairbrush? Shampoo? Whatever you want, I can get it for you."

Yasmin replied softly, "Who are you? What do you want from me? Why are you doing this to me?"

"Doing this to you? It's what you were doing to us that is the real question. I know it's not your fault; you were just doing your job. So, if you cooperate with me, I can help you."

Yasmin studied the attractive woman and her pleasant smile. She hesitated to respond. Her training had taught her not to give away anything, but… "Obviously you are here to interrogate me," she said, "But why? I have done nothing wrong."

"Abida. Let us start with that. Abida Hammami. Is that your name?" Pouri's voice was not quite so kind.

Yasmin shook her head. "You know it is. You have my passport. You have everything."

"Please don't lie to me. It will not go well for you if you lie to me. Your documents are false. The company you supposedly work for is nothing more than a front. You are a CIA spy. We know all of that. I just need you to fill in a few blanks for us."

Yasmin fought to control her emotions. She was terrified and hungry. How much more did they know? Her hands shook uncontrollably. She tried to hide her fear but could not. "You don't know that." She was on the verge of tears. "It's not true. Not true…"

Pouri stood up and made a circle around the small table, never taking her eyes off the shaking young woman. *Such a filthy, scared, little girl,* she thought. *No need to get rough with this one. Not yet anyway. A little kindness will work.*

She put her hands on the back of the chair she had just abandoned and looked down at the quivering figure in front of her. "Enough for today," she said kindly. "I will instruct Abu Salah to let you wash in the sink and to have your clothes laundered. I want you to feel good when I see you in the morning. Then we can start fresh. How does that sound?"

Yasmin looked up with tear-filled eyes and she nodded slightly.

Pouri Hoseini thought, *This is going to be an easy one.*

# CHAPTER 14

Hadi Kashmiri reflected on his conversation with MacMurphy. Of course, the driver would know where Abu Salah went and therefore where Abida Hammami (if that was her real name) was being held. But, he was Hezbollah. He would never cooperate. Not willingly anyway.

Kashmiri shook his head. He didn't quite understand what was in MacMurphy's mind but was confident he knew what he was doing. So, Kashmiri decided to spread a little of the CIA's money around to learn what MacMurphy wanted to know.

And he knew exactly how to do it.

The moment he arrived back at his apartment in Beirut, Kashmiri called a few of his close friends, including his main contact at *L'Orient-Le Jour* and a couple other journalist friends. He invited them to dinner and drinks at the iconic Saint George Yacht Club and Marina located in *Ain el Mreisse*. Its restaurant and bar had been the equivalent of a Foreign Correspondents' Club for local and foreign reporters since the 1930s. Although it had lost some of its luster since then, it was still a haven for correspondents, jet-setters, and spies.

To set the mood for the evening, Kashmiri told his guests he was celebrating a huge commission he had just received for arranging a real estate deal in Cyprus. He knew there would be several other journalists at the bar who would talk freely with a little encouragement and a toast or two in them. Thus, his pool of prospective sources would be substantial. Surely, one of them would have information on Abu Salah and his Hezbollah connections. He hoped that in a relaxed and alcohol-fueled environment, conversation would flow freely.

He was not disappointed.

Most people opened up to Kashmiri without realizing it. He was soft spoken and had a non-threatening cherubic look about him that put them at ease. He was also a good listener. One had to be a good listener to be good at elicitation. The trick was to guide the conversation with careful questions and to let other people talk. People love to talk when they have an interested listener to entertain. And they love to show off how smart they are.

During dinner, the conversation among the friends had been about general things that interested them all. Things like the economy, politics, women, and local gossip. After dinner, they headed for the bar on the circular terrace and joined up with several others, including two other local journalists and a foreign journalist from Le Monde in Paris. The newcomers had overheard Kashmiri's journalist friends digging into local gossip and couldn't help but ask a few questions of their own. Journalists. Always looking for the next headline.

Kashmiri ordered a round of drinks for the group and gently turned the conversation to Hezbollah and the terrorist acts it had committed over the years. When the name Imad Mughniyeh came up, as it always did when a discussion touched on Hezbollah in Beirut, Kashmiri ordered another round.

Meanwhile, the journalists engaged in a sort of competition, each one trying to outdo the other with stories about the murderous Mughniyeh and his cohorts and their exclusive knowledge of the events. Well-oiled with alcohol, they were on an enthusiastic roll.

Kashmiri waited for the right moment and then asked, "Remember that brute who was Mughniyeh's security guy? What was his name...Abu Saba, Sabya, something like that?"

One of the journalists replied, "Yeah, Salah, Abu Salah. Miserable bastard."

Kashmiri picked it up, "Right, Abu Salah. That's his name. A real chickenshit. Did you know the asshole was afraid to drive? Big vicious animal and he was afraid to get behind the wheel of a car."

His friend from the *L'Orient-Le Jour* chimed in, "I heard about that. He needs a driver to chauffeur him around. Maybe he's just smarter than all of us!"

The crowd laughed and Kashmiri ordered another round of drinks.

One of the journalists asked, "Is he still around? He must be pretty old by now."

Another journalist said, "Oh, he's around alright. Still doing Hezbollah's bidding. I saw him drinking tea in a café on Hamra Street a couple of weeks ago. He looked as mean and miserable as ever."

Kashmiri laughed and interjected, "Did he have his driver with him?"

They laughed again and the journalist replied, "Yup, his black Mercedes was parked right at the curb in front of the café. He's had the same driver for at least ten years. He's a cousin, or nephew, or something like that..."

The *L'Orient-Le Jour* journalist broke in, "On Hamra Street? That makes sense. The driver's father owns an English pub on Hamra Street. Near the American University. It's called Wellington's or something like that. It's in the old Mayflower Hotel. Very nice. I think he's related to the former Druze leader, Walid Jumblatt. His name is Sami something. Pretty well known and wealthy. But his son was a punk. Juvenile delinquent. A gang member, as I recall. Always getting into trouble. He ran away to Baalbeck out in the Bekaa Valley and joined Hezbollah. It was all over the gossip columns at the time."

Hadi Kashmiri smiled inwardly. The son of Sami who owned Wellington's Pub on Hamra Street was Abu Salah's driver. He could figure out the rest.

He ordered another round and relaxed.

# CHAPTER 15

MacMurphy looked out at a port on the southern coast of Cyprus. He was standing in his room on the twenty-seventh floor of the Golden Beach Hotel in Limassol. If it was on schedule, Kashmiri's ferry from Beirut would dock in about ten minutes. A delay would be unlikely as it was a beautiful, sunny day with flat seas.

He was excited. Kashmiri had been typically cryptic during their phone call earlier that morning. Both men knew all telephonic communications between Beirut and Cyprus were closely monitored by at least three security services. But the enthusiasm in Kashmiri's voice left little doubt that he would bring important information with him.

The knock on MacMurphy's door came almost an hour later. A disheveled Kashmiri stood in the doorway wearing a sweat-stained, tan suit. His tie was opened and he was mopping his balding head. "I'm sorry, Mac. There was a long queue at the taxi stand so I decided to walk over from the pier. Not a good idea. It's hot as Hades out there, and as you can see I'm not in the best shape." He placed his hands over his ample stomach to demonstrate.

MacMurphy shook Kashmiri's hand and closed the door behind him. Before he sat, the disheveled man blurted out, "His name is Walid Nassar. He's forty-one years old and lives in Beirut. And he's the son of an old friend of mine."

Kashmiri related in agonizing detail the events that led to his uncovering the identity of Abu Salah's driver. When he was through, and after MacMurphy had heaped enough praise on Kashmiri's head to elicit large toothy grins from the man, the conversation took a strange turn.

They were sitting in comfortable chairs by the window of the suite and drinking heavily iced Cokes with a panorama of the beautiful Mediterranean behind them when MacMurphy said, "Tell me more about Walid Nassar's family. The people he is closest to. Relatives and friends he sees regularly and respects."

"Well, that definitely does not include his father. As I mentioned, his father, Sami, is a good friend of mine. He's a Druze. Not a radical bone in his body. He's completely estranged from his son."

"How did Walid become radicalized?" MacMurphy leaned forward to emphasize the importance of this line of questioning.

"Sami had a younger brother. A terrific athlete. A football player. Not your kind of football. Our kind of football. You know, soccer. Anyway, he was a real tough kid. Rebellious. Always getting into trouble. Walid looked up to him. Admired him."

Now MacMurphy was very interested. "So, this uncle...what's his name?"

"Nabil. Sami could not spend much time with his kid because he was working all the time at the restaurant, so Nabil kind of took over. Then Nabil fell in with a bunch of Hezbollah thugs. He was involved in some robberies, probably to raise money for Hezbollah, got caught, and spent time in jail. That made things worse for him. When he got out of jail he was not the same person."

MacMurphy said, "He was radicalized in prison." It was not a question.

"Yes, it was a shame. His family disowned him. He was in and out of jail for another couple of years until he and some other Hezbollah members robbed a company payroll and got into a firefight with the police. Two of his friends were killed and he was struck in the spine with a bullet that left him paralyzed from the waist down."

"So, he's in a wheelchair?"

"Yes. He was quite a womanizer before then. Now he can't get it up. It left him a very bitter man from what I hear."

MacMurphy gazed out through the hotel window to the Mediterranean, thinking. He ran his fingers through rapidly graying hair. "What kind of life does he have now?"

*He's looking for vulnerabilities*, Kashmiri thought. *But he's heading in the wrong direction…*

Kashmiri knew just enough about recruitment operations to understand MacMurphy's line of questioning. "This guy is hard-core. You cannot recruit him. He's a bitter, screwed-up man. He has no life and he owes his allegiance to Hezbollah. In fact, he's on some sort of Hezbollah pension. They pay him a stipend every month because of the injuries he got in the line of duty. He owes his whole existence to them now."

MacMurphy stood up and stretched his lean frame. The sun streamed through the windows. He pulled the sheer drapes closed and adjusted the heavy drapes to cut some of the direct sunlight. Then he plopped back down into his chair.

He leaned toward Kashmiri and said in a serious tone, "Here's what I'm getting at. We need access to Walid, direct access. To do that we need to find someone who is close to him. Someone he trusts completely. Uncle Nabil seems to fit that bill perfectly."

"But what about his father?" Kashmiri asked. "They may not see eye to eye politically, but they are still father and son."

MacMurphy shook his head. "Do you think his father could talk him into helping us?"

Kashmiri was surprised. "Never."

"That's my whole point. From what you've told me, Uncle Nabil is a trusted Hezbollah sympathizer and Walid is a long-time Hezbollah operative. That's the combination we need. They will trust each other."

"I'm sorry, Mac," Kashmiri shook his head, confused. "I still don't follow you."

MacMurphy smiled. He was enjoying this. "Here's the way it works. It's like a daisy chain. At one end of the chain, we have our driver, Walid. He's the one with direct access to our target, Abu Salah who is in control of the hostage. The one we want to rescue. Are you following?"

"Okay, I've got all that."

"At the other end of the chain we have me. And right above me is you. Still following?"

Kashmiri nodded.

"But there's a gap between you and me and driver Walid and Abu Salah."

"And we need to fill that gap," said Kashmiri.

"Yes, we need a transition figure who will work with me and you to convince Walid to report back to us on the activities of Abu Salah."

"To spy on Abu Salah," said Kashmiri.

"Right, to report on him—what he says and what he does and where he goes. We need information on the welfare and whereabouts of his American hostage and for him to report that information back to me through you."

Kashmiri was confused once again. "But they would never do that. They hate America and everything American, especially the CIA."

MacMurphy leaned toward Kashmiri and spoke in a low, conspiratorial voice. "But what if it was not me pulling the strings of the operation? What if it was the Ayatollahs in Iran who wanted to know exactly, from an independent source, how Abu Salah and his Hezbollah masters were handling their very important CIA hostage?"

Kashmiri's eyes grew large and he moved to the edge of his chair. "You want me to tell Nabil that the supreme leader, the Ayatollah, wants him to get the cooperation of Walid to monitor the activities of Abu Salah?"

MacMurphy sat back and smiled broadly. "You've got it! It's called a false flag recruitment in the trade. You can just refer to me as the Ayatollah from now on..."

# CHAPTER 16

I t took fewer than six hours of skillful interrogation to crack Yasmin Ghorbani.

The poor girl had cleaned up well, but she still looked frail and stooped and defeated when Pouri Hoseini returned to the safe house for the second round of interrogations.

Pouri began her questioning in a soft, non-threatening manner, designed to get the woman talking. Pouri knew that communication was key. They discussed health issues, the treatment of women in the West as opposed to the Middle East, Middle Eastern politics, and the Iran nuclear deal that had just been finalized between the United States and its allies and Iran. Pouri agreed with Yasmin's opinions more often than not.

They formed an unexpected bond: one between two intelligent women of Middle Eastern descent against the stupidity and excesses of the Mullahs and Sharia law. They agreed that an Iranian nuclear capability in the hands of the fanatical Ayatollahs would kick off a nuclear arms race in the Middle East, and that that would be a very bad thing for the world.

Yasmin was being gently pulled out of her funk and a sparkle was returning to her eyes. She began to revel in this intellectual conversation with this perceptive woman and almost forgot who and where she was.

Until Pouri Hoseini dropped the bomb on her.

"So, Yasmin, was that what you were doing in Iran during all of those meetings with our nuclear scientists? Were you attempting to elicit information on our nuclear program in the interest of world peace?"

Startled, Yasmin looked up into Pouri's eyes and stuttered, "You know my name? I mean, you called me Yasmin. Why did you call me that?"

"Yes, Yasmin Ghorbani, I know your name. I know who you are and what you have been doing in Iran. I know you live in Nicosia, Cyprus, on Nikis Avenue and that you travel to Beirut under that name, which I suspect is your true name. You change into your Jordanian alias, Abida Hammami, when you travel to Iran and elsewhere to do your spying for the Great Satan. I know all of this."

Yasmin's reaction wavered from shock to dismay to utter fear. Was her tradecraft that bad? What had tipped them off? Why didn't her cover backstopping hold up? Had she been under surveillance in Cyprus? What about Beirut and Tehran? Did they enter her apartment in Beirut and find incriminating evidence? What about her Nicosia apartment? Did they know about her contacts in Tehran, or were they just probing? Had they identified her agents and developmentals?

But most of all, she worried about her future. What would they do with her? How long would they hold her? Would she be starved, tortured, or killed? Espionage carries the death sentence in Iran. Would she be forced to reveal her sources? Did they already have this information? What would happen?

After a long silence, Pouri rose from her chair, brushed her long hair from her face, and walked slowly around the small room in deep thought. She returned to stand over the cowering young woman with her arms crossed. She asked, "Who were your sources in Tehran? You know we know some of them, so do not try to lie."

Tears streamed down the face of Yasmin Ghorbani and dropped on her blouse. She trembled and sobbed uncontrollably. She was trapped.

"We have been talking for a long time, so I will leave you now and let you get some rest," said Pouri. "I want you to think about your situation. Think hard about your situation and tomorrow we will talk about your sources. That's all that interests me now: your sources."

# CHAPTER 17

Hadi Kashmiri had his marching orders. He now understood exactly where MacMurphy was heading with the operation. What had he called it? A false flag recruitment operation. And, in this case, the flag was Iranian.

MacMurphy had given him another envelope containing $10,000. His instructions were to convert the currency into Lebanese pounds and to deliver the money to Nabil as a recruitment bonus. Kashmiri quickly calculated the exchange in his head and decided he would need a bigger envelope; it amounted to more than fifteen million Lebanese pounds at the going rate. Nabil would think he had died and gone to heaven.

Kashmiri wasted no time. He returned to Beirut on the evening ferry and changed the $10,000 dollars into Lebanese pounds at the Beirut ferry pier. He put the fifteen million pounds into a manila envelope and pocketed the remaining fifty-seven thousand pounds. He was not stealing the money; he simply did not want to place the exact equivalent of $10,000 dollars in the envelope. He was proud of himself for thinking of that little detail.

The following afternoon he headed for the Duke of Wellington Pub at the Mayflower Hotel for lunch. He knew Sami would probably be there in his usual spot during the lunch hour, and he wasn't disappointed. Sami was sitting at the far-end corner of the bar watching people enter the pub. He recognized Kashmiri as soon as he stepped through the doors.

Sami was an elegant man with a well-trimmed, salt-and-pepper beard, a full head of curly, snow-white hair and wire spectacles perched on the end of his nose. "Hadi, my old friend, how are you?" He slid off his stool and embraced Kashmiri warmly. "Are you alone? Come sit by me."

Kashmiri ordered lunch, a draft beer with bangers and mash, and the two friends chatted. Halfway through his lunch Kashmiri steered the conversation toward family and asked about Sami's brother, Nabil.

"Nabil? He's as ornery as ever. I don't see much of him anymore." He lowered his voice and leaned in closer to Kashmiri. "He joined up with Hezbollah."

"Yes, I recall. That was several years ago, wasn't it?"

"A long time ago. It pulled our family apart. He's crippled, you know. In a wheelchair."

Kashmiri had him headed in the right direction. "How did it pull your family apart?" he asked.

Sami shook his head and removed his glasses. Thoughtfully, he said, "Because he took my son away from me. He talked Walid into joining up with Hezbollah. I lost them both to that murderous outfit."

"What a horrible shame. I knew about Nabil but not Walid. Do you stay in touch with them?"

"Nabil is not welcome in my house. Walid, well, he stops by the house from time to time to see his mother, but we do not speak much. He is still working for Hezbollah. I don't approve of that."

Kashmiri was filled with empathy for his friend. It was not just an act to elicit information. He was genuinely saddened. He reached out and touched Sami on the shoulder. Then he decided to plunge ahead with his elicitation. "I'm sorry. I'm really sorry. Where is Nabil now? I remember he was quite the athlete back in the day. Is he still in Beirut?"

"Oh yes, he's still here. He lives in East Beirut over the Al Bouchrieh Pharmacy. It's one of the few buildings over there with a lift."

Kashmiri had the information he came for. Now it was time to change the subject. "This is all too sad, Sami, let's talk about something more pleasant. Guess who I ran into the other day…"

They lingered for another hour, chatting and drinking more beer. When Kashmiri left, he turned his car east and headed for Massaken Street and the Al Bouchrieh Pharmacy.

It was in an area of East Beirut that had experienced a lot of fighting over the years. Many of the buildings remained bombed-out ruins that were pockmarked with bullet and shrapnel damage. The Al Bouchrieh Pharmacy took up the whole bottom floor of an old, narrow, five-story building that had survived the bombings, but the wounds of war remained visible on its façade.

He parked his car down the street in a spot where he could sit and watch the entrance of the building. After sitting for a while, he walked over to the building for a closer look.

The entrance to the upper floors was on the right side of the building facing the street. The glass entry door was operated with an electric fob or a key. It opened into a small foyer with an elevator and a narrow staircase on the left and four mailboxes on the right.

He returned to his car to continue his vigil.

Surveillance is nothing like the way it is depicted in movies. In the real world, it's not as easy as pulling up in a car, finding a position with a good view of the premises, and then immediately springing into action as things start happening. Surveillance is time intensive. It requires sitting and watching and watching and sitting while nothing happens. Until you take your eyes off the target for an instant and then, bam! Things start popping and the adrenaline starts flowing.

Kashmiri was slowly learning this painful lesson. It was now after seven o'clock in the evening. His butt was sore from sitting and he needed to pee. He had been there for almost four hours and had not spotted anyone in a wheelchair going in or out of the building. He considered leaving for just a few minutes to find a restroom. Just thinking about it made his urge to urinate stronger. He thought about opening his door and peeing in the gutter. There wasn't a lot of foot traffic where he was parked, but what if someone saw him?

He held out as long as he could and then decided to find a restroom and call it a night. He planned to return early the next morning with enough food to last him an entire day and a large jar to use as a urinal.

Kashmiri also rehearsed in his mind how he would approach Nabil when he spotted him. This was the difficult part. He figured he had one shot at the guy, and if he didn't do it right the first time, he wouldn't get a second chance.

He wished he could find someone to act as an intermediary and make a soft introduction to Nabil. But he knew this was impossible. Even mentioning Sami would be a no-no. He could not put anyone else in jeopardy. After all, he was dealing with a Hezbollah operative, and a pretty unsavory one at that.

If this operation went south, the only one who would suffer would be Hadi Kashmiri. He was keenly aware of that fact, and it tied his stomach in knots.

He contemplated giving Nabil an alias name but decided against it. He would have no bona fides in an alias. For anyone in Beirut who cared to check, it was common knowledge that Kashmiri was Iranian by birth, traveled frequently to Iran, kept a residence there, and had high-level Iranian contacts. Many suspected he worked secretly for Iranian intelligence, which indeed he had, and this would add credibility to his cover story. He had discussed this with MacMurphy during their last meeting, and the balance of risk versus gain tipped in favor of Kashmiri approaching Nabil under his true name.

Nevertheless, his main concern now was finding a restroom.

# CHAPTER 18

Three days had passed since the interrogator's visit. Yasmin was left alone in her prison with Abu Salah and that nasty old crone who barely spoke a word. Pouri had said she would return the next day, but she had not.

It was strange, but Yasmin actually missed talking to Pouri. She had taken the "Resistance to Interrogation" course during her CIA training down at The Farm, so she was aware of this eventuality.

In fact, the more she thought about it, Pouri had conducted a classic interrogation, straight from the Army Field Manual, in the style now used by the CIA and other United States intelligence agencies. There was no sleep deprivation, no slapping around, no humiliation, no loud music, no standing in stress positions for long periods, and no waterboarding. She had experienced all of these things down at The Farm in preparation for this moment. And she had been told by her instructors that torture could get a lot worse, especially in the Middle East.

She had been taught the difference between enhanced interrogation and actual torture, and the difference was profound. She did not fear enhanced interrogation, even waterboarding, because she knew it would not leave scars or have lasting effects. It would be uncomfortable, but she would live through it. This knowledge was enough to help most people resist.

But she did fear torture. The United States would never engage in it, but Hezbollah was holding her. With them, anything could be expected.

The frequency of her meals was erratic, but they still came at least once a day. Maybe her treatment was unusually good because Iran was pulling the strings. Probably, but Iran did not play by American rules either.

She knew Pouri Hoseini had effectively broken her down by skillfully using information against her. The only question was how much did she really know? Was Pouri bluffing about the extent of her knowledge? Almost certainly she was but how much?

Yasmin decided she had said enough, confirmed enough. From now on, they would have to pull out her fingernails to get any more information.

When Pouri returned to the safe house late in the afternoon, she was carrying two large shopping bags. She dismissed Abu Salah with a wave of her hand and dropped the bags onto the card table in the center of the room.

"Wait till you see what I bought for you," she exclaimed happily. "You've been wearing those awful clothes for far too long."

Yasmin could not help but smile. She moved from the bed to the card table and sat down in her usual spot. "You brought me clothes?" she asked.

"Yes, you need them." She pulled a brightly colored scarf from one of the bags and unfolded it. "Isn't this a pretty *hijab*? This is for when we go out together. And that's not all."

*Go out together?*

One by one, she pulled out a pair of tan slacks, a purple, long-sleeved blouse, a sequined tee shirt, a beige sports bra, a pair of matching beige panties, and two pairs of white socks. She was delighted with herself.

"I can't thank you enough," said Yasmin. She was close to tears of gratitude. *Did she really say that we would go out together?*

"You must try them on, but first I imagine you would like to take a proper bath. I don't suppose you've had a real bath since you've been here, have you?"

Wide-eyed with gratitude, Yasmin responded, "No, I would love a bath."

"Then gather up those new things and let's go." She knocked on the inside of the door and Abu Salah opened it immediately. "We are going to the bathroom. Keep an eye on things. We'll be out shortly."

Pouri guided Yasmin to the small bathroom at the end of the hall. It consisted of a white, chipped, porcelain tub, a sink, and a toilet with a stained-wood seat. The dark linoleum floor was worn through in spots. Old and cheap. But at least it was clean.

Pouri closed and locked the door behind her, went to the tub, and turned on the hot water tap. "Get out of those clothes," she said over her shoulder. "You're in for a treat."

While the tub filled, Pouri unwrapped a bar of green, scented soap and placed it in the soap dish. She squirted bubble bath into the running water. She looked back at Yasmin, who was standing nervously in her bra and panties, covering herself, looking confused as to what to do next.

"Get those off too. Do you want to bathe in your underwear?"

Embarrassed, Yasmin removed her bra and dropped it on the floor then hesitated a bit before stepping out of her panties. She stood there, nervously covering her breasts with one hand while the other attempted to cover her pubic area. Finally, she sighed and dropped both hands to her sides and just stood there watching the tub fill.

Pouri knelt beside the tub stirring bubble bath into the water. As the tub filled, she turned toward Yasmin. Her heart sank when she saw this beautiful woman standing nervously and fully exposed in front of her. Long dark hair, deep green eyes, flawless olive skin, ample rose-tipped breasts, flat, toned stomach, a trimmed patch of silky, black pubic hair, slender muscular legs, and perfect, small feet. Yet, she looked pale and too thin—something Pouri had not noticed during their interrogations. It finally dawned on her that Hezbollah was not treating Iran's hostage as well as she had requested. And there was nothing she could do to change this without creating dangerous, politically charged friction. Anger and shame washed over her. Torture, even mild food deprivation, was despicable.

*I am helping them do this to her.*

She abruptly turned away and busily resumed her task of preparing the bath. She dared not look back.

When the tub was half-full, she turned off the water and busily stirred in more bubble bath. She turned back and noticed that Yasmin had not moved. She stood there, arms to her sides, with a strange, inquisitive look on her face.

Pouri, unable to speak, beckoned to Yasmin. She slowly walked toward the tub. When she reached it, she stopped and looked down at Pouri. Their eyes met and they held their gaze. Something small was shifting between them.

Yasmin reached out a hand to steady herself and placed it gently on Pouri's head. She lifted one leg up and into the tub. Pouri reached out to assist and placed a hand on Yasmin's hip, guiding her into the tub.

Yasmin settled into the warm, soapy water and luxuriated in the release of tension that flowed out of her body. She looked over at the still kneeling woman beside her and their eyes locked once again. Yasmin slid down into the tub, submerging her entire body and dunking her head under the soapy water.

She emerged with suds and water streaming from her face and hair.

# CHAPTER 19

MacMurphy was hanging out at the pool of the Hilton Hotel in Nicosia, waiting for news from Kashmiri in Beirut. He was bored and did not like being far from the action. It was difficult not to envy Kashmiri for being in the thick of it.

Kashmiri had been surveilling Nabil's residence for two days, looking for an opportunity to approach the man. But he still hadn't seen him. Either Nabil was not at home, or he simply did not go out very often. Kashmiri had asked MacMurphy if he could make some discreet inquiries at the pharmacy and around the neighborhood, but MacMurphy rejected the idea. MacMurphy explained that inquiries of any sort often came back to bite you. No one else needed to know about their interest in Nabil.

Strict compartmentation was an absolute necessity in an operation like this. MacMurphy instructed Kashmiri to keep up the surveillance. He would just have to continue peeing in a jar.

Although MacMurphy had confidence in Kashmiri's ability to pull off the recruitment of Nabil and his nephew, he was less confident in Kashmiri's ability to carry out the surveillance. He would have liked to engage the services of a professional surveillance team, but compartmentation made this impossible. He would have to make do what he had, and that was Hadi Kashmiri.

MacMurphy also worried about what "Plan B" would be if Nabil decided to reject Kashmiri's offer. Nabil would tell his Hezbollah masters he had been approached. Then they would tell their Iranian masters, who would realize the approach was a total ruse, which would be the end of Kashmiri.

He wondered if Kashmiri realized this fact.

Hezbollah, knowing someone was planning a rescue op, would then move Yasmin to a more secure location, probably in Iran.

Everything rested on the shoulders of Hadi Kashmiri.

■　■　■

Kashmiri was on his third day of surveillance. It was a little before nine o'clock in the morning. He was pouring a second cup of tea from a large thermos bottle when the door to the apartment building opened and a man in a wheelchair struggled through.

He felt a surge of adrenaline and splashed hot tea onto his lap. He struggled to compose himself, set the thermos aside, wiped the hot tea from his lap, and bolted out of the car.

He watched Nabil Nassar maneuver the wheelchair out onto the sidewalk and turn up Massaken Street. Moments later, he entered the Al Bouchrieh Pharmacy. Heart pounding, Kashmiri tucked the manila envelope full of money under his arm and headed toward it.

He pulled open the pharmacy door and stood for a moment, surveying the interior. Nabil was nowhere to be seen. He headed up the aisle directly in front of him. At the end of the aisle, he came upon the prescription drug section. Two pharmacists in white smocks were working behind a long counter. One of them was assisting Nabil.

Kashmiri lingered in the aisle, pretending to examine the merchandise while always keeping one eye on Nabil. Nabil was dressed in black slacks and a white, tight-fitting polo that displayed his huge, muscular arms. He was a rugged man with a large, crooked nose, an easy smile and longish dark hair tussled in a carefree way.

He smiled broadly as he accepted his package from the pharmacist, who thanked him by name, and wheeled away from the counter back up the aisle toward the exit. Kashmiri hurried up the parallel aisle and met him at the front of the store. He stood between the exit and the oncoming wheelchair, reached out his hand and said, "You're Nabil Nassar! How are you? Do you remember me?"

Surprised and a bit wary, Nabil took Kashmiri's outstretched hand and replied, "You look familiar, but..."

"Of course, you don't remember me. It's been years. We used to play football together. But now I'm old and I've gained a few pounds. And I never was very good at the game anyway." Kashmiri placed his hands over his stomach and laughed. "I heard the pharmacist say your name and then I recognized you."

"Well, I've changed as well," said Nabil, pointing bitterly to his wheelchair.

"Yes, I heard about that, your accident, I mean..."

Anxious to get Nabil out of the pharmacy and away from prying eyes, Kashmiri pushed open the door and held it. Nabil wheeled himself through the door with strong arms and spun the chair around to face Kashmiri when he reached the sidewalk.

"It was a pleasure seeing you again, Mister..."

"Kashmiri, Hadi Kashmiri."

Nabil put his hand to his forehead. "That name is familiar. Hadi Kashmiri..."

"Come have a cup of tea with me, Nabil. Unless you are in a hurry to get someplace?"

"No, I should be getting back, but thank you for the invitation." He turned his wheelchair in the direction of his apartment.

Kashmiri's heart sank. "Couldn't you spare ten minutes for an old admirer?"

Nabil turned back and looked up at Kashmiri. After a moment he said, "Well...okay. I am never in much of a hurry these days." He indicated his legs and shook his head. "There's a good café just up the road." Nabil nodded in a direction further up the street.

"Wonderful," said Kashmiri. "Would you like a push?"

"No, no thank you. I'm fine."

Nabil gave the wheels a strong push and headed up the street. Kashmiri hurried to keep up. When they reached the café, Kashmiri led Nabil to a table near the sidewalk but away from other customers.

When they were seated and had ordered, Kashmiri decided to get directly to the point. He leaned forward and placed a hand on Nabil's arm. "There is actually something I would like to discuss with you, Mr. Nassar."

"Nabil. Please call me Nabil."

"Yes, of course, and please call me Hadi." He hesitated a moment to punctuate what he was about to say. "Nabil, I have a very important message for you, a message from a very important person in Iran."

Confused, he replied, "Iran? I don't know anyone in Iran."

Kashmiri smiled and nodded. "But there are people in Iran who know you. They sent me to find you. But before I get into that, I need your assurance that you won't repeat what I am about to say under any circumstance."

"But…I don't understand…"

"I will explain everything to you. But what I am about to relate to you is very sensitive. So, if you give me your word that you won't reveal what I am about to say, I can continue."

Nabil shook his head and ran his fingers through his wavy hair. "I don't know. This is very strange…"

"Look, you know my name, and you know I am Iranian. You can check me out. Ask around. My relationship with the Iranian leadership is well known in Beirut. I maintain a residence in Tehran and I travel there frequently. I help the Iranian leadership with all kinds of things outside of Iran."

"Outside of Iran? What do you mean?"

Kashmiri took a sip of tea and gently set the cup down in front of him, never taking his eyes off Nabil. "Most Iranians do not have the ease of travel I have. I am what they call an 'overseas Iranian.' I have an Iranian passport and a British passport. I can do things outside of Iran that a normal Iranian cannot. Do you understand?"

Still confused, Nabil replied, "Yes, I think so."

"Good. Now I want to be very frank with you. You can check me out all you want later. But right now you must promise not to reveal to anyone what my message is to you. If you can't agree to this, I cannot continue."

Nabil studied the man sitting across from him. He was very smooth, very convincing. He did not doubt that Kashmiri could be an Iranian emissary, but this was all very odd. He did recall having heard that Hadi Kashmiri worked for the Iranians, but that was a very long time ago.

"Yes or no, Nabil. I need to have your word before I can continue. Those are my instructions from the Iranian leadership."

"What Iranian leadership?" asked Nabil.

"This is right from the top. The Ayatollah Khamenei himself has signed off on this approach."

"The supreme leader? He wants my help?"

"He needs your help. You are the only one who can help."

Nabil's head spun. His curiosity was sparked. There was no way he could stop now. He needed to know more. After all, he could always decline whatever it was they wanted him to do.

"Okay, I agree. I will not divulge to anyone what you are about to say to me. I promise in the name of Allah."

Kashmiri sat back in his chair and took another sip of tea while he collected his thoughts. Then he leaned forward, solemnly placed both hands on Nabil's arms, and squeezed for emphasis. "That's enough for me, Nabil. I was told I could trust you, and I do."

Kashmiri reflected for another moment and then began. "A couple of weeks ago, on the orders of the Iranian leadership, your colleagues in Hezbollah kidnapped an American spy. A young woman who was collecting information on our nuclear program. She is being held in a safe house in Beirut for interrogation."

"I heard something about that," said Nabil.

"Yes, the story has been reported in the press."

"But how can I help? I am not active any longer as you can see." He indicated his wheelchair.

"You are in an excellent position to help. That is why you were selected. Her jailer is Abu Salah—you know him—and Abu Salah's driver is your nephew, Walid."

Nabil's eyes widened. "I, um, I don't understand."

"Let me explain. Ayatollah Khamenei is a very 'hands on' leader. And this American spy is extremely important to him and the rest of the Iranian leadership. And, well, this is very delicate—you must understand, a delicate matter..."

"Yes, go on..."

"Yes, a delicate matter. You see, he does not fully trust Hezbollah to keep this extremely important Iranian asset safe and secure. Especially Abu Salah, who is a bit of a, shall we say, Neanderthal. Surely, you must understand this concern. Hezbollah can sometimes be, well, a bit heavy-handed and sloppy..."

"Well, I don't know about that. But why don't they bring this spy to Iran?"

Kashmiri sensed that the hook was in. Nabil was becoming involved in the process. In a low, conspiratorial voice, he said, "Exactly. That is the plan. But we are not there yet. Hezbollah has control of this spy and is reluctant to give her up. It's a delicate issue and we must maintain some balance..."

"Balance?"

"Work with Hezbollah but keep a degree of control. To do this we need to be kept informed of Hezbollah's every move concerning the spy. That's where you come in."

"Why me? Why don't you ask Abu Salah?"

Kashmiri shook his head, "No, no, Abu Salah is the main problem. He is a thug and not to be trusted."

Nabil nodded, "Yes, indeed. He is a stupid thug. Not very bright at all."

"So now you understand." Kashmiri smiled and spread his arms wide, welcoming Nabil into the conspiracy. "Your role will be to monitor Abu Salah's movements through your nephew and report back to me.

I will in turn report your findings to the Ayatollah through his representatives in the Ministry of Intelligence."

Nabil nodded. He understood fully but had a question. "Why don't you just ask Walid? He is already on the scene."

"Great question. I actually asked them that and they said it was a matter of trust. They trust you and have confidence in you, but they do not know Walid yet. They want you to act as an intermediary between them and Walid. Walid respects you..."

"Ah, sure, I understand now. I can do that." He was excited now. He was back in the game.

Kashmiri grinned broadly and lifted the manila envelope from the seat next to him. He handed it to Nabil with both hands and a slight bow. "You will incur expenses and you deserve to be compensated for your time, so this is a down payment from Ayatollah Khamenei. You might want to share some of it with Walid. There is more where this came from."

Confused, Nabil opened the package and looked inside. When he looked up there were tears in his large brown eyes.

# CHAPTER 20

MacMurphy was bored. He had set things in motion in Beirut and they were playing themselves out while he cooled his heals in Nicosia. He decided to get out of the hotel, drive across the "Green Line" to the Turkish side of the city, and visit the majestic Bellapaix Abbey.

Throughout his many travels in Cyprus, he had frequently visited the abbey, and it never ceased to impress him and instill a sense of calm in him.

MacMurphy loved old rocks. So much history. And this pile of rocks was very old and contained a lot of history. The original site of the abbey was built by the bishops of Kyrenia as a place of refuge from Arab raids in the seventh and eighth centuries. The current structure, consisting of a church, cloister, and several outlying monastic buildings, was built in the thirteenth century. Today, Bellapaix overlooks the harbor town of Kyrenia and the Mediterranean Sea.

It was midday when MacMurphy arrived. There were no crowds of tourists in Northern Cyprus, though it was the most beautiful part of the island. He enjoyed wandering through the ruins practically alone.

Northern Cyprus was also home to several Crusader castles that MacMurphy had visited. He enjoyed walking among their ruins without being molested by hordes of obnoxious tourists. It left him free to think about Richard the Lionheart and other events that had taken place within their walls over the centuries.

Cyprus is rich in history but a sad place. The island was divided in 1974 when the Greek Cypriot population, led by Archbishop Makarios III, tried to annex the island to Greece. This did not sit well with the Turkish Cypriot population, so Turkey invaded, occupied the top third of the island, and declared a separate, Turkish Cypriot state.

Realizing that Greeks and Turks were like oil and water, the Turks then demanded that all Greek Cypriots living in the northern third of the island abandon their homes and businesses and head south to the Greek sector. All Turkish Cypriots living in the south were forced to move north to the Turkish sector. The Turks got the better part of the deal.

The United Nations then created an armed barrier along the border to keep the ethnic Greeks and Turks from killing each other. That "Green Line" barrier, patrolled by the United Nations, exists to this day. The result is that the "Turkish Republic of Northern Cyprus," which is only recognized by one state, Turkey, has remained relatively unchanged since then.

MacMurphy reflected on all of this as he wandered through the ruins of the Bellapaix Abbey, touching the ancient stones and reflecting on their history.

He ate a light lunch in the small, uncrowded restaurant within the walls of one of the monastic buildings and thought about Kashmiri's successful recruitment of Nabil Nassar. Kashmiri could not go into detail over the phone, but MacMurphy heard enough to know that Nabil was on board.

The next steps had to be carefully planned and orchestrated. It was hard enough orchestrating a recruitment operation when a case officer worked directly with a prospective agent. But, there were many extra moving parts in this operation; too many people were involved in the daisy chain. The more complicated an operation was, the easier it fell apart when things started to go wrong.

While MacMurphy trusted Kashmiri's instincts, Kashmiri did not have the training of a case officer. He was not a professional. And Nabil was only the first link in the daisy chain. Clear and secure communication still needed to be established throughout the chain. Specific questions would have to pass down the daisy chain from MacMurphy to Kashmiri, from Kashmiri to Nabil, and then from Nabil to Walid. And those promptings—questions to which the Ayatollah would reasonably want answers—had to be consistent with their cover story.

Then there was the added problem of getting the information back up the chain to MacMurphy. Would Walid's reports be accurate and timely after going through the ears and mouths of two other people?

There were so many things to consider, so many things that could go wrong, and so much room for misinterpretation.

# CHAPTER 21

The interrogations of Yasmin continued for several hours each day, but things had definitely changed. The dynamic between the two women was noticeably different.

Pouri's questions were relatively non-threatening and focused almost exclusively on Yasmin's activities in Iran. These were the very things Yasmin had vowed to conceal. So, Yasmin would talk at length about her visits without revealing anything about the handling of her main asset, XOJAZZ.

Being held in solitary confinement had its advantages; it gave the prisoner lots of time to think. And Yasmin had used her time for just that purpose.

There were certain things she knew Pouri knew, certain things she was unsure if Pouri knew, and other things she was pretty darn sure Pouri did not know.

The things she wasn't sure if Pouri knew were her developmental contacts in Beirut and Tehran. Fortunately, none of those contacts were recruited assets. And none of them knew or suspected her true CIA affiliation.

The one operation she was pretty certain Pouri didn't know about was the only recruited agent she handled in Tehran. This agent, this one case, was her *raison d'etre*, the sole reason for her assignment. And she was 99 percent certain the source had not been compromised. Aside from one hasty brush pass that took place almost nine months ago during her first trip to Tehran, she had never met directly with the asset.

XOJAZZ was a high-level nuclear engineer working at the Tehran Nuclear Research Center. He was handled with extreme care, as any denied area asset would be. This meant little or no physical contact between case officer and agent within the denied area, which in this case was Iran.

All communication with the agent was accomplished through dead drops, secret writing, chalk signals, one-way encrypted burst transmissions and other sophisticated—and some not so sophisticated—means of clandestine agent communications.

Yasmin's primary mission was to travel to Tehran, always under the cover of her alias, to scout out potential dead-drop and signal sites, provide headquarters with detailed casings of them, and then load or unload the sites and set the signals as required. Headquarters maintained parallel electronic communications directly with the asset via encrypted burst radio transmissions.

When she wasn't casing for possible sites or performing her operational tasks—which included unloading dead-drop sites of voluminous documents from XOJAZZ, photographing them and reducing them to microfiche—she lived out her cover as a Jordanian pharmaceutical representative. That cover helped expand her number of developmental contacts in Tehran. In the clandestine trade, creating this expansion was called spotting and assessing new agent talent.

Yasmin spent every waking hour of her captivity concocting a reasonable cover story to explain her mission in Tehran and Beirut. It was a story designed to lead Pouri as far away from the nuclear subject and XOJAZZ as possible. She felt confident she could pull it off, especially given the way her relationship with Pouri was evolving. As long as Pouri kept the interrogations on the present track without the use of torture or enhanced techniques, she could survive this ordeal.

As with all good cover stories, Yasmin's had to be believable and verifiable. It also had to be something that would make her presence in Iran seem less important. For example, spying on Iran's nuclear plans was an extremely sensitive issue for Iranians, but spying on Hezbollah's involvement in drug trafficking that could be linked to Iran was another thing altogether. It was even possible that the Iranian Ayatollahs would look askance at this kind of behavior from their close ally.

Yasmin decided to use this classified operation run by the Drug Enforcement Agency as the cover story for her nuclear spying. Before leaving for Cyprus, she had been briefed on the operation at headquarters and had been instructed to keep her eyes and ears open for any information about it. She also knew that portions of the operation had recently been leaked to the press, something that would enhance her story's credibility in the eyes of the Iranians. After all, most DEA operations were not all that secret anyway.

So, when Pouri hammered her for the umpteenth time about her contacts in Tehran, she dropped her head, sighed, and said, "Let me explain something to you, Pouri. Your country and mine are not so estranged on certain issues. In fact, if we just tried a little harder, we might be able to cooperate on some things of mutual concern."

"Of course," said Pouri, "but your country is bound and determined to deny us access to nuclear technology, and that's wrong, flat wrong."

"My job here has nothing to do with nuclear matters. I know nothing about that. I'm only a junior officer. This is my first overseas tour. But that's all you can think about, nuclear matters. A deal has been hammered out between our two countries and, like it or not, it is done. We are not going back on our word. And there are other things that concern us..."

Pouri stood up from behind the little table and walked slowly around the room. When she turned back, she placed both hands on the table and looked down into Yasmin's eyes. "Then what? What other things?"

"Like drug trafficking and money laundering operations run by your lackeys with your full knowledge and consent."

Pouri slapped her hand on the table. "What are you talking about? What lackeys? With whose knowledge and consent?" She sat back down heavily.

"Surely, you are aware of the recent arrests that have resulted from the DEA's Operation Cassandra?"

Pouri shook her head. "Never heard of it."

"Let me fill you in. Things are coming to a head. Unraveling, you might say." Yasmin paused to collect her thoughts. "This operation has been going on for a little over two years and I have been directly involved in it, fully involved in it."

"What's your role?"

"Finding connections between Hezbollah and Iran."

"And have you found any?"

"Nothing solid yet, but there are indications..."

"What kind of indications?"

"Surely, you've heard of some of the groups that are part of Hezbollah's External Security Organization?"

Pouri shook her head again.

"Well, to give you some background, the ESO was founded by Imad Mughniyeh. You know, the little prick who blew up the U.S. Embassy and the Marine Barracks here in Beirut. He also tortured and killed Bill Buckley, our station chief. You know who I'm talking about."

Pouri nodded. "Yes, I know who you're talking about. I'm sorry..."

"You don't have to be sorry. You just have to know that the United States has a long memory."

"But your people killed Mughniyeh. You dropped a bomb on him in Damascus a few years back."

"May he rot in hell..."

Pouri rubbed her chin and looked up. "So, what's Mughniyeh and these groups got to do with Iran? Everyone knows Hezbollah is just a bunch of thugs. Yes, they take some direction from Iran, but we can't control everything they do, can we?"

"No, but when your people are involved in and actually profit from Hezbollah's illegal activities, that's where you should draw the line."

Pouri was taking notes rapidly. When she was finished scribbling she looked up. "Continue. Which Iranians are involved?"

"I don't have any names for you yet...Look, for a long time Hezbollah has been working with several South American drug cartels, including *La Oficina de Envigado*, to supply cocaine to the U.S. and Europe.

The proceeds from this drug trade are laundered through a scheme called the Black Market Peso Exchange. Ever heard of that?"

Pouri continued rapidly taking notes and shook her head without looking up. "No. Go on."

"Well, one of the ESO groups controls other money-laundering schemes, which in turn provide both revenue and weapons for Hezbollah. This helps finance its terrorist activities around the world. I should say it supplements the financial support it receives from Iran. Can you really look me in the eye and say Iran is not aware of this?"

"I, well…I don't know…"

"That's naïve of you to say. You know the answer. And that is exactly what I'm trying to prove. Maybe you can help me do that. You see, the latest efforts against Hezbollah have uncovered a network of couriers busily transferring drug money from Europe to the Middle East. Much of this money has been traced going through Lebanon, where Hezbollah siphons off a large chunk. A large portion of what remains then moves on to Iran."

Looking up from her notepad, Pouri asked, "How do you know all this? Who are your sources?"

"The DEA and their counterparts in France, Germany, Italy, and Belgium have recently arrested several top leaders of the ESO group. This was the result of our work over the past year or so."

"Again, can you be more specific? Give me some names."

"Sure, the main guy is a creep named Mohammad Noureddine. He's a Lebanese money-launderer who transferred funds to Hezbollah through his company, Trade Point International. He has direct ties to terrorist elements in Lebanon, Iraq, and Syria. He and two of his cohorts—Hamdi Zaher El Dine was one of them, I don't recall the other guy's name—admitted that they had used criminal drug proceeds to fund terrorism and political instability in the region."

"And Iran is aware of all this?"

"You'll just have to ask them that question, won't you?" They stared at each other before Yasmin continued, "I would start by asking Foreign Affairs Minister Mohammad Javad Zarif. After all, he's a big fan of Imad

Mughniyeh. He even visited Mughniyeh's grave to pay his respects not too long ago…"

■ ■ ■

Pouri left the safe house and started walking toward her car. The air was humid and the streets were alive with the dredges of Lebanese society. Why did Hezbollah always choose the worst neighborhoods for their safe houses?

Actually, she knew the answer to that question. That's where they belong, that's where they are comfortable, and that's where their supporters live.

She reached her car, a dusty little Ford Focus rental, and the same three little urchins she had hired to watch it that morning came running toward her, hands outstretched, legs jumping with glee, throats yelling for their money. One of them began polishing her windshield with a greasy rag, smiling at her broadly, displaying a gap where his two front teeth used to be.

She gave each one of them a Lebanese pound and they took off, happily waving their newfound wealth in the air. She inspected her car, noticed it did not have any new scratches or dents, and wondered what it would have looked like if she hadn't paid the extortion.

She felt safe again when she was in her car and on her way out of the western slums. As she headed toward her middle-class *pied-à-terre* in East Beirut near the corniche, she realized she was happy to be out of that dingy prison apartment. It was strange that she should feel so liberated after leaving her place of business.

She wanted to believe Yasmin but wasn't sure if she could. Her MOI bosses in Iran were exerting a lot of pressure to finish the interrogation quickly. If she didn't gather true intelligence and finish the interrogation as soon as possible, they would replace her with one of their torturers. And she did not want that to happen.

Knuckles white on the steering wheel, she decided to take a short walk along the corniche before reporting the information she had received from Yasmin. She parked a mile away from her apartment and began walking at a brisk pace. The wind ghosted across the shimmering sea and swept past her in waves, forcing her to cross her arms and huddle as she marched. Noticing a father enjoying the view with his two young children not far ahead, she stopped and turned to glare at the beautiful water below. She looked up at the pale blue sky and felt her hand tighten on the metal railing that kept pedestrians from falling into the sea. The sky was the same color as the shirt he always wore.

When she was young, her father traveled for work and her mother frequently accompanied him. While they were away, Pouri stayed with her mother's brother, who worked from home to take care of his wife. She was soft-spoken and always very kind to Pouri when her multiple sclerosis didn't restrict her to a bed.

Looking after herself at her uncle's house suited Pouri just fine. She enjoyed inventing games only she knew the rules to. But she was not the only one.

The first time it happened, she was lying in the middle of a rug trying to spot animals in its intricate patterns. The object of the game was to find the most threatening beast and sit on it before it clawed its way through the rug's thin fibers and ate her. She was darting between a cheetah and a bear when she noticed a salamander eating a deer out of the corner of her eye. For some reason, the audacity of the small creature made her laugh, and she collapsed on top of it in a fit of giggles. That's when her uncle started screaming.

He was standing in the doorway, wearing the same black business suit and blue, buttoned-down shirt he always wore. He accused her of never shutting up, of always interrupting his work, and of making her aunt's migraines worse. She lay still as stone as he charged toward her. For some reason, her entire body went numb. She couldn't move an inch, not even when he stood over her with the belt.

He never broke the skin and always made sure the damage was superficial enough to disappear before her parents returned. He threatened to hurt her in worse ways if she ever told anyone, but she still thought of telling her parents every time they took her home. Whenever she tried, a lump would grow in her throat and words would abandon her. She hated herself for not being braver and for feeling ashamed of something that wasn't her fault.

She was slow to learn that begging and crying did not stop the beatings. But she was quick to learn that her uncle had no patience for children, especially when they accidentally dropped things, or refused to eat food they didn't like, or laughed too loudly. She tried her best to learn the rules that would keep her safe, but they seemed to change daily. Something that wouldn't bother her uncle one day would incense him the next.

Pouri learned too late that chaos has no rules.

When she was thirteen, her uncle died in a car crash. At the funeral, her mother explained that he was bipolar and that his manic episodes sometimes made him a reckless driver. To this day, she could not articulate the thoughts that had passed through her mind at that moment.

Standing over his fresh grave, Pouri decided to bury his evil along with his body. What difference would the truth make now? The damage was already done. Denying his memory the sordid pleasure of tormenting her in the future was the only revenge she could achieve.

But thoughts of her aunt still haunted her. She was never present when the abuse happened, but hadn't she heard Pouri scream? How could her uncle have kept such behavior a secret?

Maybe he didn't. Maybe her aunt's multiple sclerosis wasn't the only thing that kept her bedridden.

A child laughed, and it brought Pouri back to the present. She watched as the father shepherded his children further down the corniche. Pouri turned and started walking back to her car, lost in thought.

She wanted no part of torture. But this was a minority view in Iran's Ministry of Intelligence. Just the thought of it being applied to Yasmin made her wince. She had convinced her bosses that torture would not be necessary in this case, and so far she had been correct. At least she thought so.

The shock and feeling of despair that Yasmin exhibited right after her abduction, combined with the isolation in the days that followed, appeared to have had their desired effect. And her malnourishment seemed to aid this process. When she was allowed to bathe and change into clean clothes, her whole attitude changed. Yasmin became more cooperative, if in fact she was telling the truth.

Pouri hoped so. She knew Yasmin was probably holding some things back—this was just human nature—but she did not want to harm the intelligent woman she had come to respect and admire. No, she would not hurt Yasmin. She would not hurt anyone the way she had been hurt.

But how could she protect Yasmin from the interrogator that would surely follow if she hadn't been honest?

Well, she wouldn't have to worry about that for another two or three days. It would take them that long to evaluate the most recent information Yasmin had provided. Pouri hoped it would all check out.

# CHAPTER 22

Maggie sat across from Santos in his GSR office in Fort Lauderdale. He asked, "How's Mac doing?"

"He's still hanging out in Cyprus, probably working on his tan at the Hilton pool, eating too much and visiting old ruins."

Santos laughed, "You've certainly got his number. I'll bet that's exactly what he's doing out there."

"But while he was lounging by the pool, his asset, Hadi Kashmiri, was doing great things."

She briefed him on Kashmiri's recruiting accomplishments. Santos listened intently and when she was finished, he let out a long breath of air. "Wow! That Kashmiri guy is super. And you brought him to us, didn't you? You deserve a medal for this."

"No, the one who deserves the medal is Mac. He's the one who pulled all the strings. But we aren't there yet. We're still waiting to see what will happen after Nabil's meeting with Walid. I'm pretty confident Walid will buy the story. Nabil certainly did, but you never know..."

"You mean, that the Ayatollah is behind the whole thing?"

"Exactly, and whether the guy can keep a secret. If he starts bragging to his Hezbollah buddies, we're dead in the water."

Santos chuckled, "Interesting choice of words—dead in the water! If he takes the money, we'll be fine. Nabil will share some of his new-found wealth with Walid, won't he?"

"I certainly hope so. That was the plan. We'll find out soon enough."

Santos stood up, walked to the window and gazed out at the Intra-coastal Waterway bustling with white yachts below. "So, what's the next step? We wait?"

Maggie shook her head and joined him at the window. "No. In fact, we may be running out of time."

"What do you mean?"

"Rothmann called yesterday. He's worried, really worried. He asked a lot of questions about our progress, and I filled him in as best I could over the phone. We're both using throwaways, but still..."

"What did he say?"

"Well, he's following the intercepts, you know."

Santos nodded. "I assume we're pretty well plugged in? What did the DDO learn?"

"We're pretty well plugged in, but it could be better. He said there's a fair amount of chatter between Hezbollah and Iran, and some of it appears to be about this case. It seems that Iran is unhappy about the pace of the interrogations and wants to bring our gal to Tehran."

"Ouch, that would not be good."

"No, not at all. Hezbollah is against it. They're guarding their turf, which is good for us. It looks like they're arguing that the interrogator is Iranian, so there is no need to bring her to Iran."

Santos blanched. "An Iranian interrogator? You're sure?"

"That's what it sounds like."

"So, the Ministry of Intelligence is definitely controlling the operation. That's good news and bad news. Good news because the Iranians will probably take better care of their hostage than the Hezbollah thugs would, but bad news because it means they know they have a very important prisoner in their hands."

Maggie tucked an errant strand of graying hair behind her ear and looked up at him over her glasses. "They know what they have," she said with certainty.

"Then I'd better get out there right now."

"Not so fast! We've got some preparations to take care of first."

"What preparations?"

"Well, think about it. If you're going out there to rescue this damsel in distress, you're going to need some support."

"We need to know where the hell she is. That's what we need."

"Yes, that's the most important thing. And Mac is working on it as we speak. But once we know where she is, you guys will still have to figure out how to get her out of Lebanon."

"Yeah, you're right," said Santos a bit sheepishly. "We'll need an exfiltration plan."

"And a capture plan."

"Yes, we'll need weapons and a boat."

"Now you're thinking."

# CHAPTER 23

Walid showed up at his uncle's apartment a little past eleven o'clock in the evening. He was dressed in a traditional white *dishdasha* man-dress and black shoes. An attractive man in his late thirties, he sported longish black hair and a slender but athletic physique. He was happy to see his uncle after such a long time and they embraced warmly.

Nabil fixed them tea and they settled into comfortable chairs in a sparsely furnished living room. Walid complained that his boss demanded too much of his time and wanted Walid to be constantly at his beck and call.

"So, you are not so happy with your current work?"

"No, uncle, it is quite boring. I am nothing more than a driver for a thankless idiot. I want to be a fighter, like you were. But for the past few months I've been nothing but a flunky for this moron. You know him. Abu Salah."

Nabil flinched at the word "were." It was true, he was no longer a fighter. Just an old cripple in a wheelchair. "Oh yes, I know him. You are right. He is very strict, very old school. Not a pleasant man."

"And right now he does nothing but stay in an apartment. He is watching over someone..."

"What do you mean, watching over someone?"

Walid thought for a moment before responding, "I'm not supposed to talk about it. It's a huge secret."

Nabil nodded, took a long sip of tea and thoughtfully placed his cup on the coffee table in front of him. He looked up at Walid and said, "That's why I asked you over here. There is a problem, a very serious problem. And you and I have been asked to help."

"Help? I cannot help with anything. I'm just a chauffeur these days."

"You happen to be in a very important position right now, a very important position. That's why I've been asked to seek your assistance. I've been told what you are doing."

Walid put his hands up. "You can't know. Only a small number of cadres know, and they are all very senior Hezbollah officers. Except for me, of course..."

"Don't sell yourself short, nephew. You are very important, and you are part of a very important operation. You are a part of a small group of people who transport, guard, and feed an extraordinarily important asset, an American CIA spy. Did you know that?"

Walid squirmed in his chair and looked at his uncle with wide eyes. "I, I...How do you know this?"

"I have been told by someone much higher than Abu Salah or Abu Salah's bosses or their bosses in Hezbollah. I have been chosen to talk to you in the strictest confidence by the supreme leader himself."

"The Ayatollah? In Iran?"

"Yes, that is how far up this goes in the chain of command. The Ayatollah and his people in the intelligence directorate have asked me to speak privately with you. They chose me because I am your uncle and because I brought you into Hezbollah."

Walid's eyes grew wide in disbelief and pride. "I will do whatever he asks. I will die before I let him down. Please, you must convey to him my sincere appreciation and thanks for the trust and confidence he has placed in me and you."

"I knew you would feel that way." Nabil smiled, reached across the table and grasped both of Walid's hands. "We are in this together, you and me. No one else can know about this. Understand? May I have your pledge?"

"You have my solemn pledge, uncle. I say this in Allah's name..."

# CHAPTER 24

Maggie was no stranger to operational planning. Her many years in the operations directorate, especially the ones spent in the ranks of the lofty senior intelligence service, provided her with ample on-the-job training in the planning and execution of clandestine operations.

She knew instinctively that any rescue operation would require reliable transportation for exfiltration. And given the location of Beirut on the coast, it did not take a genius to know a yacht would be the best choice.

Flipping through the Rolodex of her mind, Maggie tried to think of a contact with access to a suitable oceangoing yacht but came up blank. Then she thought of Buck Herring, the pilot who had flown them in and out of Roatán on a sensitive exfiltration operation a few months ago. Herring was in the business of transporting people in and out of dark places without a trace, often for the CIA. He had orchestrated hundreds of infiltration and exfiltration operations for the CIA and other more nefarious clients. If anyone knew someone in the maritime field who could do the same thing, it would be Buck Herring. He had been in the "transporting" business for a long time. It was hard to walk away from such a lucrative business model. People will pay a pretty penny to appear and disappear like magic.

She called Herring and explained what was required: a yacht big enough and fast enough to carry three or four passengers and some sensitive cargo between Beirut and Cyprus black—without going through customs in either location. The captain had to be reliable, discreet, and willing to take a few risks.

Herring claimed he knew one or two people who could fit the bill, but he would need time to secure everything. He said he would make a few calls and get back to her in a day or so. Maggie asked him to be quick about it.

The following morning Herring called back.

He recommended a man he had worked with before, one who also had Agency connections. Herring explained that his friend, Nikos Fotopolous, had assisted the CIA in the capture of the terrorist Fawaz Yunis, a lieutenant of Hezbollah's Imad Mughniyeh.

The operation had taken place in international waters off the coast of Cyprus back in 1987. Maggie remembered it well. At the time, she was a junior officer in the CIA's fledgling Counterterrorism Center, working for Rothmann and Dewey Clarridge. She had watched the operation unfold from the CTC Watch Center at Langley.

Fawaz Yunis was lured by a CIA asset to Fotopolous's yacht, which was drifting in the Mediterranean a couple miles east of Limassol. The bait was a suitcase full of one-hundred-dollar bills and the promise of a huge drug deal. When the small boat carrying Yunis arrived at the yacht, he was arrested by two huge, seasick FBI agents who slammed him to the deck so hard they broke both his wrists. As they were cuffing him, Yunis looked up in fear and asked, "Are you guys Mossad?" When they replied that they were American FBI agents and read him his rights, he sighed in relief and muttered, "Thank God."

Nikos Fotopolous observed all of this in great amusement from the bridge of his yacht.

The CIA's original plan was to have two female and two male FBI agents on the yacht to welcome Yunis. The women were supposed to be wearing skimpy bikinis and waving as Yunis pulled alongside the yacht. The two bulky, male FBI agents were supposed to remain out of sight until the last minute.

But nothing went as planned. None of the FBI agents were sailors. So, even in the calm waters of the Mediterranean, they all became seasick. During the two-plus hour wait for Yunis, with the yacht gently pitching and yawing in the sea, they spent most of their time below deck in one of the two heads, taking turns puking into the toilets.

By the time Yunis arrived the two women were so ill they refused to come out of the heads. And the two men, weakened by nausea, just wanted to get the job over with as quickly as possible, hence the rough handling when Yunis climbed aboard.

After his arrest, the yacht sped back to the gray-bottomed United States aircraft carrier *Saratoga*. Yunis was then flown to Andrews Air Force Base in a military aircraft.

The arrest was the first under a new anti-terrorism law that permitted United States agents to apprehend terrorist suspects overseas without seeking approval or cooperation from other nations. Yunis was subsequently tried and convicted and remains in a federal prison serving out a life sentence.

After hearing Herring's nomination, Maggie agreed that Nikos Fotopolous was the right man for the job.

Fotopolous was in his seventies, but his years at sea had kept him trim and fit and he was still very active. His home base was Piraeus, Greece. And he now spent most of his time ferrying well-heeled tourists around the Greek Isles. But when Maggie called and offered him an opportunity to get back in the game, he leaped at the chance. Excitement and money are prime motivators for intelligence operatives. "My decks are cleared for you, Maggie," he declared.

Fotopolous was now in possession of a heavily mortgaged, two-year-old Ferretti Altura 840. It was 84.6 feet long with a twenty-foot beam, powered by twin MTU engines. Its top speed was close to thirty knots per hour and its range was 350 nautical miles, more than enough to make the run back and forth from Limassol to Beirut. It could carry up to twenty passengers, so the anticipated three or four would travel in great comfort.

Maggie looked it up. It was a beautiful, Italian-designed yacht. She would not mind spending a few relaxing days on it at all. They agreed it would be perfect for this operation.

The next item on Maggie's list was provisions. She left the food, wine, and alcohol provisioning to Fotopolous and asked Santos to secure the "special" provisions.

Santos reached out to a trusted contact, Bill Barker, who lived a few miles south in the Florida Keys, for guns and ammo. Using a blind phone, he set up the meeting with Barker, stating he was Ralph Callaway and was sent by Tom Willett. Barker recalled the names immediately and invited him down to Islamorada for a meeting.

Rothmann and Santos used the aliases Willett and Callaway a year earlier when they had reached out to Barker. Santos and MacMurphy had needed specialized arms, ammunition, and other essentials for an operation in the Golden Triangle region of northern Thailand. Barker had made a nice profit on the sale and delivery of the arms and equipment.

Santos mentioned that he was looking for equipment that was similar to what he and Bob Humphrey (MacMurphy's alias) had purchased last year. When he arrived at Barker's oceanfront home in Islamorada; Barker already had several guns lined up on his living room couch.

Bill Barker was a big, drawling southerner who was a prized covert asset of the CIA and a long-time contact of Rothman. He had come through for Santos and MacMurphy in their recent Golden Triangle gig, and he would be a perfect asset for this gig as well. Barker was an expert in small arms and ultra-long-range rifles, and he knew how to securely deliver them anywhere in the world without the normal customs red tape.

The big man ushered Santos into a long, sun-filled room overlooking the turquoise Atlantic. "Ah assembled guns like you boys got for that Thailand gig a while back. Not much has changed since then in the way of technology, so I suspect they'll do just fine for whatever y'all got in mind this time around. Of course, it all depends on what you boys are up to on this little adventure."

Santos stood in front of the couch, admiring the display and nodding in approval. "Good thinking, Bill. This looks about right." He glanced over at Barker and said with a wink, "I see you left out the ricin this time."

That quip elicited a guffaw out of Barker. During their last visit, Santos and MacMurphy had purchased many vials of ricin to poison a drug lord's shipment of heroin. "I got it if you need it," he said.

Santos replied with a huge grin, "We won't be needing your pharmaceutical talents this time around."

Neatly arranged on the couch was a magnificent collection: one Noreen 338LM Lapua semi-automatic sniper rifle with a scope and suppressor; two POF 416 5.56mm submachine guns with one hundred round C-Mag drums, suppressors, and night vision lasers; two sets of night vision goggles; two Heckler & Koch MK 23 .45 caliber handguns with quick detach suppressors and holsters; and two Russian-made *Spetsnaz* ballistic knives.

"I think you thought of everything. Well done. Can you get all of this and plenty of ammo to Piraeus, Greece, for us?"

"Piraeus? Y'all gonna do some yachtin'?"

Santos blanched.

"Never mind," Barker laughed. "I know you boys can't talk about anythin' y'all are up to. Just jerkin' your tail…"

Santos smiled and handed him a note with two addresses on it. "Send the shipment to Nikos Fotopolous at the first address in Piraeus. Throw in a couple of Kevlar vests for Bob and me, and night vision gear, and whatever else you think we may need. Send the bill to me at the second address along with your wiring instructions. We'll get you paid immediately."

"I know you boys are good for it. No problem. By the way, how's Humphrey doin'? Give him my regards."

"Bob's doing just fine. And I'm sure he'll appreciate the Lapua rifle in this batch of goodies. I didn't think of it, and I don't think we'll need it, but it will make him real happy just the same."

# CHAPTER 25

Yasmin knew something was wrong the moment Pouri walked into the safe house. Pouri motioned for her to get off the bed and take a seat in her usual place behind the card table. She spoke not a word of greeting and seated herself, head down, on the other side of the table.

Pouri seemed to be thinking about what she was about to say. Finally, she raised her head and locked onto Yasmin's eyes. Suddenly her eyes filled with tears. "They don't believe you," she said, shaking her head in disbelief. "They just don't believe you."

Yasmin reached across the table and grasped both of the woman's hands. Oddly, she felt more concern for Pouri than she did for herself. Even though she knew what this news would mean for her.

She heard herself saying, "It's okay. You tried your best. I know you did. It's okay, Pouri..."

Pouri pulled a tissue from her bag, dabbed at her eyes and blew into it. She got up slowly, walked to the side of the bed, tossed the tissue into a wastebasket and turned to face Yasmin. "I did try. I honestly did. They just think my methods were too...too gentle. They think you are holding information back...important information...I..."

Yasmin stood and went over to Pouri and enveloped her in her arms. Pouri burst into tears once again and stood there, sobbing in Yasmin's arms, rocking back and forth. For some reason, comforting her interrogator seemed natural to Yasmin. Their mutual respect had grown into the kind of admiration sisters shared. And ever since her bath, Yasmin had begun to suspect that Pouri felt guilty about interrogating her.

When Pouri had calmed down, Yasmin asked, "What are they going to do to me? What is going to happen to you? Will I ever see you again?"

Pouri looked deeply into her eyes. "Yes. So many concerns, so many unknowns. I will do my best to protect you. We still have a few days to figure something out."

"That's not a lot of time. Will they torture me? What will they do to me?"

If Pouri had been a smoker, this would have been the time to light up, inhale deeply, and exhale a long, slow stream of smoke. It would give her time to collect her thoughts and think before responding.

Instead, she gulped back a sob that emerged from deep within her and said, "They will make you admit you collected information on our nuclear program, and they will make you give us the names of all your sources. This is what they think your mission was, and they will not stop until they have all the evidence they need to back up their belief."

Yasmin shuddered. "Then you have to help me escape, Pouri. You must."

# CHAPTER 26

Kashmiri dug into an enormous steak while summarizing his most recent meeting with Nabil to MacMurphy. "So, that's where we are. We've got a clear path to Walid and Abu Salah through Nabil. Everyone's on board. We're ready to start producing information for you." He grinned broadly. "Now what's your first question?"

MacMurphy tipped his wine glass at Kashmiri. "You really came through for us, Hadi. I owe you." He thought a moment, swished his wine around in the glass and took a long sip of the oaky Bordeaux. "I don't think we have a lot of time. Let's ask Walid to create a sort of diary of his past two weeks with Abu Salah."

"What he did and where he went?"

"Exactly. We need to know where our officer is being held."

Kashmiri brushed his plate away and pushed himself back from the table before responding. "But why don't we just ask him where they are holding her?"

"Because the Ayatollah and his people would probably already know that."

"Good point. Our questions need to make it seem like we only want to check up on Abu Salah and his Hezbollah bosses."

MacMurphy nodded. "Exactly. Our interest is in Hezbollah. Their hostage is only of tangential interest. We need to keep our questions focused on Abu Salah and his activities. That's our cover story."

"I understand. It's a question of how we pose the questions to get the information we desire."

"Right, things that Iran would be interested in."

Kashmiri stood up and prepared to leave. "Okay, I'll head over to Nabil's place right now." He dropped his napkin on the table and stuck out his hand to say goodbye.

"Hold on. Let's give our guys a little incentive to act rapidly." He withdrew an envelope from his back pocket and pushed it over to Kashmiri. "Here's five thousand dollars to grease the skids a bit. Change it into Lebanese Pounds and divide it up among the three of you."

"I'll do better than that. Let's see, five thousand U.S. dollars amounts to about seven and a half million Lebanese Pounds. I'll prepare envelopes for Nabil and Walid with three and a half million pounds in each. I'll keep the spare change and then seal each envelope and address them in Farsi to 'N' and 'W' from 'Your friends in Iran.' Would that work?"

MacMurphy smiled. He was pleased at the way this operation was unfolding. Kashmiri was learning fast and he was resourceful and dependable and honest. The latter quality was especially surprising in this world of cutthroat rug merchants. "That would be perfect. A nice touch…"

■ ■ ■

Kashmiri left the restaurant and drove directly to the Limassol port. There he boarded the last ferry to Beirut, arriving a little before midnight. He decided it was too late to call Nabil that night and took a cab directly to his flat.

The next morning he addressed two plain white envelopes to "N" and "W," carefully printing his message in Farsi to disguise his handwriting, and drove to the kiosk of his favorite moneychanger. There he converted the currency, filled the envelopes, and sealed them.

Two days later, he arranged a meeting with Nabil at their usual café. Kashmiri arrived just as Nabil was maneuvering out of his wheelchair and into a chair at a quiet table. They shook hands over the table as Kashmiri sat down.

After ordering tea and French croissants, a true mix of cultures common in Beirut, Kashmiri pushed the two envelopes across the table. "Put these away."

After glancing at them briefly, Nabil reached over and stuffed the envelopes into a pocket on the side of his wheelchair. "Feels like money," he said.

"It is. Quite a bit of money. From our friends. Something to show their gratitude. They also don't want you to go out of pocket helping them. More than anything though, it's a show of good faith."

Nabil was clearly pleased and humbled by the gesture. "I will not let them down, and I can assure you that Walid will not either. He will do his best to help. Just tell me what our friends need and we will get it for them."

Kashmiri lowered his voice and leaned forward, "As you know, they have reason to believe Abu Salah is not being, shall we say, trustworthy."

Nabil nodded, intensely interested.

Kashmiri said, "They want to know where he goes and what he does. They did not give me any specifics about their suspicions, so we should just give them as much information as possible. In other words, ask Walid to note everything Abu Salah does and every place he goes. Ask him to start with the past week or so. Like a diary of sorts. That will get us started. Once they have that information I'm sure they will have more questions and follow-up requirements."

Nabil said, "I understand."

"When can you get these questions to Walid?"

"I will ask him to come over to my flat on his way home tonight. I will give him your questions and his envelope at that time."

Kashmiri settled back in his chair and took a large bite out of his croissant. He sprayed flakes of the pastry as he replied, "Excellent. And...and when can you see him again to get his report?"

"A few days, maybe...I don't know. When do they need it?"

"I got the impression they were very anxious to have this information. Maybe you could ask him to jot down just the highlights and then maybe get a report to us the following day. What do you think?"

"Well, I guess I could ask him to prepare a report during the day and pass it to me the following evening. Would that be okay?"

Kashmiri was satisfied. "That sounds like an excellent idea. I will meet you back here the day after tomorrow. Same time."

Nabil stuck out a strong, callused hand and they shook on it.

# CHAPTER 27

When MacMurphy received the news that the meeting between Nabil and Kashmiri had gone well, he immediately contacted Maggie and Santos to help coordinate the rescue attempt. Meanwhile, he hoped Nabil would deliver Walid's report to Kashmiri as soon as possible. He recalled that when the CIA was gearing up for the rescue of foreign hostages back in the 1980s, the problem wasn't how to rescue them, it was finding them.

More than one hundred foreigners were taken hostage in Lebanon from 1982 until 1992. Most of them were Americans and Western Europeans. At the instigation of Iran, Imad Mughniyeh and Hezbollah orchestrated the kidnappings. They included CIA Station Chief William Buckley and Marine Colonel William Higgins, both of whom were killed in captivity. Others were University of Beirut President David Dodge, Associated Press Chief Middle East Correspondent Terry Anderson, and an envoy for Anglican Church, Terry Waite.

Hezbollah eventually went so far as to kidnap four Soviet diplomats, but they were released a month later after the KGB retaliated by kidnapping and murdering a key Hezbollah leader. This was proof to MacMurphy and anyone else who was paying attention that swift, lethal retaliation was the key to ending these kinds of terrorist actions.

But the United States chose to dawdle and play Pat-A-Cake with Iran and Hezbollah through diplomatic channels while their hostages rotted in chains and were tortured and murdered. MacMurphy knew that things hadn't changed much since then. The CIA still tried to orchestrate a rescue while negotiations were slogging along. They spent millions on infiltration plans, exfiltration plans, lining up rescue boats, mapping out routes and stocking clandestine warehouses in Beirut full of food, arms and ammunition, medical supplies, vehicles, and other necessary gear. They even selected advance commandos, mostly of Filipino and Middle Eastern descent, who could infiltrate and blend into the Lebanese environment. They studied maps of every house, street, and back alley of Beirut.

But they were never launched. No rescue missions were ever attempted even after fastidious preparations. Why? They needed to locate the hostages before they could rescue them. And this they never could do. This one critical piece of intelligence eluded them.

This was the precise reason why Rothmann decided to enlist the aid of MacMurphy and his team on this rescue mission. MacMurphy was confident that Kashmiri's daisy chain of informants would provide that critical piece of information. He just hoped he would get it in time.

■ ■ ■

Maggie arranged for the secure transfer of $100,000 to Nikos Fotopolous in Piraeus. The money, which came from a numbered account in the Banque Credit Suisse in Bern, Switzerland, an account that had previously been set up by MacMurphy under the alias Frederick Martin, would be a down payment for the indefinite rental and provisioning of the yacht.

Fotopolous agreed to move the yacht to Limassol as soon as he received Bill Barker's shipment. Santos in turn was biting Barker's ankles to get the shipment out to Fotopolous as soon as possible.

To get the shipment to Fotopolous without the knowledge of the authorities in the United States or Greece, Barker flew the arms to Canada via private aircraft where he arranged for a Ugandan diplomat to accept delivery. The diplomat placed the shipment into a diplomatic pouch and sent it on to the Ugandan embassy in London via a commercial flight. Upon arrival in London, the shipment was loaded onto a lorry and driven across the European Union to Piraeus by an embassy staff member. The shipment arrived safely at the dock where Fotopolous's Ferretti was tied up. The whole process took less than a week from the time it left Islamorada in the Florida Keys.

Once the arms and all the provisions were safely aboard, Fotopolous charted a course for Limassol, Cyprus. As requested, he left his two crewmembers on the dock and traveled alone. He told no one what his destination was.

# CHAPTER 28

Three days after Kashmiri gave money to Nabil, the informant called Kashmiri and excitedly requested to meet at their café. Once there, Nabil explained that Walid had come to his apartment late the previous evening. "He said it was the first chance he had to break away from Abu Salah and that Abu Salah was 'busting his balls.' He said, 'He treats me like I'm his personal servant. He wants me with him twenty-four-seven. He can't even wipe his ass without my help!'"

Kashmiri laughed as Nabil continued, "I told him that the Ayatollah's people in Tehran were very pleased he had agreed to help and that keeping tabs on Abu Salah was an extremely high-priority issue."

Kashmiri was anxious. "Did you give him the assignment we discussed?"

"Yes, I explained that they did not tell me why they distrusted Abu Salah but that they clearly do. And I also explained the diary."

"What did he say?" asked Kashmiri.

"He said, 'That's very easy.'" Nabil pushed back in the booth and awaited Kashmiri's praise.

"Excellent work, Nabil. Now we are all on the same page. When can we expect him to complete his first report?"

"He told me there was no need for a report. He said that for the past couple of weeks they've done nothing but guard someone in an apartment in South Beirut. They bring food and other supplies to the apartment and supervise changing guards. That is all they do. He said he spends most of his time just sitting in his car in front of the apartment, waiting for Abu Salah."

Kashmiri looked puzzled. "Just one address?"

"Actually, there are two addresses. The first one was on Old Saida Road in the southeast quarter of Beirut, but then they moved to Lailake Road. That is still in the southern quarter but further west, very close to the airport."

Kashmiri knew Beirut well. For the most part, East Beirut was the Christian Quarter, West Beirut was Sunni Muslim, and the southern suburbs were Shia Muslim. The middle downtown area was the Green Line no-man's land. It made sense that Hezbollah and Iran would choose to operate in the Shia section. "Can you be more specific?" he asked. "What's the house number?"

"Yes, the building is number 67. I have been in the neighborhood. It is in a very bad part of town. Very run down with lots of damage from the fighting that took place there."

"Did Walid describe the building to you?"

"Yes, of course. I asked him that. It's an old building with three stories and an apartment on each floor. They use the apartment on the second level."

"Has Walid ever been inside the building?"

"He said he's been in the lobby to deliver food and packages but never upstairs. He said Abu Salah would never permit that."

"Has Abu Salah ever discussed with Walid what he does inside the apartment?"

Nabil shook his head. "You have to understand…my nephew is just a flunky for Abu Salah. He drives the car and does what he is told. Abu Salah does not confide in him or discuss things with him."

"So, let me get this straight," said Kashmiri. "Walid has no idea what is going on inside the apartment or who is inside it. Is that right?"

"Let me put it this way. He has not been told anything about what's going on in the apartment, but he is not stupid. He has eyes and ears. He knows they are holding someone prisoner in the apartment. And he thinks it's a woman."

Kashmiri blurted out, "Why does he…" and then he caught himself. "Sorry…"

Nabil laughed. "I told you, he brings them supplies—mostly food but other things as well. One time he brought a bottle of Midol tablets and a box of Tampons." Nabil sat back to let that sink in.

"Okay…but what if those things were for one of the jailers or someone else in the apartment?"

"I don't think so. Walid said the only people connected with that apartment are Abu Salah, a grouchy old woman who is well past the age of menstruation, and three rotating male guards who remain out front or in the lobby at all times. Oh yes, and then there's another woman who comes and goes. She appears to be an interrogator. She drives her own car and never spends the night there. She wouldn't need to have that kind of stuff delivered to her."

Kashmiri was excited. "Why does he think she's an interrogator?"

"He said that's the way it looks. She is Iranian, he thinks. She dresses and looks like an Iranian. Middle-aged woman. Quite attractive. Occasionally, she brings packages up. Stays there for hours at a time but doesn't come every day."

Kashmiri had to fight his emotions. He knew he had hit the jackpot for MacMurphy and could hardly restrain himself. But his cover story was the activities of Abu Salah. He took a deep breath, calmed himself, and continued along that line of questioning. "Walid clearly has a keen eye. The Ayatollah will be pleased to know this sensitive assignment is in such capable hands. But now we are completely off topic. When does Abu Salah arrive and when does he depart?"

Kashmiri continued along these lines for another half an hour, feigning interest until he eventually called the meeting to an end. He congratulated Nabil on a job well done and asked him to keep asking Walid for similar updates about Abu Salah.

In truth, he couldn't wait to get out of there so he could call MacMurphy and get back to Cyprus.

# CHAPTER 29

MacMurphy watched through the windows of the Larnaca Airport lounge as the Cyprus Air flight from Athens touched down. While the plane taxied to its gate, MacMurphy walked to the arrivals section to meet Santos.

The first thing MacMurphy noticed was the week's worth of dark beard growth on Santos's face. Other than this unshaven, scruffy quirk, he looked the same. He wore familiar blue jeans, a blue blazer with gold buttons, and a white button-down shirt. Like MacMurphy, he was a bit preppy in his dress. But the man with three advanced engineering degrees from MIT still could not completely disguise the powerful physique beneath his tailored Brooks Brothers exterior. And the beard only added another dimension to his already threatening appearance.

As Santos walked, he towed a black leather valise small enough to fit in the overhead of the plane. Checked luggage was just one more thing to worry about these days.

MacMurphy was happy to have Santos back in the field with him. He had excellent case officer skills, but he had a knack for getting himself into dicey situations, sometimes of his own making. Whenever that happened Santos always seemed to be there to bail him out and save the day.

Once, while they were successfully tracking a vicious drug lord in northern Thailand, MacMurphy let his guard down by celebrating too much and trying to pick up an attractive American tourist. He had drunk way too much wine and cognac and was out of control. Santos managed to get him safely back to their hotel, but later, in the middle of the night, the druggies came looking for them. Santos heard them but could not rouse MacMurphy, who was snoring loudly in an adjacent room in an alcohol-induced slumber. Santos managed to slip out of his room in his undershorts and ambush the thugs as they were in the process of breaking into MacMurphy's room. Santo's quick action saved them that time and many others.

It wasn't just loyalty. It was mutual respect and dependency. They had been through a lot together, and each one felt he needed the other to succeed.

The two friends embraced warmly in the terminal and headed out to the parking lot. Once in MacMurphy's rental car, MacMurphy briefed Santos on the details of the operation during their hour-long drive up to Nicosia.

"Everything's falling neatly into place," he said. "Fotopolous is bringing the yacht down to Limassol from Piraeus along with the provisions and the arms and ammunition you ordered from Barker. We'll be ready to launch as soon as the Ferretti arrives."

"Do we have a plan to get our gal out of there, or will we just wing it like those child recovery jobs?" Santos asked sarcastically.

MacMurphy winced.

"Just kidding." Santos knew that planning was one of MacMurphy's strong suits. He told anyone who would listen that careful planning was the key to success in any operation. But he also knew that the ability to wing it when all else failed was a gift that only the very best case officers possessed. Sometimes things just don't go the way they are planned. "I guess the main thing we need to know is whether she's still at that 67 Lailake Road address."

"We think she is, but you know how that goes. If they decide to move her, they won't announce it in advance. That's what they did last time," said MacMurphy.

Santos thought a minute, looking out the window at the bleak, dusty Cyprus countryside zipping by. "I guess we'll have to do our own casings. The info we have is pretty sketchy."

"Yes, it is. I wish we could talk directly with Walid, but we actually know quite a bit: small building, target apartment on the second floor, one guard at the entrance. And the only people in the apartment are Yasmin Ghorbani, Abu Salah, an old woman in a full, black *burqa* and occasionally the interrogator. We should be able to handle that."

Still concentrating on the dusty, Middle Eastern landscape, Santos reflected, "Sounds almost too easy. Makes me nervous..."

"Would you rather have it the other way?"

"No, but I want a firsthand look myself. I'll feel a lot better then. When's the yacht supposed to get here?"

MacMurphy slowed and pulled onto the off-ramp toward central Nicosia. "Day after tomorrow. I'll give him a call later on the satphone to confirm the exact time. The Ferretti cruises at twenty-plus knots per hour, so unless he hits heavy seas, which is unlikely at this time of year, he should arrive on schedule. As soon as he gets here we'll load up and be on our way."

"We're going in black, right?"

"Black as pitch..."

# CHAPTER 30

Pouri backed away and looked quizzically at Yasmin. "What do you mean, help you escape? You know I cannot do that. I have a husband, two children, and a career. You want me to throw all that away for you?" She softened her tone when she saw Yasmin's terrified eyes. "I would like to help you, and I will do whatever I can to protect you. But you must understand it is not me who is in charge. There are lines I cannot cross. There are limits...

"Hezbollah is in charge of your security, and Iran is in charge of your interrogation. And Hezbollah and Iran do not see eye to eye on everything. Even their goals are different. Hezbollah would like to ransom you for money or a trade while Iran wants you as an intelligence source and possibly a bargaining chip later on. They want to milk you dry and then trade you for some concession or prisoner or whatever..."

Yasmin smiled sadly and said, "Looks like I'm between the proverbial rock and a hard place."

Pouri squeezed her hand. "You certainly are..."

Yasmin pulled her hand back, sat up straight, and asked, "Okay then, you're the expert. What can I expect from now on? Don't pull punches. What's going to happen to me?"

Pouri answered thoughtfully, "I think they will move you to a new location very soon. You have been here almost two weeks. It's time to move. That's Hezbollah's *modus operandi*."

"And what about you?" Yasmin asked.

"I don't know. They are not happy with me. I think they will replace me with another interrogator."

Yasmin flinched and shook her head. "How did it come to this? Iran and America were close allies not that many years ago. Now we are bitter enemies."

"I remember—or at least I remember hearing my parents speak about it—the way things were before the revolution. I was a little girl when the Shah was overthrown and Ayatollah Khomeini returned from exile in Paris. Suddenly everything changed. The move from a westernized nation to a fanatical religious country was swift. The religious police would beat women in the streets for wearing western style clothing. Western music was banned. Then there was the war with Iraq and millions died. It was horrible."

Yasmin nodded, "One of my history professors described it as the most egregious foreign policy mistake made by America in the twentieth century. The Shah was far from perfect, but compared to the Ayatollah he was a saint. The cruel vengeance the Ayatollah reaped on his people was unbelievable."

"But it was predictable," said Pouri. "One only had to look into the eyes of Ayatollah Khomeini to see a hatred and a lust for vengeance. All of the pictures of him demonstrated that. Under his rule, my parents' lives changed forever. They were an educated, westernized couple and were suddenly thrown back into the Stone Age."

"And from a foreign policy perspective," said Yasmin, "America lost its closest ally in the Persian Gulf. Overnight, an ally that had maintained peace and stability in the gulf region with arms purchased from the U.S. was turned into an adversary that needed to be boxed in and contained by American forces, which were sent into the region at great expense."

"And look at the entire Middle East region today," said Pouri. "It's true that when America sneezes, the rest of the world catches cold."

"Then why not join me and try to make things better?" asked Yasmin with a wink.

"Always thinking like a CIA case officer, aren't you?" replied Pouri with a laugh.

"Well," countered Yasmin, "it's worth considering if things get really bad. Just a thought to keep in mind..."

# CHAPTER 31

imassol Marina was certainly not Monaco or Nice, but it did have its share of huge, white luxury yachts lined up in slips reaching far out into the harbor. One of those yachts had arrived in the early morning hours. It was tied up at the end of one of the docks, waiting to be assigned a more permanent slip. The name of the yacht was Theano, in honor of its owner's daughter. It was a sleek, cream-colored Ferretti Altura 840.

Nikos Fotopolous lounged behind the wheel on the flying bridge. He thoughtfully puffed on a cigarette while waiting for the customs inspector. The yacht had performed well during the trip and he was happy to be able to relax.

Fotopolous was a familiar figure in Limassol, having visited frequently over the past forty years. And he was not concerned about the cache of arms and ammunition in his yacht's hold. The customs inspectors were all old friends. Some gentle conversation, a smoke, and a one hundred Cyprus pound note passed along through a handshake would keep the inspector from looking any further than the main cabin.

The inspectors knew that well-healed passengers needed their supply of hashish and cocaine, and they figured a little recreational pot and snuff was not hurting anyone anyway. They would never suspect a cache of weapons and ammo, which was just as well.

After passing the customs check and moving the Ferretti into an assigned slip, Fotopolous went below to take a well-deserved nap. His passengers were expected to arrive around mid-afternoon. He would need rest before setting out for Lebanon.

■  ■  ■

Santos and MacMurphy arrived at the marina at three o'clock in the afternoon. They parked their rental car in the marina lot and headed for slip number 102. They were dressed similarly in tan shorts, boat shoes, and light-colored polo shirts. Each man pulled a piece of luggage and carried a backpack slung over one shoulder. Just two dudes on their way to a cruise around the Greek islands; one was lanky and gray-headed, and the other was shorter and square with an unkempt dark beard.

They found *Theano* near the end of the pier. She was backed into her slip with a ladder leading directly onto the after-deck. Santos called out to Fotopolous, who quickly appeared from below deck, looking refreshed and ready to go.

He was dressed neatly in a white captain's uniform and cap, which contrasted with his unruly shock of longish gray hair, deeply tanned, weather-beaten face and bare feet. His eyes were pale gray and deeply creased from years of squinting into the sun. He sported a bushy, salt-and-pepper moustache and a four-day-old beard. They later learned that Fotopolous shaved only once a week—on Sunday mornings before church. That was, of course, when he was able to attend. If not, he would just let it grow for another week or two until he could attend.

Santos and MacMurphy dropped their packs on the deck and greeted Fotopolous warmly, briefly talking about mutual friends like Maggie Moore and Buck Herring and generally playing the "do you remember so-and-so?" game. MacMurphy made a point of praising Fotopolous for the key role he played during the Fawaz Yunis capture a few miles off the same Cypriot coast thirty-some years ago. The comment drew a huge grin and a proud, "aw-shucks" response from the old sailor. It cemented their "we're all members of the same secret group" affiliation.

Fotopolous gave them a quick tour of the yacht and showed them their cabins. After MacMurphy and Santos stowed their gear they all gathered around the table in the spacious, air-conditioned main cabin to discuss plans.

Fotopolous served a couple of cold beers from the fridge while Mac-Murphy briefed him on the kidnapping, telling him just enough to allow him to perform his function effectively but not any more than was necessary. A strict adherence to the need-to-know policy.

"The short story is that Hezbollah grabbed one of our officers off the street about three weeks ago. She's a young woman and doesn't have a lot of operational experience. We believe she's being held in a safe house in the southern suburbs of Beirut."

Fotopolous nodded.

"We have the address. It's an apartment building just east of the airport. We need to get there, grab the woman and get out. That's the bones of our plan. How we accomplish it is largely up to you. Your main job is to get us into Beirut without anyone knowing and to get us the hell out of there when we're done."

Santos added, "You will need to drop us off somewhere where customs and immigration will not present a problem. And then we will need to get from the drop-off point to Beirut and back again."

MacMurphy looked directly into Fotopolous's pale eyes. "Can you do that?"

Fotopolous removed his cap, scratched his mane of white hair, replaced the cap, and said, "Yeah, what the hell, I think I can handle that…"

# CHAPTER 32

The crossing from Cyprus to Lebanon was uneventful and slow and quite pleasant, giving the team plenty of time to fine-tune their plans. Fotopolous spent a good portion of the voyage on the satphone, arranging things for their arrival. It was time well spent.

The night they arrived, they could see the distant lights of Juniyah to the north and Beirut to the south. The pulsating light at the end of the Dbaiyeh Marina breakwater, their destination, lay directly in front of them.

Fotopolous had chosen a small, private marina close to the larger Dbaiyeh Marina because it had little commercial activity and contained mostly pleasure yachts, many of which belonged to American diplomats from the nearby United States Embassy. It also had no immigration and customs office, and the dock-master's office was unmanned during the evenings. Foreign visitors were supposed to report their arrivals and departures to the main office in Beirut. There was a phone on the main dock for that exact purpose, but few people bothered with this detail.

The *Theano* gently rolled and pitched as it approached the coast of Lebanon. It moved silently at not much more than idle speed. Fotopolous eased the yacht around the breakwater and into the quiet marina. He skillfully docked the *Theano* at the end of one of the finger piers, and MacMurphy and Santos helped him tie off.

Santos jumped down onto the pier and MacMurphy hefted the two heavy bags down to him. MacMurphy turned to Fotopolous, shook his hand in thanks, and followed Santos down to the dock. The two hurried down the pier to the parking lot where a late-model Toyota Land Cruiser, rented by one of Fotopolous's trusted contacts, awaited them.

Santos reached under the left, front wheel-well and retrieved an envelope taped to the top of the tire. It contained a set of car keys and two hotel key cards.

Santos drove while MacMurphy adjusted the car's GPS to guide them down Seaside Road, past central Beirut, and on to the Coral Beach Hotel and Resort. The hotel was located on the beach and was just three miles west of the Beirut Rafic-Hariri International Airport. It was also close to their target address on Lailake Road in the southern Shia neighborhood.

Less than an hour after walking off the *Theano*, they pulled into the parking lot of the five-star hotel and proceeded directly to adjacent rooms 420 and 422 for a well-deserved rest. Their rooms had been rented and paid for in advance by the same Fotopolous contact who had rented and planted their vehicle.

MacMurphy couldn't help but think, *Nice job, Nikos*…

# CHAPTER 33

The phone jolted MacMurphy awake.

"Mac, this is Maggie. Did I wake you?"

"Of course, you did. It's...what time is it?"

"It's eight-thirty in the morning, your time. Sounds like you arrived okay. Are you in the hotel?"

MacMurphy sat up and tried to clear the gunk from his brain. He was always like this in the morning. His deepest sleep came in the early morning hours and he always hated getting out of bed. In this respect, he was like a teenager. "Yes, we arrived early this morning. What's up?"

"I wouldn't normally bother you so early, knowing how much you like to sleep, but this is important. Edwin just called to warn us that they may be getting ready to move our friend."

"What!" MacMurphy struggled to absorb the information. He knew that as the DDO, Rothmann had access to NSA intercept information and that the CIA was monitoring this situation closely. Something discussed between Iran and Hezbollah must have tipped him off. "Do we have a timeframe?"

"That's all he knows."

"Okay, we'll get out there ASAP. Is there anything else?"

"Just be careful."

"Always. Thanks, Maggie. Keep us posted. Bye..." MacMurphy hung up and phoned Santos's room but there was no answer. He knew

Santos was an early riser and was probably down in the dining room having breakfast. He quickly showered, dressed, and entered the downstairs dining room in twenty minutes. Sure enough, he found Santos chowing down on an enormous American breakfast of fried eggs, ham, sausage, toast, orange juice, and coffee.

Santos looked up as MacMurphy approached. "Well if it isn't sleeping beauty. You must have gotten hungry. Food's great here. Just like back home."

MacMurphy slid into a chair across from him. "You better eat fast. We've got a problem." He brought Santos up to speed as he wolfed down a couple slices of toast with butter and jam and ordered a large coffee and a banana to go.

Soon they were in the Land Cruiser heading toward 67 Lailake Road. The morning traffic was heavy and it seemed like every other driver was leaning on his horn, creating a cacophony of street noise. Only a few traffic lights were working in the run-down, working-class neighborhood, which created gnarled traffic jams at various intersections.

The Land Cruiser was a good choice. They sat up high with a good view of the surrounding traffic. And SUVs like Land Cruisers were abundant in Beirut, especially white ones that were cooler in the summer heat, like the one they were driving.

They found the address without any difficulty and made a slow pass in front of the target building. MacMurphy took several photos of it through the car windows as they passed.

Walid's description proved accurate. It was a narrow, three-story building wedged between an auto repair shop and an electronics store. People passed by but they saw no one entering or leaving the building. The entrance door was closed and there was a button on the door jam, which was probably used to buzz the door open from the outside. The door was solid wood with no windows.

The street teemed with cars, trucks, pedestrians, shoppers, bicycles, and generally the dregs of humanity. To say it was a lower-class neighborhood would be generous.

Santos looked over at MacMurphy and shook his head. MacMurphy nodded in agreement. They both understood that this surveillance was going to be a bitch. There were no other westerners in sight. They were going to stick out like dogs in a horse race.

Finally, MacMurphy said, "We can't get out of the car. We're just going to have to keep circling around."

"Yup, the minute we step out from behind these tinted windows, we'll attract a crowd. Doesn't look like there's any good place to park either," said Santos.

"Maybe something will open up." MacMurphy thought a moment and then added, "Damn, this is bad. We really need an indigenous surveillance team on this job."

Santos nodded in agreement as he maneuvered the large SUV through traffic. "What about bringing Kashmiri on board? We need someone on the street, and he would certainly blend in. The need-to-know principle might have to be relaxed in this case."

"Yeah, I think you're right. He's probably still in Cyprus but he could get over here in a day. I'll give him a call. Meanwhile, let's keep circling the block and taking photos. Something might change."

MacMurphy called Kashmiri, confirmed that he was indeed still in Cyprus, asked him to meet them at their hotel the following morning in a rental car and advised him to dress like a poor native.

They continued their surveillance in vain. During one pass, they noticed a man in a white man-dress with a full beard smoking a cigarette in front of the entrance. But aside from that, there was no activity. The problem was the time between each pass. Each circle took ten to fifteen minutes and they only had the entrance in sight for about a minute each time.

Before too long, MacMurphy said, "I think we need to give this a rest for a while. We're going to attract attention if we keep this up much longer. Let's drive to a more metropolitan area near the airport, get something to eat, and buy you one of those *dishdasha* man-dresses. That beard you're sprouting looks pretty good right now, and you might be able to pass as an Arab if you keep your mouth shut. What do you think?"

At first Santos scoffed at the idea, but the more he thought about it... "Lunch is a great idea, and maybe the man-dress isn't such a bad idea. I'm glad we'll have Kashmiri with us, though. He's the real deal and we may not have a lot of time left."

# CHAPTER 34

MacMurphy and Santos drove west, skirted north around the airport, and turned onto Ouzai Highway, which ran north and south along the coast. They located a modern shopping mall where they grabbed a quick lunch of falafels and beer and found a department store that sold all sorts of things, including a whole line of fashionable *dishdasha* man-dresses.

"Looks pretty good on you," said MacMurphy. Santos had exited the changing room modeling a white *dishdasha* robe with black piping.

"Really?" said Santos, mock posing in front of a tall mirror.

MacMurphy leaned toward him and whispered, "Actually you look pretty much like a terrorist. Great cover for action."

"You need to get one too. Look, you can conceal a whole armory of weapons under one of these things." He demonstrated the roominess of the robe and was careful to keep his voice down. They were drawing attention from gawking customers and staff.

MacMurphy laughed. "Good idea." He signaled for the hovering, little sales clerk, also dressed in a *dishdasha* robe, to come over. He asked, "Do you have one just like this in my size?" He thought for a moment and then added, "And how about a couple of matching, what do you call them, beanie hats?"

"*Kufi*," said the sales clerk. "It's called a *kufi*."

Santos rolled his eyes. "Whatever…"

Fed and purchases made, they headed back to Lailake to continue their sporadic surveillance. On their second pass, they saw the same bearded man squatting in front of the building smoking a cigarette.

"You think he belongs in that building?" asked Santos.

"Could be," said MacMurphy. "Maybe one of the guards."

"I'm really afraid we're going to heat this place up if we keep doing this for much longer. Why don't we limit our passes to one an hour, each time coming from a different direction?"

"Yeah, this is too risky. Damn!"

They continued their surveillance at the new pace and noticed lights in a window facing the street came on at dusk. Later, during a pass a few minutes before eleven in the evening, the lights went out. This was a good indication that at least one of the apartments was occupied.

They saw the bearded man in the white *dishdasha* robe several times, always squatting and smoking in the same place. But aside from these sightings they noticed nothing unusual, nothing to give them a clue as to whether Yasmin Ghorbani was inside.

They decided to knock it off for the day and put a full press on tomorrow when they would have Kashmiri and his vehicle at their disposal and would be wearing their own *dishdasha* disguises.

■ ■ ■

They were up early the next day and grabbed a quick breakfast before meeting Kashmiri in the hotel parking lot. They hardly recognized him. He was leaning against a dark gray Nissan sedan and was dressed like a Shia cleric in a black robe and turban. His usually well-trimmed moustache and goatee were surrounded by two day's worth of stubble.

MacMurphy did a double take and then approached him. "You look like a Mullah, Hadi."

"I just hope I'm not asked to say any prayers. I'm a Coptic Christian. How do you like my *dulband*?"

"What's a *dulband*?"

Kashmiri touched his head. "My hat, my turban."

"I like it!" MacMurphy laughed and motioned in Santos's direction. "Hadi, this is my partner, Culler Santos."

They shook hands. Kashmiri looked thoughtful and then remarked, "Culler? That's an unusual name..."

Santos started to reply but MacMurphy interrupted him. "It's a nickname. He got it when he was a kid growing up in a rough neighborhood south of Boston. He enjoyed kicking the crap out of bullies. He used to say his goal in life was to cull the world of all the assholes. That's still his goal: hence the name Culler. It just stuck."

Kashmiri laughed, "Well, pleased to meet you, Culler. That's an admirable goal and I'd like to help you achieve it."

Grinning broadly, Santos said, "Well, you just might get your chance, Mr. Kashmiri. If we're lucky, that is..."

"I'm feeling pretty lucky. So, what's the plan, gentlemen?"

"I'll brief you on the way over," said MacMurphy. Then he turned to Santos and said, "Let's change into our robes in the car. Hadi and I will follow you over. Let's make one pass so I can point out the address to Hadi and then meet up at that gas station at the southern end of Lailake."

■ ■ ■

It was a few minutes past seven o'clock in the morning and the roads were already beginning to fill with rush hour traffic. As planned, MacMurphy, Kashmiri, and Santos rendezvoused at the gas station and gathered between their two vehicles.

"Okay, here's the plan," said MacMurphy. "Hadi, take your car and find someplace to park in the area. Then walk around as if you're shopping, but try to keep the target apartment in sight. If you see someone like that guy I told you about—the one we think may be a guard who smokes in front of the building—try to approach him. Ask him about the building or for directions. Something like that. The goal is to find out what he is doing there and what's going on inside."

Kashmiri nodded. "I understand."

"Culler, I'll drop you in the neighborhood. Walk up and down the street on the opposite side of the target for as long as you can. Try to coordinate with Hadi so that one of you has the target in sight at all times. I'll try to do the same thing after I've found a place to park. We'll coordinate with our cell phones."

Santos nodded and said, "Let's do it."

■ ■ ■

The boredom of surveillance sets in fast. The hours tick by without anything happening. Annoyances stack up. Impatience builds. Then a single movement releases an avalanche of adrenaline.

The rush occurred three hours into their surveillance. Kashmiri was the first to notice a woman in a headscarf drive by the safe house in a dark Ford Focus. She squeezed into a tight parking place a few meters past it. Something about the way she slowed and looked at the building as she drove past made him notice.

He watched the woman exit the car, speak to a couple of young kids who ran up to greet her and then walk back to number 67. She hit the buzzer on the door jam, pushed open the door, and entered the building.

Four minutes later, a white Range Rover Evoque parked behind the woman's Ford Focus. A young man in a white *dishdasha* man-dress stepped out of the SUV and removed a black duffle bag from the passenger seat. The street urchins swarmed him as he locked the car.

He had a strange smile on his face as he crouched down to speak to them. When he gestured to his bag, the children's eyes grew wide and they backed away from him. Free to move again, he straightened and walked to number 67 without any further delay. Like the woman, he pressed the door-jam buzzer and stepped inside.

# CHAPTER 35

Three days had passed since Pouri's last visit, so Yasmin did not know what to expect when Pouri stepped into the room with trembling hands. She got up from the bed as Pouri closed the door behind her. "What is it?" Yasmin asked.

Pouri noticed Yasmin was wearing the clothes she had brought her, including one of the colorful *hijabs*. The sight of it almost made her cry. "I tried my best. I really did. But there was nothing I could do. Iran wanted a new interrogator, someone more effective. And Hezbollah offered one of their best. I've heard of him. He's psychotic. And he's broken every person he's tortured." The words poured out of Pouri, and her hands shook worse than ever.

Yasmin felt something colder than ice slide down her spine. "How much time do we have?"

"He'll be here any minute," Pouri said as she crossed the room to hold Yasmin's hands. She ignored the tremors her hands sent up Yasmin's arms. "You have to tell him everything. He will not hesitate to kill you and make it look like an accident to cover his ass with Iran."

Tears welled up in Yasmin's eyes. "I can't. Too many people would die. And I can't betray my country."

Pouri realized her hands were no longer the source of Yasmin's shaking. She had never seen the woman look so afraid.

The sound of a door opening and a chair scraping cut through the silence. Pouri immediately wiped the tears out of Yasmin's eyes and backed herself into a corner. She crossed her arms to keep her hands from shaking as the door to the interrogation room opened. Panic leapt into Yasmin's eyes as the man standing in the doorway smiled at her. He was younger and shorter than she imagined he would be, and his dark eyes did not blink.

"What are you doing here, Miss Hoseini?" the man asked, without taking his eyes off Yasmin.

"Supervising this interrogation, Bashir." Pouri said.

"And Iran sanctioned your supervision?"

"My superiors will understand my precaution. It would be unwise to leave one of Iran's most valuable assets alone with you for too long. Your reputation precedes you."

He finally broke eye contact with Yasmin to flash Pouri a rack of perfect, white teeth. "It usually does." He turned his attention back to Yasmin as he closed the door and latched it behind him. Then he dropped the duffle bag in his hand. The sound of metal hitting wood cried out as the bag landed on the floor.

An hour into the interrogation, Pouri felt like throwing up. Bashir was in no hurry to finish the job, which only made his actions more sickening. After a brief, half-hearted attempt to make Yasmin talk without force, he dove straight into intimidation tactics. When those failed to elicit a confession, the torture began.

It started slow and simple. If Yasmin remained silent after he asked a question, he would pull her hair or twist her arm behind her. That continued until Bashir looked bored. Then he switched tactics.

Pouri watched in horror as he stripped Yasmin naked, bound her wrists with rope, and zip-tied her ankles together. He punched a hole through the ceiling with a hammer and hung her by the wrists from a metal pipe close to the hole. Yasmin's face twisted in agony as her entire body weight started to crush her wrists' delicate joints.

Bashir paused to watch her tremble. He asked her a few questions about her contacts in Iran. When she whimpered in response, he removed two black boxes and a coil of wires from his bag. One of the boxes looked like a small car battery. The other was a modified inverter generator. He connected the boxes with wires and unraveled a coil of electrodes that he clipped to Yasmin's toes. Tears slid down her cheeks when she noticed the electrodes were wired into the generator.

"What the hell do you think you're doing?" Pouri asked from her corner. Her voice was dangerously low.

"Nothing she can't handle. Girls much younger than her have survived worse," Bashir said as he walked back to the generator. Something like a chuckle skulked down his throat. "Well, for a while," he said, before crouching down and flipping a switch on the generator.

Yasmin's whole body convulsed and twitched as she screamed. The sound was mangled and inhuman. It matched the look on Bashir's face.

He flipped the switch again, cutting the electrical current, but she still twisted wildly from the rope. Bashir straightened and felt an explosion of pain hammer his head and knock him over. Pouri stood over him, breathing hard. Her feet were planted apart and her fist still hung in mid-air. Incredulous, he looked up at her with a hand on his forehead where she had punched him.

"The fuck—"

"Get out. I don't care who sent you."

Livid, Bashir pushed himself up and strode over to Pouri until they stood face to face. "I finish what I start."

"You can't be trusted to extract information without killing our asset." Pouri grabbed a fistful of his robe and rammed her face against his so that his neck bent back and his eyes were unnaturally close to hers. "So, you will not touch her again." Her voice was indescribable.

Rattled by Pouri's uncomfortable proximity and predatory grip, Bashir shoved her away. His eyes were wide yet menacing. He glared at her for what seemed like hours. Neither one of them broke eye contact. The only sound in the room was Yasmin's uneven sobbing. Finally, he turned and started to pack his bag.

"Iran will send one of its own to replace you. Tell that to whomever you need to." Pouri said as she crossed her arms and watched him unclip the electrodes from Yasmin's toes. He shoved them in his bag, strode past Pouri, and slammed the door on his way out. As soon as she heard him leave the apartment, Pouri grabbed a chair and slid it under Yasmin's feet, hoping to relieve some of the weight from Yasmin's wrists while she looked for something to cut the rope with. The chair wasn't quite tall enough to reach Yasmin's feet, which was just as well. The entire lower half of her body was numb from the electric shock.

"I swear I will help you escape. I don't know how. But I will never be complicit in this again," Pouri said with a tremor in her voice as she continued her search.

# CHAPTER 36

MacMurphy had found a place to park three blocks past the target address. He sat there with the windows up, engine and air conditioning running. He planned to stay there as long as possible before making another loop past the target apartment.

His phone rang. "Hadi here. I think we have something."

"What's up?" said MacMurphy.

"I'm directly in front of the target. A woman drove past very slowly and then parked a few meters down the road. She spoke to some kids when she got out of the car and then walked right past me. She went into the target. She's attractive, probably mid-forties, and I'm pretty certain she's Iranian."

"How do you know that?"

"She's dressed like an Iranian. And I heard her talk to the kids. She asked them to take good care of her car and to watch it carefully. Her accent is definitely Iranian."

MacMurphy was excited. He was pretty sure he could guess who this woman was but wanted confirmation. "Who do you think she is?"

"If I were a betting man, I would say she's the interrogator. She sounds educated, upper class. What other role would she have in there?" He reflected for a moment and then added, "Unless she's going to one of the other apartments."

"That's a possibility, but we haven't observed any activity in the other two apartments. No lights. Nothing. I think we've got something here."

"There's more. A young man, probably late twenties, parked behind her and also entered the target. He looked like a local, and he carried a duffle bag. He talked to the kids, but he spoke quietly and I didn't catch what he said."

"Maybe they are beefing up their security and need more supplies. He could be another guard."

"That sounds possible."

"Stick as close as you can. I'm going to call Culler."

They hung up and MacMurphy quickly made his next call. Santos answered on the first ring.

"Did you get a look at the woman and man who just entered the building?" MacMurphy asked.

"Yes, but not too closely. I'm on the other side of the street. But the woman walked right past Hadi. She went in at exactly four minutes past ten."

"Yes, Hadi got a very good look at her. We think she's the interrogator. Hadi heard her speak. He says she's upper-class Iranian. He didn't hear the man talk, but Hadi thinks he's a local. Probably another security guard."

"Then they're in there. So, let's go get our gal. I'm ready if you are."

"Hold on. Let me think." MacMurphy's mind was churning out options. If they went in now they would be going in blind. They had not learned very much from their surveillance. At the very least, she was guarded by the bearded guy at the main entrance, Abu Salah, the old woman, the interrogator, and the security guard. But what if there were others? If they waited to gather more information, she could be moved and they would miss this opportunity. He and Santos were carrying sidearms, but maybe more firepower would be needed.

Then it came to him. "What if we grabbed the interrogator? We could wait until she leaves and then grab her before she gets into her car. Just like Hezbollah. We could interrogate her about the security situation inside the building, and maybe we could even swap her for Yasmin Ghorbani. No, probably not. That would be too complicated. Take too long. But..."

"We can do that. We can grab her, get whatever information we need and then go in there tonight or tomorrow and get our gal. That's brilliant."

"Okay, I'll give Hadi a call and then I'll spin by and pick you up so we can work out the details. How long do you think she'll be in there?"

"Beats me," said Santos. "But I'll head over to her car right now in case she decides to make it a quick visit. Those little kids are hanging out over there, probably watching the car, but they shouldn't pose any problems."

"Okay," said MacMurphy, "I'm on my way."

# CHAPTER 37

Santos and MacMurphy decided to keep the plan as simple as possible—the KISS principle.

Kashmiri would hover near the target building with his eyes on the entrance and his phone at the ready. Santos would hang out near the interrogator's car and MacMurphy would try to park the Land Cruiser as close to it as possible. When the interrogator exited the building, Kashmiri would call MacMurphy. When she reached her car, both Santos and MacMurphy would grab her, carry her to the Land Cruiser and beat it out of the area. Fast and simple.

Almost two hours passed before they saw any movement. The young man suddenly walked out of the building and made a beeline to his car. Kashmiri noticed that he still carried his duffle bag and that the children guarding the Iranian's car moved further down the street when he approached. As soon as the Range Rover sped off, Kashmiri called MacMurphy and told him what had happened. It was difficult to make heads or tails of the young man's actions. They eventually decided that there had been some sort of miscommunication about which supplies he was supposed to bring to the safe house. But that theory was debunked when he never returned.

The hours dragged on and it was hot. On one of his passes, MacMurphy handed a bag of falafels and bottles of water to Kashmiri and Santos. They refused to take their eyes off the building even for a moment. But, they were beginning to attract attention in the neighborhood. Kashmiri did a better job of explaining his presence than Santos, who would simply growl at anyone who approached him.

The only routine movements they noticed were the smoke breaks the bearded guard took every hour. During those times, Kashmiri would move down the street to avoid contact with him. Then, a few minutes after four o'clock in the afternoon, a man replaced the bearded guard. The two men stood in front of the door for a few minutes, chatting and smoking. When they finished their cigarettes, the new guard entered the building while the old one walked to the adjacent auto-repair garage, mounted a moped, and departed the area.

Kashmiri noticed the new guard wore a white *dishdasha* robe, like the old guard. But he was larger and had less facial hair than his predecessor. Kashmiri reported this to MacMurphy.

The hours ticked by and the shadows grew longer. Eventually, MacMurphy found a suitable place to park the Land Cruiser. The spot was three or four car lengths in front of the interrogator's car.

When he exited the vehicle to join Santos and Kashmiri on the street, one of the kids watching the interrogator's car ran over to him, jabbering in Arabic. MacMurphy figured he wanted money for watching the car. Without saying a word, he pushed a fifty-pound Lebanese note in the little urchin's hand and slapped the fender of the Land Cruiser to indicate he wanted his car watched. The kid got the message and yelped with glee in the direction of the other children. They all hurried over to the Land Cruiser to gawk at the money in their friend's hand.

MacMurphy walked up the street toward Kashmiri, who was stationed at the front of the building. He whispered as he passed and motioned for Kashmiri to move to the other side of the street. Then he stationed himself near the far side of the adjacent electronics store. He glanced at his watch: 5:20 p.m. The interrogator had been inside for more than seven hours.

Kashmiri was the first to notice the door open and the woman exit. She turned in the direction of her car, head down, searching for something in her purse. She paused, pulled out some change, closed her bag, and continued on her way, oblivious to the surveillance.

Kashmiri motioned to MacMurphy but it was unnecessary. He fell into step behind her, walking rapidly to catch up. Kashmiri crossed the street and headed for the woman's vehicle.

Santos was already standing next to her car. He watched as the woman approached with MacMurphy close behind.

■ ■ ■

The first thing Pouri noticed as she approached her car was that there were no kids there. She looked around and saw them leaning against a large, white SUV parked a few cars up the road. She called to them and they came running over. She met them at her car and gave them some money. They darted off again, back in the direction of the white SUV.

She had her keys in her hand and was about to open the car door when a tall man in a white *dishdasha* robe approached. He spoke softly to her in English, grinning broadly. "Excuse me, ma'am, could I ask you for a huge favor?"

She turned and stared up at the handsome, pleading face looking down at her. She answered in English, "I…um…well, sure. What can I help you with?"

MacMurphy continued to smile, displaying even, white teeth and dark, warm eyes. He was non-threatening. Just a man, a foreigner, who needed some sort of assistance. She leaned back against her car, at ease now that the initial shock of the interruption had passed.

Santos watched the scene unfold from the other side of the car. He decided to lie low and let MacMurphy finish whatever it was he was doing. He had no idea MacMurphy was just playing it by ear, trying to put the woman at ease and get her into the Land Cruiser with as little noise as possible.

MacMurphy said, "I don't speak Arabic; I'm an American. And…well, those kids over there…" He motioned to the kids standing near the SUV.

"I gave them some money to watch my car...I saw other people do it. Would you help me talk to them? That's my car up there."

Pouri glanced over at the kids standing next to the SUV and said, "Sure, they watch my car all the time. It's a racket. If you don't pay them, you risk getting your car scratched. How much did you give them?"

"Fifty pounds."

She blanched as they started walking slowly toward the SUV. "Fifty pounds! That's way too much. You're going to drive the market up!"

MacMurphy shook his head in shame. "I know, but I didn't have any small change and I was afraid they'd do something to the car if I didn't pay. It's okay. They can keep the money. Just tell them that they need to split the money equally among themselves and to share it with their families. And not to expect that much money again in the future..."

"Good idea," said Pouri.

She was shaken up, but she still managed a small smile. When they reached the Land Cruiser, Pouri began speaking with the urchins. Standing behind her, MacMurphy motioned for Santos to get into the back seat and for Kashmiri to get into the driver's seat.

Pouri finished with the kids and they went running off, screeching with delight. She turned to MacMurphy who was standing beside the left rear door. Kashmiri walked around and got behind the wheel and Santos slid into the backseat on the other side.

Pouri noticed that the driver was a native and asked, "Why didn't you ask your driver to interpret for you?"

MacMurphy shook his head and said, "He barely understands a word I say. We've been getting lost all day." He opened the back door and motioned her over. "My friend Rick can tell you all about it. He's a cab driver back home. Getting lost in a hired car is particularly funny to him."

When she leaned into the doorway, MacMurphy shoved her inside and slid in after her, trapping her between him and Santos. "Let's go, Muhammad," he ordered, slamming the door behind him.

# CHAPTER 38

Pouri was too shocked to scream or resist. Two sets of powerful hands grasped each of her arms. She could hardly move, but, oddly, they were not hurting her.

MacMurphy spoke softly in reassuring tones. "Don't be frightened. We are not going to harm you. You will be fine. We just need to talk with you. You are not in any danger at all. Do you understand?"

Pouri nodded. She was close to tears and trembling, but she quickly understood what was happening. These were Americans. They would not harm her. Somehow, they must have found out where Yasmin Ghorbani was being held and had grabbed her for a prisoner swap. It all made sense, perfect sense.

*Fine, so be it*, she thought.

Kashmiri excitedly weaved the Land Cruiser through the heavy rush hour traffic.

"Slow down, Muhammad. We've got plenty of time. Let's not attract any attention," said MacMurphy.

"But where are we going?" he replied.

*Good question*, thought MacMurphy. He hadn't given this much thought at all. Where could they go? He looked over at Santos who simply shrugged. "Just keep driving cautiously, Muhammad. I'll tell you where to take us in a moment," he said.

MacMurphy turned his attention back to the frightened woman. He could not help but notice how attractive she was—large, dark eyes, full lips, fine nose, perfect alabaster skin, and a slim figure. Really, a fine looking woman. Her vulnerability added to her allure. But now that he had her, where was he going to hide her? How was he going to use her?

The most obvious option was to use her in a one-for-one trade for Yasmin. But first he needed to interrogate her, find out who she was and what the Iranians had planned for Yasmin Ghorbani. He would move on from there.

Then his training kicked in.

*Wait a minute.*

Nothing less than an officer in VAJA, the Iranian Ministry of Intelligence, would be qualified to handle such a sensitive interrogation. Given her age and the importance of this assignment, she most likely was a fairly senior VAJA officer. He started thinking of her as he would any new intelligence source.

Kashmiri continued to drive aimlessly, generally heading in the direction of the coast and their hotel, while Santos sat quietly next to the interrogator. He released her arm but remained coiled and ready to grab her again if she made any sudden moves.

MacMurphy also released her arm. He continued to speak to her in a quiet, reassuring manner. His first question was very important. "Can you tell me what your plans were for this evening?"

"I do not understand. Why do you want to know what my plans were?"

"You were getting into your car. I suspect you were going home at the end of the day. Is that correct?"

"Yes, I was heading home, back to my apartment."

"Do you have any family at your apartment or perhaps a roommate?"

She was puzzled. "No, I'm on temporary duty here in Beirut. There is no one."

"What are your plans for tomorrow? Do you have to check in with anyone?"

She relaxed a bit and flashed him a knowing smile. "Oh, now I get it. You want to know if I will be missed by anyone. Is that it?"

He returned the smile. "Yes, I need to know how much time we have before people come looking for you."

She thought for several moments. She had regained her composure and was evaluating her circumstances. She looked up into his eyes and carefully considered her response. Her main objective was figuring out how to help Yasmin while still guaranteeing her own safety.

Finally, she said, "Look, I'll be honest with you. I have been recalled to Tehran. They are not happy with my work here. I was planning to return to my apartment, pack up my things, and call the airline for a flight out tomorrow. I will tell you the truth. I'm not happy with this outcome."

MacMurphy took it all in. He glanced over at Santos who looked surprised but not displeased with the way things were going.

"What's your name?" MacMurphy asked.

She looked up at him again for a long time, considering. Finally, she took a deep breath, exhaled, looked directly into his eyes, and said, "My name is Pouri Hoseini. I am a mid-level officer at the Iranian Ministry of Intelligence. My husband is a senior officer at the Ministry of Foreign Affairs. I have two grown children—a boy and a girl."

"And you are here for..."

"I was sent here by my ministry to interrogate an American CIA officer named Yasmin Ghorbani, also known as Abida Hammami."

"Where is this American CIA officer?"

Pouri looked at him quizzically. "You know the answer to that question already. Are you testing me?"

"Please just answer my question, Miss Hoseini."

"She's being held at 67 Lailake Road in a safe apartment on the second floor. It's about thirty meters from where you picked me up."

"What's her condition? How long will they keep her there?"

"She'll be there for a while. They like the location. And she is...recovering." She looked up at him again. "Hezbollah sent a torturer to interrogate her. It should have never happened, but Iran was impatient and heard he had never failed to break a hostage."

MacMurphy turned in his seat and placed his hand on her shoulder, turning her toward him. "Is she okay?"

"Yes, I stopped him before any permanent damage was done. But Iran will send someone else. And I can't guarantee his replacement will use methods that are any less revolting." Her eyes welled up with tears. She looked deeply into his eyes, dropped her head, and said, "I do not want her to be hurt again."

MacMurphy glanced over at Santos and then sat back in his seat, thinking. Suddenly, the young man and his duffle bag made too much sense. They had been driving for almost an hour when MacMurphy's instincts told him he had a willing and cooperative source.

*Manna from heaven. But what do I do with her?*

Santos interrupted his thoughts. "Let's bring her back to the hotel."

MacMurphy considered their options for a moment and nodded. "Yes, good idea. Muhammad, let's go back to the hotel." Then he turned to Pouri and said, "We're going to trust you. Will you trust us?"

"Of course," she replied. "Do either of us have a choice?"

"Not really," said MacMurphy.

# CHAPTER 39

They drove in silence back to the hotel. MacMurphy needed to think. He broke the silence when they entered the hotel parking lot. "Muhammad, pull over there in the corner and park away from the other cars. Rick, you and I need to chat a bit. Miss Hoseini, please stay in the car. We won't be long."

She said, "Don't worry. I'm not going anywhere."

MacMurphy and Santos walked a short distance away from the car until they reached the edge of the lot. MacMurphy said, "I think we just struck gold. This is beyond our wildest expectations. I don't know what went on between this woman and Yasmin in that safe house, but I think we've got ourselves a potential recruited source. I think Yasmin may have recruited the woman. What do you think?"

"You may be right. Unless she's playing us, and I don't think she is. I think she's decided to throw in with us. We may have just solved some of her problems—being recalled and all that."

"Yes, maybe," said MacMurphy. "We need a safe house and someone to watch her while we go back there and get Yasmin. How are we going to do that?"

Santos nodded. "Yeah, not an ideal situation. But you always say security and production are like a teeter-totter. We're just going to have to relax security a bit to take advantage of this situation. We should just take her up to our rooms and hide her there and debrief her until we come up with a better plan."

"You're right. That's about all we can do right now. But we can't leave her up there alone. What if she has second thoughts? We need to watch her twenty-four-seven. We can't do that and rescue Yasmin at the same time."

"Can we use Hadi?"

MacMurphy shook his head adamantly. "Absolutely not, we've exposed him too much already. We need to keep Hadi away from her from now on. He's too vulnerable and too valuable."

Santos said, "Then we need to call in reinforcements."

MacMurphy shook his head again. "We don't have any reinforcements. We're it."

"Yes, we do," said Santos. "We have Maggie. She can babysit Miss Hoseini and debrief her. That'll leave us free to do our thing."

"Great idea!" MacMurphy hesitated, "But wait, it's going to take Maggie a couple of days to get out here. And we need to get Yasmin out of there immediately."

Santos said, "You're always looking for perfection. We've got some time. Iran won't miss Hoseini or be able to replace Hezbollah's interrogator for at least a couple of days. And you heard what she said. They have no plans to move Yasmin anytime soon. They like the location."

MacMurphy nodded. "Maybe, but Rothmann said they were planning to move her soon. And that info came straight from intercepts. Maybe the DDO's info is better than Hoseini's."

"Or not," said Santos. "Do we have a choice?"

# CHAPTER 40

Santos and MacMurphy walked back to the Land Cruiser and escorted Pouri into the hotel through a side entrance. She offered no resistance, and to show her cooperation she made an effort to hide her face as they walked to their rooms.

Once Pouri was safely in MacMurphy's room, he instructed Kashmiri to drive to the safe house with her keys, move her car into the long-term parking garage at the Beirut-Rafic Hariri Airport, and return to the safe house to keep it under sporadic vehicular surveillance until further notice.

Santos called Maggie and briefed her on the capture of Pouri Hoseini. Maggie relayed the information to Rothmann and told him their plans. He informed her that the intercepts continued to indicate Hezbollah was planning to move their captive to a new location, a location that seemed to be within a kilometer of the current safe house. She booked the next available flight to Beirut.

Meanwhile, MacMurphy and Pouri settled into comfortable chairs around a coffee table in room 420. Santos opened the door between room 420 and room 422 and joined them. The debriefing—no longer an interrogation given the cooperative nature of the conversation—was already in progress. MacMurphy was questioning Pouri about the security at the safe house.

"There really isn't very much," said Pouri. "Hezbollah believes that keeping a low profile in the neighborhood and using trusted assets is preferable to employing a large guard force. There is a security manager named Abu Salah, an older woman who has never identified herself, and a couple of other guys who, I believe, stay downstairs near the entrance at all times. Hezbollah controls the whole building, but I do not know what's on the floor above or below the safe house. They appear to be empty, but I could be wrong."

"Hezbollah's probably got the right idea about security," said Mac-Murphy. "Cloaking an action is often far better than displaying a large force. At least that's the way intelligence officers tend to think."

Santos had ordered room service in room 422. So, when he heard the bell ring, he got up and crossed into the other room, closing the door behind him. A few moments later, he returned with a tray of food, which he placed on the coffee table. The meal consisted of spaghetti and meat sauce, salad, warm rolls, and a bottle of Chianti. It was a little after nine o'clock in the evening and the three of them were ravenous. Santos figured comfort food was called for.

They dug into their meals but continued to talk. Rapport between the three of them was excellent and increased as Pouri slowly relaxed. Yasmin's torture had shook Pouri to her core. But she felt relieved knowing that her conversation with the Americans would help Yasmin and, hopefully, lead to her rescue.

Eventually, the wine and fatigue caught up to Pouri. She decided to have a little fun with her captors. "So, you're Rick," she said, indicating to Santos. "And our driver is Muhammad. But who are you?" she asked, looking at MacMurphy.

Without hesitation, MacMurphy said, "I'm Ralph."

"Do you have a last name, Ralph?"

"Let's just leave it at Ralph for now, okay?"

She smiled knowingly. "Rick and just Ralph. Could those be aliases by any chance?"

Santos laughed and MacMurphy said, "Of course they are. You know the drill."

"Indeed I do. I have another question."

"Shoot," said MacMurphy.

"Yasmin admitted she was a CIA officer, so I assume you guys are also CIA. Is that correct?"

MacMurphy hesitated for a moment before answering. "Yes, you can assume we're both CIA."

"Hmm…When did the CIA get so bold as to try to do what you guys just did?"

Santos said with a grin, "There are a few of us left."

"Okay, but when this is all over, I would like you to tell me who you really are—your true names. Is that too much to ask?"

"Not at all, Pouri…May I call you Pouri?" said MacMurphy.

"Of course you can…Ralph."

"Then you can call me Mac from now on."

"Mac…That suits you…"

"And his name is Culler."

"Culler…That's an unusual name…"

Santos replied, "It's a nickname, a real nickname. It's a long story…"

She laughed and sat back from the table, looking first at MacMurphy then Santos then back at MacMurphy. Seemingly satisfied, she said, "I believe you…both of you. It's not important, but…I think you understand…"

"We do," said MacMurphy. Santos nodded.

She held out her wine glass and Santos topped it off. She swirled it around, looked deeply into the glass, toasted them both, and took a long drink. When she set the glass back down, she exhaled a long breath and said, "Now that we understand each other, I want to tell you what I want out of this. Is that okay?"

Santos and MacMurphy nodded. MacMurphy said, "Of course it is…"

"I know how the game is played so just hear me out. If you accept my terms, we will move on. If you do not…well, things will be more difficult. Understood?"

They nodded again.

"I will agree to cooperate fully with you. I will agree to a thorough debriefing while I am still in your custody. Moreover, I will agree not to try to escape. But at the end of it all, when you have Yasmin back, you must release me unharmed and in a manner that does not put my future with VAJA in any sort of jeopardy."

Her glance went from MacMurphy to Santos, who both nodded agreement. She continued, "I have a husband, two children, and an extended family back in Tehran. I want them to be safe. I also want to continue my career in the Ministry of Intelligence after all of this is over. I won't be able to do that if the ministry suspects I've been cooperative with you."

Santos and MacMurphy looked at each other with raised eyebrows and again nodded, this time more emphatically.

"So, I will agree to be your fully recruited and totally cooperative asset both now and after I return to Tehran." She paused to let that settle in. "But you will have to protect me."

"Of course, we'll do everything in our power to protect you," said MacMurphy. "That's our job…"

She nodded. "One more thing. Beginning immediately, I want a salary of one hundred thousand dollars to be placed in a U.S. bank—under an alias of course—every year from now until I can no longer continue my work against Iran. At that time, I want resettlement for me and my immediate family in the U.S." She sat back in her chair as if to say, "This discussion is over," and took another long drink of wine.

MacMurphy looked over at Santos who shook his head and shrugged. Then MacMurphy said, "I think we can give you what you ask for and more, but I must tell you that this decision isn't mine to make. I'll have to propose it to headquarters for a final decision. However, I can't imagine why they would not agree to your terms."

She looked deeply into his eyes and said, "Fair enough. You just better make it happen, Mac."

"I will, Pouri."

"Oh, there is one more thing," she said. Guilt twisted her insides. Fear and horror had paralyzed her until it was too late to stop the worst of Yasmin's torture. She hadn't flipped the switch, but she had stood by and watched as someone was abused and dehumanized the way she had once been. Pouri felt responsible for what had happened to Yasmin, and she wanted to make some sort of amends. "I know very well the importance your CIA would attach to the recruitment of a penetration of the Iranian VAJA. The recruiting officer would receive a promotion and an award and maybe even a cash bonus. Isn't that right?"

They both nodded and MacMurphy said, "But that's not important to us, Pouri."

"No matter," said Pouri. "I want you to promise that all credit for my recruitment will go to Yasmin. The reason I came to the decision to cooperate with you is all because of her—due to the long discussions we had during her interrogations. She made me realize just how bad my life under the Ayatollahs really is. And she made me crave something better: to live freely. You understand..."

# CHAPTER 41

M aggie arrived the following evening and went directly to her hotel room before calling MacMurphy. "I'm in room 303, Mac. Come on by and tell me what's been going on."

He was in his room with Santos and Pouri. MacMurphy excused himself to brief Maggie. Before he left he turned to Pouri and said, "You are going to love Maggie. She'll stay with you while Culler and I go get Yasmin back."

Pouri fired back, "You still don't trust me."

"No, and you know full well why I can't. Consider it protection. That and I don't want to spend another night on the couch listening to you purr away in my bed." He closed the door behind him without waiting for a response.

MacMurphy updated Maggie on what had transpired since their last conversation. She sat there transfixed as he related the stories of Yasmin's torture and Pouri volunteering to serve as their agent inside of VAJA after her return to Iran.

"My god. Yasmin," Maggie said, covering her mouth with her hand. After a few minutes of stunned silence, Maggie removed her hand and said, "We have to get her out of there as soon as possible. What would have happened if Miss Hoseini hadn't intervened? I can't even think it. You did an excellent job recruiting a penetration of VAJA. The DDO will be very pleased when I report to him."

"Hold on, Maggie, let's get the story straight. Yasmin recruited her. She was all prepped when we got a hold of her. The capture accelerated things a bit, but she had already made up her mind to make the jump at some point."

"Okay, okay, I got it. And you have enough information to move ahead with the rescue?"

"You can never have enough info. But I think we're okay. Pouri didn't know much. But based on what she said and our own surveillance, I think it's safe to assume there's not an army of guards waiting for us."

Maggie yawned and rubbed her eyes with two hands. She was jet-lagged but still excited to be in the midst of the operation. She asked, "When do you plan to go?"

"Tonight. No sense hanging around here any longer, especially since Rothmann believes they may move her soon."

Maggie said, "Didn't you just tell me Miss Hoseini thinks the place is just fine and that they will elect to stay there?"

"That's what she thinks, but the DDO thinks differently. I don't want to take any chances. We've got all the information we're going to get so we might as well move out ASAP."

"Okay, I'll call Rothmann and get him up to date. When are you going to leave?"

MacMurphy checked his watch. "It's a little after nine now. I'll check in with Hadi and tell him to be prepared to back us up around two o'clock tonight. Meanwhile, we should all try to get some rest. I'll bring Pouri down to your room. I don't think she'll try to do anything, but sleep lightly just in case."

■ ■ ■

Santos and MacMurphy had their gear spread out on the bed in front of them. They were dressed alike in black running shoes, blue jeans, and tee shirts.

Together they donned their light Kevlar vests. Next, they selected their handguns, Heckler & Koch MK-23 .45s, equipped with suppressors.

They unscrewed the suppressors, slipped them into their pockets, and slid the pistols into holsters on their belts.

On the other side of their belts was a Russian-made *Spetsnaz* ballistic knife. Santos used the same knife against a drug courier in the Golden Triangle about a year earlier. It looked like a normal fighting knife but when a release button was pressed, the blade flew out of the knife with enough force to penetrate a two-by-four twelve feet away. Santos swore by it. Silent, accurate, and deadly.

Next, they donned nearly identical, dark-colored, short-sleeved shirts. They were comfortable and long enough when untucked to conceal the holstered knife and handgun.

All that remained on the bed was night-vision gear and two POF-416 automatic sub-machine guns with one-hundred-round drums full of 5.56mm ammunition. The guns were equipped with suppressors and infrared lasers that were invisible at night unless you were wearing night-vision goggles. With night vision, a shooter could see a green line emanating from the rifle.

The drums had been loaded by hands wearing latex gloves to assure there were no fingerprints left on the cartridges. This was a precaution often forgotten by criminals, who landed in prison when their fingerprints were found on spent cartridges.

Santos and MacMurphy put a lot of rounds through similar POF guns in the Golden Triangle. The guns performed well, had an ample supply of ammo without reloading and never jammed.

They slipped the guns and night-vision headgear into backpacks and slung the backpacks over their shoulders. They were ready to go.

# CHAPTER 42

On their way to the safe house, MacMurphy called to touch base with Kashmiri one final time. Kashmiri, parked directly across the street from the safe house, reported that he had observed no movement from that location over the past three hours.

He informed MacMurphy that before parking in that spot his surveillance had consisted only of drive-bys every half-hour or so, and he could have missed something during that time. He stated the last activity had occurred around four o'clock in the afternoon when a guard walked outside for a smoke break.

Santos and MacMurphy drove into the area right before two o'clock in the morning. The neighborhood was quiet and, aside from the occasional automobile or motorcycle, deserted.

They drove slowly past the safe house and noticed no activity on the street. They recognized Kashmiri's car parked across the street and drove past it so he would know they had arrived.

The pair pulled into a parking space on same side of the street as the safe house, just a few car lengths away from the spot where they had abducted Pouri. Santos cut the lights and they sat there for a moment in silence, screwing the suppressors onto their .45 caliber H&K handguns.

Santos broke the silence. "What are we waiting for?"

MacMurphy said, "I don't think we should carry the POFs out on the street. They could attract attention. Let's go in light and fast."

They adjusted their night-vision goggles and switched the dome light to the off position so the lights would not turn on inside the car when the doors opened. Then they nodded to each other and exited the vehicle from both sides, gently closing the doors behind them.

They hurried back up the street and stood in front of the safe house door, observing the area around them. MacMurphy hit the button to buzz the door open while Santos positioned himself to be the first one in, pistol at the ready.

Nothing happened.

They looked at each other with raised eyebrows and MacMurphy hit the buzzer again. Still nothing.

Santos tried the handle. Locked.

Nervously, they looked up and down the street. Nothing. MacMurphy motioned to Santos to shoot out the lock, which he did with two well-placed, silent .45 caliber rounds.

Santos pushed through the door and into the foyer with MacMurphy close at his heels. Still nothing. The place was dark and silent. The only furniture was one small wooden chair just inside the door.

MacMurphy moved to the apartment door to their left, put his ear to it and listened. He shook his head. He looked up the stairs, clearly illuminated by the green-tinted night vision, and signaled Santos to follow him. They moved up the stairs silently.

They reached the second-floor landing, glanced around, and focused on the apartment door to their left. They noticed an identical small wooden chair by the door and nodded to each other.

MacMurphy put his ear to the door and listened. After a moment, he looked back at Santos and shook his head again. Santos reached his hand out toward the door handle but MacMurphy signaled him to stop. He then motioned for them to check out the third floor before entering the second-floor apartment.

They moved up the stairs and stopped on the landing in front of the apartment door. MacMurphy put his ear to the door. Still nothing, not a sound.

Santos tried the door and it opened. They moved inside and quickly determined the apartment was empty—not a stick of furniture. Satisfied, they went back down the stairs to the second floor and stood once again at the entrance.

MacMurphy listened again at the door, indicated to Santos that there was still no noise coming from the apartment and tried the doorknob. Locked.

Santos aimed his .45 at the lock and looked up to MacMurphy for approval. MacMurphy nodded and Santos shattered the lock with two silent rounds. MacMurphy pushed through the door and entered the room, scanning it with his .45 at the ready.

They found themselves in a long, narrow living area. At one end was a kitchen-dining room. Two closed doors to their left presumably led to bedrooms. They moved down to the kitchen area. Dishes were in the sink and an unwashed frying pan sat on the stove. From the look and smell of it, it was recently used.

One open door near the kitchen led to a rather large bathroom with a toilet, sink, and tub. Used towels were scattered about and the soap dishes were full.

They were getting that fluttery feeling in their guts. Something was badly amiss.

They approached a door they hoped led to a bedroom. Santos stood at the ready while MacMurphy listened for a few moments and then tried the knob. It opened into a recently used bedroom. The single bed was unmade and the closets were empty with the doors open and there were no personal items in the room.

They returned quickly to the main room and tried the other bedroom door. It was locked but Santos quickly opened it with two poofs from his .45 caliber key. They burst inside and found a small, unmade, single bed, a card table, and four chairs. There was a hole in the ceiling, and the closet was bare. The only evidence that it had been used as a prison was the barred and blackened window that opened to the street below.

Santos and MacMurphy stood in the middle of the room, long guns hanging loosely at their sides. They looked around again in disbelief. When their eyes met, Santos shook his head and MacMurphy simply said, "Fuck…"

# CHAPTER 43

When they were back in the Land Cruiser and safely out of the area, MacMurphy called Maggie. He explained what happened and told her they were on their way back to the hotel where they wanted to meet with both her and Pouri.

Maggie wanted to know more but MacMurphy cut her off. He told her he would brief her in the room shortly. "Just get up, get dressed, and maybe order some coffee," he said.

On the way back to the hotel, they commiserated over their bad luck. They were thoroughly disheartened and discouraged. Monday morning quarterbacking was not going to help.

Santos tried to make MacMurphy feel better. "They obviously moved out sometime between four o'clock in the afternoon, when Hadi observed the smoker out front, and around eleven o'clock in the evening, when Hadi took up his stationary position across the street. It must have happened in between one of his drive-bys."

"Yeah," said MacMurphy, "they just got lucky, real lucky. We needed proper surveillance. Anyway, now we deal with the cards we're dealt."

They drove the rest of the way back to the hotel in silence. By the time they pulled into the hotel parking lot, MacMurphy had moved beyond his initial despair and was fully focused on turning this unfortunate event to his advantage.

They locked most of the guns and ammo in the rear of the Land Cruiser, taking only the handguns with them, and then returned to their rooms to change into more comfortable clothes—shorts and tee shirts—before heading to Maggie's room.

Pouri and Maggie were also dressed comfortably in shorts and colorful blouses. Pouri was not wearing a *hijab* and MacMurphy could not help but notice how beautiful and well-coiffed her hair was. He also noticed she wasn't wearing a bra under her flimsy silk blouse.

Santos and MacMurphy settled into the two chairs beside the coffee table. Maggie sat at the desk, prepared to take notes, and Pouri sat on the side of the bed. Santos served coffee while MacMurphy started his briefing. His voice was dispassionate, setting out the facts exactly the way they happened.

When he finished and focused on Pouri and said, "It's important now to know for certain whether you're with us or if you're still considering things."

"No, I've made up my mind. As long as you agree to protect me and resettle my family in the United States when all of this is over and it's safe to do so, I'm with you all the way." She looked directly into his eyes without flinching.

"We will do everything in our power to do that. You have my word on that," said MacMurphy. He looked over at Santos and Maggie and they voiced their agreement.

MacMurphy continued, "We have one and only one requirement for you now. You know what it is."

Pouri nodded, "Of course I do. I will do everything I can to help you locate and rescue Yasmin."

MacMurphy reached over and dropped the car keys and parking ticket into Pouri's hand. "Then you are free to go. Your car is in the long-term lot at the airport. The space is written on the back of the ticket. I'm sure you can come up with some story to explain your delayed return."

"I don't even think I've been missed. But I can come up with an excuse. Don't worry."

Maggie said, "What about commo?"

MacMurphy said, "Pouri, we don't have time to give you an elaborate clandestine communications plan just yet, so we are going to rely on throwaway phones for the time being. Maggie, you'll be Pouri's main point of contact. Give her your phone number. Pouri, purchase a pre-paid phone as soon as you can and notify Maggie. Even if you don't have information to report, work out a schedule with Maggie to call her at least once every few days, just so we know everything's okay with you. Understood?"

They both nodded.

MacMurphy said, "Good, now let's get some sleep. We've got to start back at ground zero tomorrow. Let's all think about that."

He stood up and reached out his arms to Pouri to say goodbye. She slid off the bed and embraced him warmly. "Good luck, Pouri. And thanks again for all of your help."

She gave him an extra squeeze and he could feel the softness of her breasts against his chest. Then she pushed back gently and looked up into his eyes. "Just get Yasmin back safely. That is all I ask."

# CHAPTER 44

Pouri left the hotel early in the morning. She took a cab to the airport, retrieved her car, and returned to her apartment to pack. She then drove to the airport, turned in the rental car, and took an afternoon flight back to Tehran.

Santos, Maggie, and MacMurphy met in the hotel coffee shop for a late breakfast and to discuss their next steps.

"All I can say is thank god we still have Kashmiri and our link to Walid Nassar," said MacMurphy. "Walid should know where they've moved Yasmin. I'll meet with Hadi later this morning and tell him to meet with Nabil and put him on it."

Maggie placed her granny glasses on her head and wagged a finger at them. "I just hope they don't notice those shot-out locks at the apartment building anytime soon. Didn't you guys ever attend the locks and picks course down at The Farm?"

Santos grinned. "Sure we did, and so did you. And you know damn well that opening locks with a pick isn't like how they do it in the movies. It takes time to manipulate a lock. Sometimes a long time, and we couldn't risk that."

"I guess so," said Maggie, "but I still worry about the damage you guys did there. If they notice it—and they will the moment someone goes back in there—they will know a rescue attempt was made."

MacMurphy said, "Maybe they'll think it was a robbery attempt."

"Right," said Maggie with a bemused look on her face.

"Anyway," said MacMurphy, "it's done. Let's put it behind us. We'll find out where Yasmin is from Abu Salah's driver and then we'll go get her."

Santos rolled his eyes. "And we'll work out the details as we go."

"Nobody said this was going to be easy," said MacMurphy.

"Okay, knock it off," said Maggie. "What do you want me to do?"

"Well," said MacMurphy, "your baby-sitting job is over. You can either go back home and tend to business there or stay here and help with surveillance."

Santos said, "We could throw a black *burqa* over you to help you blend in."

"I'd rather do that," she said. "You boys definitely need some adult supervision, and Christy and Wilber can manage things just fine back in Fort Lauderdale."

"Done," said MacMurphy. "Call the DDO later this morning and brief him. I'll do the same with Hadi. We've got no time to lose."

# CHAPTER 45

MacMurphy's phone call to Kashmiri was brief. "They've moved her out of the Lailake apartment. We don't know where she is and need to find her. Please contact Nabil and find out where she is. Give him another envelope. I'll reimburse you."

Kashmiri met with Nabil that same afternoon at their usual café. He was seated in a booth at the rear of the café when Nabil came wheeling in. They greeted each other and Nabil used his powerful arms to lift himself out of the wheelchair and into the seat across from Kashmiri.

Kashmiri got right to the point. "We've got a problem. They moved out of the apartment at 67 Lailake Road. They did it last night without consulting Tehran. The Ayatollah is very upset and believes either Abu Salah has gone rogue or Hezbollah is directly defying Tehran's orders. This is very serious, Nabil."

Nabil was wide-eyed. He shook his head in disbelief. "They are crazy," he exclaimed. "Why would they do such a thing?"

"Because they are all thugs and can't be trusted. That is why we contacted you in the first place. Your help is more important to us than ever before." He pushed a fat manila envelope across the table to Nabil. "This is a bonus for you and Walid. It is to underscore the importance Tehran places on your cooperation, especially now."

"Certainly, you can count on me. I'll call Walid right away and meet with him as soon as he is able."

"Do it right now. I can't emphasize enough the importance of this."

■  ■  ■

It was after midnight when Walid walked into his uncle's home. Nabil had been sitting up watching old TV reruns while he waited. They embraced and Walid sat down in a chair across from his uncle. He immediately apologized for being so late. "I'm sorry, Uncle. I know it is terribly late, but they have kept me very busy. I'm sorry to keep you up so long, but you said it was very urgent, so I..."

"They called me," said Nabil. "Tehran asked me, 'What's Abu Salah up to? What's he doing?' They said he moved the CIA hostage without their approval. They were frantic."

"Oh, my...I didn't know." Walid was confused. "I thought Abu Salah was just obeying orders. He doesn't do anything without orders."

"Orders from Hezbollah, perhaps, but not from Tehran. They were taken completely by surprise. They do not know what's going on. What happened?"

Still confused, Walid said, "I wasn't given any notice. I was waiting in the car down the street as usual. And Abu Salah came over and told me to pull up in front of the apartment building and wait. Several minutes later he came down with the old woman and the hostage in between them. At least I'm pretty sure it was the hostage. They got into the back seat and he told me to drive away."

"How do you know it was the hostage?"

"Because they were leading her, one on each arm. Then again, she looked unsteady as she walked. But—"

"Did you see her face?"

"No, she was covered from head to toe in a black *burqa*. I only saw her eyes and they were frightened."

"Did they speak? Did you hear her speak?"

"Not the hostage. She was sobbing. She never said a word."

"Where did you take them?"

"When they got into the car they blindfolded her. They did not want her to know where we were going. Abu Salah just indicated to me to drive and keep driving. That is what I did. I just drove around the city. Occasionally he would indicate to me to turn left or right."

"How long did you do this...drive around?"

"About thirty, maybe forty minutes."

"And then?"

"And then he directed me to a building. We drove to a small bungalow next to a gas station, about two or three kilometers south of the Lailake address."

"Is that where you let them off?"

"Yes, they hurried her out of the car and up the path and into the house."

"And then what happened?"

"Well, I waited there for a while. I was starving. I had not eaten. Then Abu Salah came out and sent me to get food for everyone. When I returned I just waited there, afraid to move in case Abu Salah wanted something."

"What time did all of this happen?"

"We left the Lailake address at around six. I was just about to leave and get some dinner when Abu Salah came over to me. Then we drove to the new place. We got there a little before seven. Then I got the food and waited there until around eleven when Abu Salah came out and told me to go home. He stayed there all night. I got home around midnight."

Nabil sat back for a moment wondering if he had covered everything, if there was anything he had forgotten. "Oh yes, I almost forgot. How stupid of me. What is the address of this new place, this bungalow?"

"I don't know the address. I didn't notice. But I can tell you how to get there. It's pretty simple."

Nabil wheeled into the kitchen and returned with a pad of paper and a ballpoint pen. He handed them to Walid and said, "Draw me a map please."

Walid spoke as he drew a rough map on the pad. "Here's the old address. From there you drive south and then cut over to Hadi Hassan Nassrallah Road over here to the west. I am sure you know it. It's a big thoroughfare."

Nabil nodded.

"Then you continue going south until you come to the end of the road, just past the entrance to the Hadath Branch of the Lebanese University. Here. Then you turn right and go a short distance to the end of that street. Then take a right again onto this little street. There is a small gas station—just two pumps and a garage—here on the corner. You cannot miss it. Just past the gas station, set back from the road, is the bungalow."

Nabil studied the map for a moment, thinking. He said, "Who is with the hostage?"

"Abu Salah and the old woman. They are stuck there until I go back in the morning. They have no automobile."

"Did you eat with them in the house?"

Walid laughed. "No, of course not. They do not trust me to go in the house. I ate my food in the car. I never went into the other places either."

Nabil nodded. "So, right now, the only people in the bungalow, as far as you know, are the three of them?"

"Yes, the old woman, the hostage, and Abu Salah."

"What about the guards? There were guards at the other place, weren't there?"

Nabil reflected a moment. "You're right. Three guards rotated at the front entrance of the other place. Maybe they will come tomorrow. I do not know. But there were no guards at the bungalow when I left."

Walid got up to leave. He leaned over to offer a goodbye embrace to his uncle when he suddenly remembered something and pulled back excitedly. "Oh, I almost forgot. I don't know if this is important because it doesn't concern what we have been talking about, but it is very...I don't know..."

"What is it?"

"I overheard Abu Salah speaking on his cell phone. He was very excited and spoke too loudly. It sounded like he was getting instructions from someone very important in Hezbollah. A man was telling him about a plan to ambush the American ambassador's motorcade, and he wanted Abu Salah to participate in the attack."

"What? Are you sure? When will this happen?"

"I'm not sure, but he mentioned the American ambassador had scheduled a meeting with some Syrian officials near a place called Aanjar on the Syrian border. Abu Salah was very happy. He said, 'Don't worry. The sonofabitch will never make it to Aanjar.' Those were his exact words. He was very excited."

# CHAPTER 46

They were not taking any chances.

Yasmin's wrist was handcuffed to a metal cot in a small bedroom at the rear of the bungalow. Moving her wrists was agony, so she tried her best to keep them still. The feeling in her legs and feet had finally returned. The muscles in them felt sore and irritated, but any feeling was better than the numbness she had feared would never completely wear off. She wore a black *burqa* over her clothes. It stank of a body odor that was not hers.

She tried to remove the *burqa*. But with one hand chained to the top of the cot, she could not get it all the way off. So the smelly garment ended up hanging painfully from her wrist to the floor. She guessed it belonged to the old woman. Black *burqas* were her uniform.

Yasmin looked around the little room. There were two small windows, both of which were boarded up with plywood. The walls were papered in a gaudy floral pattern of yellows, purples, and greens. The paper was stained and peeling and the oak flooring was uneven and warped.

Like her previous prisons, the only furniture in the room, aside from her bed, was an old wooden table and four matching chairs. Her blindfold had not been removed until she was in the room, so she had not seen the layout of the rest of the house. But she knew they had walked her through the entrance and down a hall to her room.

She could hear the muted sounds of a TV or radio coming from down the hall behind her. She surmised that there was a kitchen or living room at the front of the house and that this was where the sounds were coming from. She could also hear the distant sounds of aircraft flying low overhead, which led her to believe she was still fairly close to an airport.

She had been there for about an hour, trying to get her bearings, when the old woman entered the room with a plate of food and a tall glass of lukewarm tea. Yasmin resisted the urge to cry out in pain when the woman unlocked the handcuff from the bed and let the *burqa* fall to the floor. The woman stilled the swinging handcuff in an iron grip, and Yasmin couldn't stifle the small scream that escaped her throat. Unfazed, the woman asked if Yasmin wanted to use the restroom before eating.

Yasmin nodded. The woman led her down the hall past Abu Salah, who stood menacingly by the door, to a small bathroom. The old woman accompanied her, never releasing her end of the handcuffs, while Yasmin did her business. Then she brought her back to the bedroom. At the table, Yasmin sat down and the woman attached the handcuff to the back of a nearby chair. To distract herself from her throbbing wrists and legs, Yasmin stared hard at her food and tried to think of other things.

*At least they are feeding me three times a day. But why all the extra precautions?* Yasmin thought.

Yasmin sat eating her meal with one hand while the old woman sat across from her, staring up disinterestedly at the ceiling or across the room. Neither spoke. Abu Salah had closed the door but she sensed he was not far away.

She gingerly pushed the food around on her plate but could not eat much. Her stomach would not stop fluttering in trepidation. Yasmin knew this was the beginning of a new phase of her captivity and feared the worst. What was going to happen to her? Was anyone looking for her? What were her CIA colleagues and the rest of her government doing to gain her release?

Yasmin was well aware of her NOC status and that she had no immunity, and this added to her dismay. She was afraid Pouri wouldn't be able to keep her promise and was anxious about who would replace Bashir. Obviously, Iran would send someone who could do what both Pouri and Bashir had failed to do, someone with more extreme methods.

Yasmin shook and she stared hard at her food.

# CHAPTER 47

MacMurphy briefed the team on his late-night telephone conversation with Kashmiri while they ate breakfast in the hotel coffee shop. He led with the news of the planned Hezbollah attack on the American ambassador's motorcade. When he finished, he shook his head and said, "That's all we know. But we can fill in some of the holes ourselves. I don't think the ambassador has multiple upcoming meetings with the Syrians, not in Lebanon anyway. And the distance he will have to travel—it's what, a three- to four-hour drive to the border?—should help us narrow down the intended attack date." He turned to Maggie expectantly.

Maggie sat there stunned before answering. "Holy crap! We need to get this to the DDO as fast as possible. He'll be able to figure out if the information is correct and, if it is, the date of the meeting."

Santos said, "And if it is good info, all the ambassador has to do to prevent the attack is cancel his meeting. If he doesn't actually have a meeting scheduled, we'll know the information is bad."

MacMurphy completed his briefing on the location of the new safe house and said, "We won't know how difficult this surveillance is going to be until we get out there and take a look. Hadi will join us at the site later this morning. Let's grab our surveillance duds and get out there ASAP. We'll meet at the Land Cruiser as soon as Maggie finishes her call with Rothmann."

They met at the car twenty minutes later and headed toward the new safe house. MacMurphy drove while Santos navigated from the hand-drawn map spread out on his lap. Maggie sat in the back seat, awkwardly pulling a black *burqa* over her street clothes.

As they headed south down Nassrallah Road, Santos remarked, "Hey, this surveillance might not be too bad. This is a good neighborhood. Lots of shops, restaurants, and relatively upscale buildings. Not like that other slum."

Maggie said, "Yes, that's the entrance to the Hadath Branch of the Lebanese University coming up on our left. We'll do fine in this neighborhood. Lots of students and middle-class people walking around."

"Turn right at the next street," said Santos, looking down at the map. "Go to the end and turn right again."

MacMurphy turned and proceeded down the paved, two-lane road, lined on both sides with three-story, red-brick apartment buildings. They guessed they were in a section of student housing. At the end of the road, the pavement ran out and so did the nice neighborhood.

He made a sharp, right U-turn onto a dusty, unpaved, pothole-infected road that ran parallel to the road they came in on. The small gas station, surrounded by a junkyard filled with an acre or two of rusting automobiles and trucks, was on their right. To their left, on the other side of the road, they saw empty fields dotted with scrubby trees, polluted with garbage, and pockmarked with the occasional squatter's hut. The huts were built mostly of corrugated roofing, old metal signs, and a few two-by-fours. A bit further down the road sat a dilapidated, pea-green-colored cottage. Their target.

"*Merde!*" said MacMurphy. "This is impossible!"

"Jesus, how are we going to hang around here without attracting attention?" said Maggie. "There's no traffic and, aside from the natives, there's no one on the street."

MacMurphy drove a bit further down the road and came to a dead end. "Sonofabitch..."

An old woman in a black *burqa* stepped out from behind one of the shacks and stood staring at them while picking at her nose with her pinky finger. MacMurphy struggled to turn the Land Cruiser around. The woman's mangy dog began barking incessantly.

"What do we do now?" said Maggie.

"We get the hell out of here," said Santos.

MacMurphy said, "Maggie, shoot as many pictures of the cottage as you can when we pass by."

Afraid to roll her window down, Maggie took photos through its tinted glass instead. She kept shooting until MacMurphy pulled onto the pavement of the main street and turned back toward the university.

■ ■ ■

They gathered back in MacMurphy's room at the hotel. "Well, that was disappointing," said Maggie.

"That's an understatement," said MacMurphy.

Santos sat reviewing the photos on Maggie's camera. "Wait a minute." He turned the camera toward them and scrolled through the photos. "Do you see what I see?"

Maggie said, "I see a bunch of dark photos of a crappy, pea-green bungalow sitting out in the middle of a junkyard. That's what I see. Good location for a prison."

"Look more closely," said Santos.

"I see it," said MacMurphy. "You're talking about the backside of the apartment buildings along the road we came in on."

"Yes, they look out over the rear of our target."

Maggie said, "You're right. Observation posts. A whole row of them. Maybe we're back in business. Let's get Hadi Kashmiri on it right away. We need a real estate agent."

# CHAPTER 48

MacMurphy briefed Kashmiri on what they had seen and described the apartment buildings in detail.

"I know exactly what you're talking about. I was just there. Actually, I am still here. I just pulled back onto Nassrallah Road and I'm heading north."

"Well, turn around," said MacMurphy, "and check out those apartment buildings. We think they may be rentals for students and others affiliated with the university."

"You're probably right. Makes sense..."

"See if there's a rental office someplace. Inquire about the availability of units. See if you can rent one with a view of the bungalow from its rear windows."

"I'm heading back there right now."

Kashmiri pulled an illegal U-turn in front of the university, scattering a bunch of students crossing the road with their noses in their phones, and headed back to the apartment complex. When he reached the complex, he drove past slowly and looked for a rental agency sign or a concierge apartment. Finding nothing, he parked his car and got out.

He walked up the sidewalk in front of the apartments. There were eight buildings on each side of the street, all connected and numbered consecutively from the corner of Nassrallah to the end of the paved road. Buildings four through eight on the right side probably offered the best view of the target house, and he guessed the higher the number the better.

Dressed in a black robe and turban, he could pass for a Shia Mullah. The moustache and goatee surrounded by several days' growth of stubble rounded out his disguise. He lingered in the area, walking up and down the street in front of the buildings, scoping it out.

He stopped two young students coming toward him and asked politely, "Excuse me. I am looking to rent an apartment in the vicinity. Is there a rental office nearby?"

The gawky male student, dressed in black skinny jeans and a black tee shirt, gave the female student a vague look and shrugged. Dressed in a bright red *hijab*, the cute girl responded, "There's a bulletin board in the student union building with a listing of available units here and elsewhere around the campus. You should try there first. Otherwise you will have to rent through one of the real estate agencies, and that will cost more." She paused and added, "But I don't think there are any apartments available at the moment."

"You are very kind. Very helpful," said Kashmiri with a slight bow. "Do you live here?"

The skinny kid started to respond but she answered first. "Yes, we both have flats here. He shares with three other boys and I share with two girls." She waved her arm in the direction of the building behind them. "Most of the apartments along this street are occupied by students. It's very convenient to the campus." She nodded in the direction of the university at the end of the street.

Kashmiri thought for a moment and added, "You said all of the apartments are probably rented. Do you think anyone would be willing to sublet an apartment? I would only need it for a few weeks. Just till the end of the summer."

The girl responded, "I guess that would be possible. The summer is almost over and a lot of the students are taking a break before the fall semester begins."

Kashmiri asked, "Okay, perhaps you can do me a favor and find something for me. I will pay double rent to the occupants and give you a handsome commission for your efforts. I only need the apartment until the fall semester begins, just a little less than a month. Could you do that?"

The girl's eyes grew wide, "How much would you pay for my flat?"

"Where is it?" he said.

"Building five, third floor. Right there." She pointed at the building behind her.

Kashmiri quickly calculated. It was three buildings from the end. An ideal observation post, as long as it didn't look out on the street.

"Is it in the front or rear of the building?" he said.

She gave him a puzzled look. "What difference does it make?" She continued, "Actually, all the apartments go from the front to the back. The living-dining area is in the front, overlooking the street. The kitchen is in the middle and the two bedrooms are in the back. There are two apartments on each floor separated by the staircase."

"It doesn't really matter. I'm just curious. May I see it?"

The young woman glanced up at her companion, who shrugged again. "Sure, I'll show it to you right now." The boy waved goodbye and continued walking down the street in the direction of the campus while she led Kashmiri back in the direction of her apartment building.

They walked together up the three floors and she opened the door to her apartment. He feigned interest while she showed him the sparsely furnished living-dining area and kitchen. When they got to the two small bedrooms at the rear, he walked directly to the window and looked out.

The view across the junk-filled field looked down on the backside of the pea-green bungalow approximately one hundred meters away.

He turned toward the young woman and said, "This will be fine, but I have a few conditions. If you accept my conditions, I will pay you ten million Lebanese Pounds to rent this flat from today until the first of September."

The girl's eyes grew wide. That was more than five thousand dollars for a little over three weeks. She nodded excitedly.

He continued, "But you and your flatmates will have to vacate the apartment tomorrow and not discuss the rental with anyone. You will simply give me the keys and disappear for the next three weeks. I will meet you, and only you, back here at six o'clock tomorrow evening and give you the money. What you tell your flatmates is your business, but no one can return to the apartment before September first. Is that understood?"

"Yes, yes of course," she sputtered. "I understand. We will not return. We will not bother you."

# CHAPTER 49

Maggie was sitting at a desk in her hotel room, reviewing notes, when Edwin Rothmann called her throwaway phone.

Rothmann said, "You guys are definitely on to something. The State Department is furious. The meeting between our ambassador and the Syrian foreign minister was very closely held within the department. They want to know how we found out about it. It's supposed to take place a week from today in—you nailed it—Aanjar."

Maggie said, "I don't understand why they're throwing such a hissy fit. The State Department never could keep secrets. Anyway, all they have to do is cancel the meeting." She paused and then added, "We're not going to tell them where we got the information, are we?"

The DDO hesitated before responding. "Of course not, but...well, there's a lot of pressure..."

"Please, Ed, tell me this is going to be okay. They're not thinking of doing anything stupid, are they? They won't put our source in jeopardy..."

"I'm doing everything I can, Maggie. But you know what I'm dealing with. This administration is like *The Gang That Couldn't Shoot Straight*. They're a bunch of amateur morons and they really don't understand our business."

"What's the worst-case scenario?"

"They're talking about making a démarche to the Syrian government. They want to show the Syrians how smart we are. That we know everything going on in the region. They want to poke the Syrians in the eye..."

Maggie almost shouted. "They can't do that. That could mean the end of our source. How long will it take them to figure out who leaked the information?"

"I don't know. But my first priority is protecting our sources and methods. You know that and I know that. And that's exactly what I'm going to do. The man you guys recruited may not be at the highest level and he may not be aware that he's working for us, but he's still the first and only penetration of Hezbollah we have. I'm hoping we'll be running him far into the future. Long after this job is history."

■ ■ ■

Maggie, Santos, and MacMurphy gathered in MacMurphy's hotel room to plan their next steps.

Santos said, "I can't believe State is even considering a démarche to the Syrians. They must know what that could do to our source."

"We live in different times," said Maggie. "I wouldn't put anything past this administration."

"The simple solution is obvious: cancel the meeting," said MacMurphy. "I still don't understand why they don't just do that."

"Maybe they will," said Maggie. "Cooler heads might prevail."

Santos shook his head. "Don't count on it."

MacMurphy said, "Okay, let's move on. If anyone can handle the State Department, the DDO can. Let's let him work his magic while we work ours. Hadi Kashmiri has come through once again. He'll be by later this afternoon to pick up another bundle of cash. I am planning to give him ten thousand dollars—five for the apartment and five as a bonus. What do you think?"

They nodded in agreement.

He continued, "The students will be out of there by six, so I suggest we go over there around nine tonight and set up shop. That'll give us one night of observation and all day tomorrow. Then, depending on what we learn, I think we should plan to go in and get our gal tomorrow night."

"Sounds like a plan," said Santos. Maggie nodded.

"Culler and I will wait here for Hadi. Can I ask you, Maggie, to run out and get us some provisions for a couple of days?"

"Sure," said Maggie.

"Don't forget the wine and beer," said Santos. "And cognac for Mac…"

"Oh, I almost forgot," said MacMurphy, turning to Maggie. "Would you also pick up a couple of black man-dresses for Culler and me? Maybe a couple of those little black hats as well. They'll be good camouflage for us while we're crawling around out there in the junk yard."

"Two *dishdasha* robes and two *kufi* hats for my boys. Got it. No one will see you out there…"

# CHAPTER 50

Things were not going well for Edwin Rothmann back in Washington. The Department of State had dug in it's heals over the démarche. It showed little regard for the source of the information and felt it could gain leverage with the Syrian government by showing how omnipotent and well informed they were.

The CIA's objections, championed by the DDO, had brought the question to its boiling point with neither side willing to compromise. Eventually, it went all the way to the president for a decision.

The president, the actual leader of *The Gang That Couldn't Shoot Straight*, ultimately sided with the Department of State. He thought sticking his finger in Syria's eye was a great idea.

For the first time in his thirty-plus years in the CIA, the legendary DDO was actually considering resigning in protest over the government's handling of the matter.

■ ■ ■

Pouri made it back to Tehran without arousing anyone's suspicion, but she was not welcomed back with open arms. After all, she had ultimately failed to break Yasmin. They felt she had been too soft.

The powers that be in the Ministry of Intelligence were absolutely certain Yasmin was developing, and perhaps even running, assets

connected with the Iranian nuclear program. And since the results of
Pouri's interrogations did not fit this narrative, they considered the interrogations a failure. They planned to replace Bashir with a more aggres-
sive interrogator, but his arrival had been delayed due to a bureaucratic
kerfuffle within the ministry.

The final insult came when Pouri was not even asked to meet and
brief her replacement.

*Screw them.*

And that is exactly what she planned to do.

# CHAPTER 51

Maggie watched as Santos and MacMurphy cleaned, checked, and loaded their weapons.

"Boys and their toys," she said to no one in particular.

"Men and their tools," said Santos without looking up.

"Those assault rifles look heavy," said Maggie.

"Actually, the rifles are pretty light," said MacMurphy. "It's the suppressor, scope, and especially the ammunition drum that adds the weight."

Thinking Maggie was actually interested in such things, Santos added, "It's a trade-off. These drums carry one hundred rounds of ammo. I'd much rather carry a little more weight than have to change thirty-round magazines in the middle of a firefight."

"Hmm, I guess that makes sense," she said and returned her attention to CNN news on the TV.

MacMurphy removed their communication gear from a box on the bed and flipped one of the cigarette-pack-sized units to Santos. "Let's check these out before we leave. They're fully charged. I don't think we need call signs."

They slipped them into their shirt pockets, adjusted the earpieces and attached the mics to their lapels. "Let's use channel two," said Mac-Murphy. "Testing, testing. Do you hear me?"

"Loud and clear," said Santos.

"Got you too," said MacMurphy.

They turned them off, removed the earpiece and lapel mics, and stuffed them back into the box. "I think we're ready," said MacMurphy.

"Let's go over the checklist one more time," said Santos. "I'll read. You stuff the duffel."

MacMurphy smiled and set a large, green duffle bag by the bed. "Shoot."

Santos read from their list. "POF assault rifles with full Beta C-Mags, suppressors, scopes with infrared lasers, night-vision gear with head mounts, commo gear, *Spetsnaz* ballistic knives, MK23 .45 caliber handguns with two extra mags each, leg holsters, binoculars with night vision, and Kevlar vests."

MacMurphy sounded off "check" as he placed each of the items in the bag and then said, "You forgot something."

Santos checked his list one more time. "What?" he said.

"Our camouflage: the black beanies and black man-dresses Maggie bought for us."

"Of course. We don't want to go out there without making a fashion statement."

Maggie shook her head. "Boys..."

■ ■ ■

They pulled up in front of the apartment buildings at exactly nine o'clock in the evening and parked. The neighborhood was dark and quiet. Several dim street lamps illuminated the sidewalk in front of the buildings.

They spotted Kashmiri's car parked a few spaces in front of them. Kashmiri, still wearing his Mullah garb, drifted out of the shadows, and approached their vehicle.

"Bless you, my sons." He hesitated a moment after looking into the Land Cruiser and added, "And daughter."

"You frightened us for a moment there," said MacMurphy. "We thought you were a member of the religious police."

Kashmiri quipped back, "If I were, you'd be busted. Cover up your head back there, woman."

Maggie scrambled for her *hijab* and wrapped it around her head. The men were wearing their black *dishdasha* robes and *kufi* hats. Maggie wore a black *burqa*.

Kashmiri smiled. "Now that everyone is decent you can follow me. Things are pretty quiet right now but let's try to get up there without being seen."

They scrambled out of the Land Cruiser and retrieved their bags from the back. Santos, the strongest of the bunch, carried the duffle bag. They followed Kashmiri up the walkway to building five. They took the stairs two at a time to the third-floor landing and stood there, huffing and puffing, while Kashmiri unlocked the door. Once inside they closed the door and dropped their bags on the floor. Santos and MacMurphy hurried to the rear of the apartment to check out the view.

Both bedrooms were identical. They were small with two twin beds, a night table and a dresser with four drawers. Bright, flowered curtains covered the single window looking out over the field and junkyard.

The apartment was clean and neat, albeit sparsely furnished. It smelled of disinfectant, an indication that the young women took pains to clean it thoroughly before their renters arrived.

Santos looked over to MacMurphy. "Looks pretty good to me."

"Yeah, we couldn't do much better than this. Looks like about one hundred meters to the back of the house. If we have to shoot from here it would be an easy shot with the Lapua and certainly doable with the POF."

Santos looked at him quizzically. "You're not thinking about a sniper op, are you? We didn't bring the Lapua. We are not going to be shooting from these windows. We're going to assault that rathole and kill those assholes up close and personal."

"Just thinking aloud. Alternatives...you know."

# CHAPTER 52

Abu Salah could not believe what he was hearing.

He stood nervously at the end of a long conference table. He was not asked to take a seat. Sitting at the other end looking up at him menacingly was Sayyed Hassan Nasrallah, the much-feared secretary general of Hezbollah. His deputy, Sheikh Naim Qassem, and two other Hezbollah officials that Abu Salah did not recognize flanked Nasrallah. Another man, dressed in a brown, western-style business suit, sporting a scruffy, salt-and-pepper beard, rounded out the table. Abu Salah guessed the latter individual was Iranian, although he was not introduced.

Nasrallah, dressed elegantly in a black turban and a dark gray robe, gazed over steel-rimmed glasses with an icy stare. "How could you let this happen? It is you who leaked the information. You are either in league with the Americans or incredibly stupid. Which is it?"

Abu Salah's knees shook. He wanted to sit or at least put his big hands on the table, but he did not dare. He did not understand what was happening. He sputtered, "I...I don't know...I didn't tell anyone."

"Of course you didn't," said Qassem. He spoke softly, although his dark, piercing eyes belied his mild tone. His well-manicured, white beard trembled as he spoke. "You have simply been careless. Think back. To whom did you reveal your mission?"

"I would never...I never told anyone. I have been loyal for more than forty years. I..."

"Enough," said Nasrallah. "We believe you. You have proven your loyalty countless times. Nevertheless, the information came from you. You were the leak. Of that I am certain."

Qassem leaned back in his chair and fixed Abu Salah with a steely gaze. "There have been two related incidents. The first occurred a few days ago when we moved the hostage to the new location."

"Yes, sir, the move went well. We were not followed. No one saw us..."

"Shut up and listen." Qassem looked over at Nasrallah, who nodded. He continued, "Someone tried to rescue the American spy shortly after you moved her to the new location. We found the lock on the front door shot out. The apartment where we held the hostage was breached in the same manner. The entry occurred sometime between when you moved the CIA spy and when the char force arrived to clean the apartment the next morning."

Abu Salah's eyes grew wide. He started to speak but Qassem cut him off. "Your tradecraft was sloppy. We trusted you, but somehow the Americans learned of the location and attempted a rescue. It was your responsibility to ensure this never happened. Do you accept the responsibility, Abu Salah?"

Abu Salah nodded. "Yes, sir. I accept responsibility. It was my fault. I just don't know how..."

Nasrallah said, "Of course you don't. But it does not stop there. There is more."

The trembling in Abu Salah's knees increased to the point where he feared he would fall, and he felt a mounting urge to urinate. "More?"

"Much more," said Nasrallah. He glanced over at Qassem and waved for him to continue.

"You were brought into our plans to ambush the U.S. ambassador's motorcade, were you not?"

Abu Salah nodded. His head dropped to his chest and he shut his eyes.

Qassem said, "Look at me." Abu Salah looked up and Qassem locked onto his eyes. After a long moment he continued, "We were notified this morning by our Syrian friends that the Americans filed an official protest against the Syrian government. They discovered our plans to ambush the motorcade near Aanjar. How do you think they learned about this?"

Head on his chest, Abu Salah shook his head in disbelief. He began to shudder. He could not speak.

"Do you know what I think?" said Qassem. "I think the same source who told the Americans about the location of the hostage told them about our ambush plans. And I think that source obtained the information directly from you, Abu Salah."

Abu Salah's head spun. He was certain he had told no one. Perhaps CIA surveillance had picked up the location. That was a distinct possibility. He had taken great care to avoid surveillance, but you never know.

The ambush was another matter. He searched his memory. He had learned about the plans through a phone call with Abu Umar, Hezbollah's chief of operations. The call occurred just a few days ago. They had not spoken about it since, and he had not mentioned it to anyone. He was going to attend a planning session tomorrow evening.

He was explaining this to Nasrallah and Qassem when it dawned on him. He stopped mid-sentence and stood there, mouth open and eyes wide.

"What is it?" asked Nasrallah.

He shook his large head. "It's…the only time I ever discussed the ambush was during that brief telephone conversation with Abu Umar. It was in the late afternoon and we had just delivered the hostage to the new location. I was walking from the house to my car when Abu Umar called. I was very excited about being asked to join the ambush team. During the conversation, I looked up and there was Walid, my driver. He looked surprised. He had overheard my end of the conversation. I immediately lowered my voice and turned away, but…"

Nasrallah and Qassem exchanged glances. "What did Walid overhear? What did you say?" asked Nasrallah.

"I…I cannot recall exactly. We talked about the ambush location and the U.S. ambassador and his motorcade. I do not know exactly what

I said but that is what I discussed with Abu Umar. Walid heard whatever I said. I am certain of it. I am so sorry. So very sorry..."

Qassem leaned over and whispered into Nasrallah's ear. Nasrallah nodded. The others sat there in silence, deferring totally to the Hezbollah leaders. The Iranian glared menacingly at Abu Salah.

Nasrallah removed his steel-rimmed glasses, cleaned them with the sleeve of his robe, and set them back on his rather large nose. He looked up at Abu Salah and said thoughtfully, "Then you have a problem, Abu Salah. And I suggest you take care of it swiftly. I also suggest you get the hostage to a new location as fast as you can. If your driver is the Americans' source, and I believe you when you say he probably is, everything we have done with the hostage up until now has been compromised. Do you understand what I am saying?"

Abu Salah bowed deeply, "I do, sir. I understand completely."

"Then get out of here and take care of it. You have no time to waste."

# CHAPTER 53

Abu Salah turned and hurried through the double doors of the conference room and down the four flights of stairs to the street. When he hit the fresh air, he stood for a moment, took a huge breath, and let the air out slowly. He scanned the street and noticed his car parked halfway down the block. The car was running and he could just make out Walid sitting behind the wheel enjoying the air conditioning.

He had to think.

Abu Salah reached into the pocket of his *dishdasha* robe and pulled out a pack of cigarettes. He lit one, sat down on the steps, and exhaled a long breath of smoke. Better.

He knew what he had to do. The question was how to do it. He had grown quite fond of Walid over the years, but he had no compunctions about what he was about to do to him. Walid was a traitor, pure and simple. And for the Americans no less. It was inconceivable, but true.

He sat there on the steps, smoking and thinking and watching the car. When he finished the cigarette, he flipped it into the street, stood up, and walked slowly away from the building.

By the time he got to the car he knew exactly what he was going to do. Abu Salah pulled open the door and slid into the back seat behind Walid, startling him.

"Oh, it's you. I'm sorry, boss. I was dozing," said Walid.

Abu Salah concentrated on acting natural. He felt like taking Walid's slender neck in his large hands and strangling him right then and there.

Instead, he said, "I'm glad you are well rested. I have another mission to accomplish before the day ends. Go north up to the Jounieh-Beirut Highway and head toward Jounieh. When we get to Jounieh, wake me and I'll give you further directions."

Walid looked back at Abu Salah through the rearview mirror. "Sure, boss. How long will we be in Jounieh?"

Abu Salah felt like slapping him down with a curt response, but instead he said, "Not long. Maybe an hour or so. Then you will be free to go home."

"Okay, thanks, boss."

They drove in silence for the next hour and a half. Abu Salah feigned sleep in the back seat but his mind was racing. Occasionally, he would open his eyes a crack and focus on the back of Walid's well-coiffed head. He continued to refine his plan until he knew exactly what he would do, step by step, when they got to their destination.

"Excuse me, boss. We're entering Jounieh."

Abu Salah sat up and looked out the window as they drove through the bustling coastal resort town. To his left, the setting sun shined across the sparkling waters of the Mediterranean Sea. The coastline was lined with marinas, their moorings filled with clean, white yachts, rough fishing boats, and barges. To his right, a mountain range stretched across Lebanon through the Bekka Valley and far into neighboring Syria and beyond.

"Turn left onto Seaside Drive at the next intersection. Continue up the coast toward Kfar Yassine. I'll tell you when to stop."

"Will do, boss," said Walid.

When they hit Seaside Drive, Walid said, "There is some beautiful country out here. I have an aunt who works at the Casino Du Libon. It's just a few miles up the road."

His employer grunted in response, a signal that Walid took to mean, "Shut up and keep driving."

Abu Salah scooted up in his seat for a better view of the road. "See that sign up there for the scenic overlook?" he said, "Pull off the road right there."

The car's tires crunched on the gravel as Walid pulled onto the side of the road. Abu Salah looked around the area to make sure no one else was around and said, "Go all the way to the end up there, beyond the fence, and pull up to the edge facing the water."

Walid did as he was told. He parked near the cliff's edge and pulled on the emergency brake to ensure the car would not roll.

"This is really beautiful, boss. They picked a great spot for a rendez-vous. Who are you meeting here?"

"You ask too many questions, Walid. Now it's my turn to ask you some questions." He pressed the barrel of a snub-nosed .38 caliber revolver against the back of Walid's head. "Do not make any sudden moves, or this .38 might go off and splatter your brains all over the windshield. We wouldn't want that, would we?"

"No sir, I..."

"I will tell you when to talk. Tell me when you started working for the Americans."

Walid was in shock. "I...I...what are you talking about? I do not know any Americans. I never met an American in my life. I..."

"Don't lie to me, Walid. You told the Americans where we were keeping the CIA spy, and you told them about our plans to ambush the U.S. ambassador's motorcade. Didn't you? Didn't you?" He punctuated each question with a jab to the head with the barrel of the revolver.

Walid's mind spun, seeking to understand all of this. Then it came to him. "Wait. Wait, Abu Salah. Let me explain. I did not tell the Americans. I told our friends. I was helping the Iranians keep track of their hostage."

Abu Salah was confused. He smacked Walid on the side of his head with the pistol and said, "Don't lie to me. That is outrageous. Do you really expect me to believe a story like that?"

Blood seeped out of the scalp wound, matting the long black hair on the side of Walid's head and staining the shoulder of his white robe. He pleaded, "You must believe me. I was helping the Ayatollah. It is his hostage, not ours. The CIA spy belongs to Iran, not Hezbollah. They just wanted me to keep them informed. That is okay, right? You would do the same..."

"Enough!" screamed Abu Salah. "You are lying, lying, lying…" He punctuated each word by smashing his revolver into the side of Walid's handsome head. He heard the skull crack and blood spurted across the car. Walid slumped forward, unconscious. Or dead. His arms fell limply to the floor.

Abu Salah sat back in his seat. His breath came in gasps. His right hand and arm were covered in blood. He wiped the blood off his arm and onto the car seat and used a handkerchief to clean his revolver and hand. He looked around again to make sure there were no witnesses. Satisfied there were none, he stepped out of the car and shut the door behind him.

He stood by the side of the car for another few moments, catching his breath and inspecting his clothing. Seeing no blood on his *dishdasha* robe or anywhere else on his body, he opened the front door, took the car out of park, released the handbrake and pushed the car toward the edge of the precipice.

He pushed harder and harder, his shoes slipping on the gravel. The car slowly gained momentum and rolled over the side, plunging down toward the rocks eighty meters below. He watched as it crashed and rolled and crashed again, finally bursting into flames.

Satisfied, he pocketed his pistol, stepped back away from the cliff and began walking casually toward the Casino Du Libon about a half-mile up the road. From there he would take a taxi back to Beirut. His stomach growled, but he ignored it. He needed to quickly find a new safe house for the hostage, and that wouldn't be an easy task.

But as he walked up the road, he could not get one thought out of his mind: *How in the world did Walid come up with such a ridiculous story?*

*Strange, very strange…*

# CHAPTER 54

Santos and MacMurphy sat side by side at the window of the observation post. They had turned off the lights and closed the door. Through their night-vision binoculars, they continued to observe the bungalow. They started their surveillance over an hour ago, but so far there had been no activity. Everything was quiet. The lights in the bungalow were on, but they could not see the front of the building.

Santos lowered his binoculars and rubbed his eyes. "What do you think?"

"Too early to tell. Someone's definitely in there, but I wish we could see the front of the house."

"Yeah," said Santos, "maybe we should get a closer look."

"I'm beginning to think the same thing. No car out front, lights on...someone's in there with our gal."

"If our gal's still in there."

"Christ, don't even think about it. She's got to be there."

"There's one way to find out. This looks like a perfect time to get out there."

"No, not yet. Still too early. Let's take turns watching and resting. I'm all for going tonight, but not until the lights go out and everyone in the neighborhood is asleep."

"You're right. I guess I'm a little too anxious to kill those bastards."

"Hang on a few more hours and you'll get your chance. I'll take the first shift. Go get some rest."

■ ■ ■

All too soon, Santos felt someone shaking him awake.

"It's almost two o'clock in the morning, Culler. Time to get ready," said MacMurphy.

Santos rubbed his eyes and sat up. "Why didn't you wake me for my shift?"

MacMurphy laughed, "You looked so peaceful lying there. Like a little boy in a sumo wrestler's body."

"Yeah, yeah, I love to sleep. The only time you sleep is when you pass out drunk."

"I haven't done that in a while."

"Congratulations." He changed the subject. "Any change?"

"No movement. But the lights inside the bungalow went out about an hour ago."

"Okay, I'll go wake Maggie…"

When Santos returned with Maggie, they donned their gear, secured their weapons, checked their communications equipment one last time and prepared to leave. MacMurphy looked over at Maggie and said, "Keep an eye on us. If you see anything suspicious, just turn the lights on in the bedroom and open the curtains. We'll look up here periodically."

"Okay," said Maggie. "Keep my boys safe." She gave each of them a big, motherly hug. As they left the apartment she called out in a hushed voice, "Bring her back safely to me. Good luck!"

Santos led the way down the stairs to the first level and then out the back door of the building. Once outside they flipped down their night-vision goggles and adjusted their POF rifles for night shooting. They sighted their rifles down range and watched the green lasers, invisible to anyone not wearing night-vision gear, dance across the field in front of them. The special operations guys called the lasers "the green line of death." Just set the end of the green line on the target and pull the trigger. Target destroyed.

MacMurphy whispered into his mic, "You circle around to the right. I'll go to the left."

"Okay," said Santos.

They moved out in low crouches and headed toward opposite sides of the bungalow. The night was clear and dark with a quarter moon. This, combined with their dark robes and hats, helped conceal them. But they still had ample light to fully illuminate their night-vision gear.

They reached the back of the cottage and crouched down even further. After a few moments of quiet listening, MacMurphy whispered, "See anything?"

"Dark back here. But there's a light up front."

"Let's go around."

"Roger that."

They moved cautiously down each side of the building. When they reached the side windows near the front of the bungalow, they stopped.

MacMurphy said, "Lights on this side. TV on. That's it. You?"

"Same. Can't see movement. Let's turn the corner."

"Wait!" said MacMurphy. His lapel mic was so close to his mouth he could have swallowed it. "Movement."

MacMurphy leaned back against the building, trying to make himself as small as possible. He heard the door open then close and the screen door slam shut. He sat still and listened. Someone had come outside.

He heard the scuffing of a chair on the porch and then the clicking of a lighter.

*Must be the smoker*, he thought.

He dropped down into the prone position and peered around the corner. A dim porch light flashed into his night vision, blinding him for a moment. When his sight adjusted, he saw the smoker leaning back in a chair under the light, smoking a cigarette.

He pulled back and whispered into his mic. "Smoker outside. Stay back while I take him out. As soon as I shoot, come around front where I can see you."

"Roger that."

MacMurphy looked around the area one more time, took a deep breath, and pulled himself past the corner. The man was sitting there, peacefully blowing a trail of smoke up at the sky.

He trained the green line on the smoker's ear and fired. Two silent 5.56 mm rounds caught the smoker in the left ear and the top of the head, blowing him off his chair and down in a heap. The plastic chair skittered across the porch.

MacMurphy jumped up and moved swiftly to the front of the bungalow. He dropped down once again on the lawn with his sights on the door. Santos came out from his spot on the other side of the building and did the same. The green lasers from both rifles flickered on the bungalow door.

They waited and listened. Nothing. After a few moments, Santos said, "My turn. Cover me."

"Go for it."

Santos ran up to the door in a low crouch. He stepped over the smoker's body on the porch and stood beside the door with his back to the building, listening.

Still nothing.

He moved quietly to a window on the left side of the door and peeked past the curtain. Seeing nothing, he moved to the other side of the door and did the same. Still nothing.

His earpiece crackled, "Got anything?" He looked in the direction of MacMurphy and shook his head.

Santos's earpiece came alive again. "Okay, I'm coming up."

MacMurphy ran up to the building and positioned himself on the other side of the door. He looked over at Santos and nodded for him to go ahead. Santos opened the screen door and let it rest against his back while he tried the main door. The knob turned. He pushed the door open and slipped quietly into the room. MacMurphy caught the screen door before it slammed shut and followed Santos into the room, gently closing both doors behind him.

Their night vision gave the room an eerie green tint. The lasers from their assault rifles danced around the room in front of them. To their left was the TV and a couple of ratty easy chairs. A small dining table with four chairs stood on their right. In front of them was a hallway. The rest of the room was clear.

Santos moved out first and MacMurphy followed him into the hall. A partially open door cut a line into the wall on their left. Santos pressed his back to the section of wall next to the door and pushed it open slowly with his foot. The door squeaked open on rusty hinges, making both Santos and MacMurphy cringe.

Santos eased into the room and scanned it. It was a bathroom. He saw a tub, sink and toilet, but otherwise it was empty. He glanced back at MacMurphy who nodded and then moved toward another door on the right side of the hallway. Santos followed.

MacMurphy stood next to the door and tried the knob. He turned it slowly until he felt the latch open and then gently pushed the door open. Hearing nothing, he moved through the door and into the room with his rifle at the ready.

He was met by two loud gunshots and a punch to the chest, which knocked him back into Santos. He reflexively touched off two silent rounds. They darted wildly into the ceiling as Santos shoved him aside and sent a short, silent burst of 5.56 mm rounds into the chest of the shooter. In the last reflexive action of his life, the shooter fired another loud shot at nothing in particular and slumped into the corner of the room.

"You okay?" whispered Santos.

Checking his Kevlar vest, MacMurphy replied, "I think so. Man that hurts. Damn! He creased my arm, too. Sonofabitch."

Santos checked MacMurphy's left arm and found an inch-long, burn-like wound oozing blood. "Could've been worse. Let's go. We're not done. There should be more of them. And they're definitely awake now…"

MacMurphy quickly tore a strip of fabric from his robe's hem and used it to bandage his arm. Then they stepped back into the hall and moved toward the back of the house. The only remaining room lay at the end of the corridor. When they reached the door, they flattened themselves against the wall at either side of it, Santos on the right and

MacMurphy on the left. MacMurphy winced when the edge of his cut brushed against the wall.

The knob was closest to Santos and he tried it. Locked. He looked over at MacMurphy, who said, "Shoot it."

Santos fired and kicked the door open and heard a woman scream, "She's got a gun!"

He dove through the door and hit the ground rolling. In an instant, he assessed the situation. There was a cot to his right with the hostage in it and someone moving at the rear of the room. He instinctively fired a long burst at the movement. At the same time, MacMurphy turned into the room, saw the dark figure, and fired a long silent burst at it as well.

The figure was slammed back into the wall by the force of the bullets and fired two wild reflexive shots from a 9mm pistol before falling face down on the floor, quite dead. MacMurphy rushed toward the black figure and kicked the pistol away from the body. It was the old woman, dressed in a full, black *burqa*.

Santos stood up and went to the sobbing hostage. He found her lying half off the cot, trying to take cover behind the bed even though she was restrained by a handcuff that tied her arm to the metal headboard.

He looked into her terrified eyes and said, "It's okay, Yasmin. We're here to take you home."

# CHAPTER 55

Rather than waste time searching for the key to the handcuffs, Santos shot the chain and pulled Yasmin off the cot. She fell into his arms sobbing. Tears flowed down her face.

"He always gets the girl," said MacMurphy to no one in particular.

Santos said, "That's a switch."

"Okay, let's hurry," said MacMurphy.

He turned and ran down the hall and out the front door with Santos and Yasmin close behind. MacMurphy almost tripped over the smoker as he bounded off the porch. Regaining his balance, he rounded the building and headed back toward the observation apartment in a crouch.

They reached the back door to the building and MacMurphy wrenched it open for Santos and Yasmin. All three of them bounded up the stairs and came face to face with a widely grinning Maggie. She almost knocked Santos over in her effort to get to Yasmin. Maggie threw her arms open and embraced the young woman tightly. "My god, I'm so happy to see you, Yasmin." Tears ran down Maggie's face.

That broke the logjam of emotions in Yasmin and she began to shudder and sob. The two women stood embracing and crying, wracked with emotion. With its chain still attached, Yasmin's handcuff rattled on her wrist. In that moment, she barely noticed the pain it caused.

MacMurphy heard sirens in the distance and figured someone must have heard the shots and called in an alarm. He interrupted the reunion.

"We've got to get out of here. Let's gather our gear and vacate." He turned to Santos. "Culler, keep the .45 but get the rest of our gear into the duffel bag and meet me downstairs *tout de suite*."

He turned to Maggie. "Throw everything that doesn't belong here into a garbage bag and follow Culler down to the Land Cruiser. I'll be waiting in the car." MacMurphy pulled his man-dress over his head and grunted when the fabric pulled at his makeshift bandage. He began removing his Kevlar vest more carefully. Then he picked at a bullet hole just under his heart, pulled out a flattened .38 slug and handed it to Maggie. "The bastard could shoot," he said.

Santos quipped, "He shot twice—double tap. Close range. Only one hit. Not so good…"

"What do you mean? He also grazed my arm, and it hurts like hell! That's not too shabby."

MacMurphy dropped the vest on the floor next to his man-dress, turned on his heal and bounded down the stairs. Santos ran into the back bedroom and began stuffing rifles and ammunition into the duffle bag. Maggie led Yasmin into the kitchen and began to sweep paper towels, paper plates, and other sundry food items Santos and MacMurphy had bought for their surveillance into a large, black garbage bag. Yasmin helped as much as she could.

They all met moments later at the door. Everyone took one more look around the apartment, locked the door behind them, and headed down the stairs. Santos led the way with the duffle bag slung over his shoulder. They hesitated for a moment on the front stoop until they spotted the Land Cruiser with MacMurphy at the wheel. Moments later, they were in the car.

They heard loud sirens turning the corner behind them. MacMurphy looked into his rear-view mirror and saw two police cars, lights flashing, coming toward them from the direction of the university. He yelled, "Everyone down."

They flattened themselves on the bottom of their seats as the two police cruisers sped past, went to the end of the road, and turned onto the dirt road leading to the bungalow. MacMurphy made a sharp U-turn, tires screeching on the pavement, and headed back up the street to the intersection. He switched on his lights just as he turned north onto Hassan Nassrallah Road. Once he hit the main road, he slowed. Traffic was light at this time in the morning, but there were still a few cars on the road. That made him feel more comfortable.

If he could just blend in and go with the flow of traffic until he got to the Dbaiyeh Marina, all would be well.

# CHAPTER 56

The sun rose slowly above the horizon, casting a golden glow over the Mediterranean. They pulled into the marina, the Land Cruiser's wheels crunching on the gravel surface of the parking lot. MacMurphy pulled up to the main pier where the *Theano* sat idling with its engines growling and sputtering in its slip.

The marina was quiet and dark; it had not yet awakened.

Fotopolous waved at them from the stern. He was barefooted, dressed all in white, and sported two weeks' worth of a beard. Clearly, he had not attended church since his arrival in Lebanon. He flipped an unfinished cigarette into the water and helped Maggie and Yasmin over the rail and onto the stern of the yacht. They spoke in hushed tones.

"Wait," said Santos, "let me get that cuff off." Yasmin held her arm out over the stern while Santos manipulated the lock with a paper clip. She winced as he worked. After a few moments, the cuff fell off and Santos dropped it into the water. He looked up at her and smiled, rubbing her wrist gently. "Better?"

She looked at him with a thankful grin on her face. "You're the best, Culler. Really you are…"

MacMurphy interrupted, "We need to move. Take good care of them, Nikos. Drop them off in Limassol and then beat it back here. Culler and I have some cleaning up to do before we can leave."

"We've got clear seas," said Fotopolous. "I'll be back in a couple days. Throw me those lines, will ya?"

MacMurphy unhooked the stern lines while Santos ran up to do the same at the bow. They tossed the lines onto the deck as the *Theano* gently pulled away from the dock and turned toward the harbor exit. The yacht accelerated slowly in the harbor, but by the time it reached open water it was fully planed and running flat out, trailing the sea with a long white wake.

The women stood on the afterdeck and Maggie waved, but Santos and MacMurphy were already in the Land Cruiser heading back toward the Coral Beach Hotel.

■ ■ ■

The first thing MacMurphy did when they arrived at the hotel was dress his wound properly. Then he called Kashmiri. He briefly explained what had happened and told Kashmiri to take the next ferry back to Cyprus and wait there until further notice.

After he hung up the phone, MacMurphy started to pace in his room. He was too wound up to sleep. His mind raced. The police surely had found the bodies in the bungalow. They would investigate, and it would not take long before Hezbollah and Iran found out what happened and open their own investigation.

*Did we cover our tracks well enough? What links could incriminate us?*

The police investigation might lead back to the observation post in the apartment building, but that would probably end right there. Perhaps, the students could identify Kashmiri, but he had used an alias and was disguised as a Mullah when he met them. Clues leading to the rest of the team would be hard to come by.

Nevertheless, the Hezbollah investigation was another story. They would question the driver Walid and Walid would talk. He would give up his uncle Nabil, and Nabil would give up Kashmiri, whom he knew in true name. MacMurphy's mind spun with alternatives.

*Okay, Kashmiri is out of town and back in the relative safety of Cyprus. But that may not be enough. Hezbollah has long tentacles—certainly long enough to reach into neighboring Cyprus.*

Regardless, Kashmiri would never again be able to travel freely between Cyprus, Lebanon, and Iran. MacMurphy might even have to arrange his relocation to the United States, which would be an expensive and delicate proposition the Agency would not be happy to hear.

While pondering all of this, MacMurphy heard his phone ring.

"Mac, this is Hadi. I just received some unsettling news. Walid is dead. Killed in a car accident. It'll be in all the papers tomorrow."

"What! Dead? What do you mean? Start from the beginning…"

"I don't know much. I heard it from one of my journalist friends. They just found his body. He said, 'Walid Nassar, age thirty-four, was found dead in his car at the bottom of a cliff between Jounieh and Kfar Yassine.' That's a direct quote."

Still in shock, MacMurphy said, "Was he murdered?"

"I asked that same question. He said they were looking into it, but it looked like he just drove off the cliff near an overlook. The body was badly burned. They don't suspect foul play yet, but there will be an autopsy."

"As soon as you get to Cyprus give Nabil a call. See what you can elicit from him." MacMurphy was thinking fast. "Just tell him you have a message to pass on to Walid and see what he says."

"Will do. This doesn't look good, does it?"

"Not good at all…"

# CHAPTER 57

As Kashmiri boarded the ferry to Limassol, Abu Salah stood stiffly in front of Nasrallah and Qassem at Hezbollah headquarters. The two other Hezbollah officials were absent, but the scruffy Iranian, wearing the same ill-fitting brown suit, sat silently at Qassem's side.

Abu Salah tensed and mentally cursed cab drivers with every filthy word he knew. His cab had broken down halfway to Beirut, and it had taken him all night to get home. He was collecting supplies for the hostage move when he received Nasrallah's summons.

After a long stare over his steel-rimmed glasses, Nasrallah said, "I congratulate you, Abu Salah. You took care of Walid very swiftly." He gestured toward a chair at the end of the table. "You may take a seat if you like."

Slightly relieved, Abu Salah sat down and immediately felt some tension seep out of his body. If he kept the focus of the conversation on Walid, perhaps he could still relocate the hostage before Nasrallah found out she was still in the same safe house. "Thank you, sir. I made it look like an accident. No shots were fired and the car burst into flames when it hit the rocks."

Qassem stroked his manicured beard and asked softly, "I hope you spoke to him before killing him. That is why we are here. We would like to hear what he said in his defense."

Abu Salah nodded and looked over at the Iranian before speaking. He turned back to Nasrallah and said, "Walid admitted everything. He said he was the source of the leaks about the hostage."

Qassem said, "So, he admitted to being an American spy. Everything fits now."

"Not exactly, sir." Abu Salah looked back at the Iranian. "He denied working for the Americans. He said he could never do that."

"Then who was he talking to?" asked Nasrallah. "The French? English?"

Eyes still on the Iranian, Abu Salah said, "No, sir. He said he was helping Iran, the Ayatollah to be exact."

"That's absurd," shouted the Iranian. He banged his fist on the table. "That's the craziest thing I have ever heard."

Nasrallah looked back and forth from the Iranian to Abu Salah. "I don't believe it either. Why would Iran want to spy on us? We tell them everything. And in this case, we were simply doing what they asked. It was their hostage."

Abu Salah said, "That's what I said to him, but he was adamant that he received a message from the Ayatollah and that Iran did not trust us."

"Enough!" shouted the Iranian. "Who delivered this supposed message from the Ayatollah to Walid Nassar? Who?"

Abu Salah was confused. He glanced at Nasrallah and Qassem who stared back at him quizzically. It was a good question. They waited for him to respond. "I...I didn't...everything happened so fast...I..."

Qassem held up his hand. "Stop! Everyone stop." Then, in a tone so soft they all struggled to hear it, he continued, "Relate to us what happened, Abu Salah. From the beginning. Do not leave anything out."

Abu Salah began to explain exactly what happened after he left the conference room the previous day. When he got to the part where he pulled out his revolver at the cliff side, he paused. "And then I accused him of working for the Americans, which he denied vehemently. He claimed he did not know any Americans and had never even talked to one. He said he hated them."

"But he admitted to working for someone, didn't he?" said Qassem.

"Of course he did. He begged me to believe him. He said he was helping the Ayatollah. He reminded me that it was Iran's hostage, not ours. He said he was just doing the Ayatollah a favor by keeping them informed. He said I would do the same."

The Iranian asked, "Would you? Would you accept a clandestine relationship with Iran if you were asked?"

Abu Salah dropped his eyes. "I don't know. I mean…my first loyalty is to Hezbollah—of course it is—but the Ayatollah is our friend, our mentor…"

"So, you might," said Nasrallah.

Abu Salah was confused. "No! I would tell you, sir. I would come to you for advice and…"

The Iranian said, "This is going nowhere. I can tell you gentlemen unequivocally that we would never do such a thing. We trust you explicitly."

The comment drew raised eyebrows from both Qassem and Nasrallah, who glanced at each other knowingly. Nasrallah removed his glasses, polished them and set them back on his nose. He said to the group, "Let's not get sidetracked here. The point is Walid Nassar may have thought he was talking to our Iranian allies, but clearly he was not." He turned to Abu Salah. "You are not aware of what happened last night while you were in the Casino du Liban, are you?"

Confused, Abu Salah stuttered, "I…um…I…"

"Of course you are not aware." Nasrallah was dead serious. His eyes burned into Abu Salah's. "You are not aware because you did not check in on our hostage this morning. Isn't that right, Abu Salah?"

"Yes, sir. I'm sorry. My taxi broke down halfway to Beirut. I got in early this morning and did not go out there because you summoned me here. I came immediately when you called…"

"And it was your decision to keep a light guard force with the hostage, wasn't it?"

Abu Salah did not like the questioning's new direction. He suspected something ominous was about to drop. "I…um…yes, sir. Sometimes it is far better to use cover and concealment and to restrict knowledge of something than to use a large guard force to…you understand…it's a matter of profile…"

"I understand the concept." Nasrallah's tone was professorial, even gratuitous. "You kept a low profile with the hostage. But last night, while you were gambling and ogling the women at the casino, your hostage was rescued and three people were killed. What do you think about that, Abu Salah?"

Abu Salah's eyes widened and he began to tremble. He could not speak. His mouth opened but no words came out. Then, "I…I wasn't sir. I wasn't gambling at the casino. I only went in to wait for a cab. I was trying to get back to Beirut as fast as possible. I…"

Nasrallah continued, "So, now there is little doubt concerning who Walid Nassar was talking to and who killed your guards and rescued the American spy, is there, Abu Salah?"

Abu Salah gazed down at his large, trembling hands and replied, "No, sir."

"Then I have one final question for you, Abu Salah. Listen very carefully. The question is who was Walid Nassar's interlocutor?"

Abu Salah looked up from his hands. He felt a sensation of doom deep in his gut. His mind raced for a proper response but there was only one answer. Finally, he dropped his head to his chest and said in a barely audible whisper, "I don't know, sir. I…"

"You killed him before you learned who his contact was, didn't you, Abu Salah?"

"Yes, sir. I am so sorry. I didn't ask…"

# CHAPTER 58

The *Theano* skimmed across the flat Mediterranean Sea at a steady twenty-five knots per hour. Fotopolous could not have asked for better weather for the 250-kilometer crossing from Dbaiyeh Marina to Limassol, Cyprus. He pulled into the Limassol marina with plenty of time to clean up and make it to his favorite Greek restaurant, Dionysus Mansion, for dinner. He could already taste their superb chicken souvlaki. He had not eaten a decent meal since he left Cyprus and felt he deserved a treat. He might even shave for the occasion...or not.

He invited Yasmin and Maggie to join him, but they declined. They were anxious to get to Nicosia right away so they could be at the United States Embassy when it opened the following morning.

■ ■ ■

The next day, Maggie arranged for CIA Station Chief Susan Monaco to meet her and Yasmin. Sue had been a protégé of Maggie's when Maggie headed the Cyprus, Greece, and Turkey Branch back at Langley several years ago. Sue would expedite their return to the United States, though Yasmin did not have a passport, and notify the DDO of their arrival via a back-channel cable.

Later that same day, Yasmin and Maggie boarded a Cyprus Air flight to Athens and an onward American Airlines flight to Dulles Airport in northern Virginia. They were met at the airport by none other than

Edwin Rothmann himself. Maggie spied Rothmann immediately upon entering the international arrivals area of their terminal. He was hard to miss; he stood well over six feet tall, weighed more than three hundred pounds, and walked with a characteristic limp. She waved at him, grinning widely, and his face lit up when he saw her.

He moved toward them, parting the crowd with his familiar John Wayne gait. Maggie threw herself into his big arms and he enveloped her, lifting her off the ground. Yasmin stood to the side, watching and grinning from ear to ear. The DDO noticed her standing there and motioned her toward him. Then he was holding both of them in his massive arms. They all fought to hold back tears. Finally, Maggie caved and Yasmin followed suit. They stood there in the middle of the airport masses, hugging the big man and crying.

Finally, they broke apart and Rothmann led them outside to the VIP parking area where his car and driver were waiting. He directed the driver to take them to the Crown Plaza Hotel at Tyson's Corner. The hotel was close to the CIA headquarters campus, which sat secluded in the woods only a few miles down Chain Bridge Road in Langley.

When they pulled up in front of the hotel Rothmann said, "I know you would like to get some rest and do a little shopping since you're traveling so light. So, I'm going to make this easy on you." He handed Maggie an envelope. "There's five thousand dollars in there. Knock yourselves out. Everything's on me. Well, the company actually. I'll send the car for you tomorrow afternoon around four o'clock."

Maggie said, "That's very thoughtful, Ed. Thanks. What's the plan for tomorrow?"

"Once you've rested and gotten what you need, get ready to meet with me and maybe a few others in my office tomorrow afternoon."

"Wait a minute," said Maggie. "I'm retired and, well, I work with Mac now. And Yasmin's a NOC. Do you really think it's...?"

The big man laughed. "Always questioning me, Maggie. Just like old times."

"No...I just mean..."

"I know. Let's just say we're going to bend some rules. I'll see you both in my office tomorrow at four thirty. Okay?"

They both nodded and hugged Rothmann one more time before exiting the car and walking into the hotel.

■ ■ ■

The next day, the two jet-lagged women rose early, ate breakfast in the hotel coffee shop and set out for the Tyson's Corner shopping mall to pick up some essentials and new clothes. Maggie hadn't changed clothes since Yasmin's rescue and Yasmin still wore her captivity rags.

After shopping, eating lunch, and taking a short nap, they walked downstairs and waited until the DDO's car picked them up. They drove down Route 123 and turned left into the CIA headquarter compound. The driver flashed his badge at the main checkpoint and they continued down the wooded road toward the original headquarters building.

Just before the main entrance, they turned left into the lower garage reserved for VIP guests and very senior CIA officers. The car stopped in front of the elevators. The driver instructed them to take the elevator up to the seventh floor. When they reached it, the elevator doors opened and two young security guards met them. The guards, both former Marines, were dressed in dark business suits and sported identical close-cropped haircuts.

The guards greeted them by name and slipped red visitor badges hanging from chains over their heads. Then the marines escorted them down the hall to the reception area of the DDO's office.

When she saw them, Rothmann's tall, thin secretary jumped up, threw her glasses on her desk, and bounded toward Maggie. "Maggie Moore! Do you remember me? I'm Kathy Barnett."

"Of course I do, Kathy. It hasn't been that long." The two women embraced warmly. "You look great and you made it all the way up to the big job! I'm so happy for you."

"Thanks, Maggie. I had a lot of help from you." She turned to Yasmin. "And you must be Yasmin Ghorbani. I've heard so much about you. You are so brave." She gave Yasmin a hug.

The door to the DDO's office swung open and a grinning Rothmann filled the doorway. "I was wondering what the commotion was all about out here. Why didn't you tell me my guests had arrived? Come on in, gals."

As he ushered the women into his office he called back to his secretary, "Kathy, please hold my meetings and calls till we're done."

"Will do, boss," said Kathy Barnett.

Once inside the office, Maggie scanned the room. She shook her head, "My, my, Ed. You haven't changed a thing about this office in the ten years you've been here."

"Has it been that long? I guess it has." Rothmann was the longest serving DDO in the Agency's history. "Well, why redecorate when I'm comfortable with what I've got? I don't like change so much anymore anyway."

One wall of the bright, seventh-floor office consisted of floor to ceiling windows overlooking the building's magnificent front entrance and the woods beyond. In front of the windows, a sitting area was constructed out of two couches and three comfortable chairs that were arranged around a coffee table. At the far end of the office, there was a small conference table, which the DDO used as his desk. The big man liked to spread out.

He motioned for the two women to sit on one of the couches as he sat in a chair next to it. "Yasmin, I'm so happy to finally meet you in person," he said. "And I want to be the first to congratulate you on how you handled your imprisonment and interrogations and, most of all, how you used your training to turn your interrogator to our side."

Yasmin looked puzzled. "I...um...I never...I mean..." She shook her head and looked over at Maggie.

Maggie said, "You were instrumental in the recruitment of Pouri Hoseini. The conversations you had with her during the interrogations softened her up. Mac just had to pop the question. After he kidnapped her, that is. She is ours now. A fully recruited, willing agent reporting out of Tehran." Maggie held up her cell phone. "She's right on the other end of this phone."

Rothmann rubbed his knee, stiff from an old injury, and stretched out his leg. "The recruitment of Pouri Hoseini is a signal achievement, Miss Ghorbani. Outstanding work for a young officer. You engineered our first penetration of the Iranian Ministry of Intelligence."

"But I..."

"No buts about it," said the DDO. "It's your recruitment. There's a promotion and an award in it for you and I'm bringing you inside. No more NOC in the wilderness. We're going to fix you up with official cover and your next job will be right here at headquarters. I am assigning you to the Near East Division's Nuclear Proliferation Branch with primary responsibility for handling Pouri Hoseini. Sound okay?"

Yasmin stuttered, "Yes, sir. I mean, thank you, sir. That's wonderful, sir..."

He turned to Maggie. "Maggie, I hesitated about bringing you into this building. Your team—you, MacMurphy, and Santos—are my secret weapons. You know what I mean..."

"I do, Ed. I wondered, but..."

"Sometimes we just have to bend the rules a bit. It should be okay. You're a bona fide annuitant and there's no reason why I can't consult with you from time to time. The other guys, Culler and Mac, are different, so just keep your connection with them to yourself. Don't mention it to anyone while you're here. Okay?"

Maggie replied, "Goes without saying, boss. But...we've got to figure out some sort of cover story for the Near East Division guys to explain how I came into contact with Pouri Hoseini."

The big man turned in his chair and adjusted his bum knee once again. "You two work up a simple story. Everyone knows about Yasmin's rescue, but no one knows how we got her out." He turned to Yasmin. "The team who rescued you is top secret. Understand? You never met MacMurphy or Santos. You don't know who killed those guards and managed your escape. I want you to forget their names. All you know is that you passed on information about Pouri Hoseini's willingness to cooperate with Maggie Moore.

"You also need to work with the Near East Division to come up with a decent commo plan—something more secure than a cell phone—for handling Hoseini out of Tehran. That's your first job. Come back in the morning through the main entrance. A Near East Division officer will meet you and arrange your integration back into the system."

He turned his attention to Maggie. "I want you to hang around for as long as you're needed. We'll get you a green annuitant's badge. I want Yasmin's transition into the Near East Division to be smooth and secure, and I want a steady stream of reporting from Pouri Hoseini to begin immediately."

Rothmann paused, switched gears from professional to friend, smiled, and said, "And how about dinner tonight, just you and me?"

Maggie smiled. "You're on, Ed."

# CHAPTER 59

Maggie and Rothmann met in the lobby of the Crown Plaza that evening. She wore a new, light summer dress with matching high-heeled shoes. Her graying, auburn hair was pulled back into a neat bun, and her signature granny glasses were nowhere to be seen. She even wore make-up for the occasion.

Rothmann greeted her with a hug and a kiss on the cheek and then pushed her back, holding her shoulders with both hands. "My, my, Maggie. You look great."

She blushed. "I thought you liked the disheveled look."

"I do, I do, but...well, I like this look as well."

She tucked her arm in his and asked, "Where are you taking me, big guy?"

"It's only a block away. We're going to walk. It's called Da Domenico—my favorite restaurant in northern Virginia."

"It's mine too! I love their double-cut veal chops."

"Me too. And if we're lucky, one of the brothers will serenade us with a little opera."

She laughed. "Aren't they great? They've owned the place for as long as I can remember, and I've been going there for more than twenty years."

"I guess everyone in the Agency knows Da Domenico and the opera-singing owners."

She changed the subject. "How's the leg coming along? You seem to be limping worse than ever."

"I don't know. It's certainly not getting any better. I've already had one knee replaced and now it's time for the other. Too much football, too many parachute jumps, and the shrapnel doesn't help much either."

"You're an old warhorse, Ed. When are you going to take the plunge and retire like me?"

"Soon, very soon. The Agency has changed a lot since 9/11 and not necessarily for the better. It's becoming just another bloated bureaucracy run by timid politicians and lawyers. That's why I need people like Mac and Santos, people who understand the business and who can get things done the old-fashioned way."

He changed the subject. "By the way, how is business these days at GSR?"

"Excellent, we're actually making money. Our *CounterThreat* publication is our bread and butter and we're keeping busy doing deep background and due diligence investigations. All in all, our cover is holding up well. We're turning a small profit in the black. That said, we've recently run into some difficulties with a couple of child recovery operations."

Rothmann frowned. "How so?"

"Well, recently Santos got arrested in Belize and Mac had to go down there to bail him out and smuggle him out of the country. In another case, the whole team, including two pilots, got arrested in Roatán. They spent a few days in the slammer before we were able to straighten things out with the authorities."

"That's not good. Maybe you guys should consider sticking to more mundane operations like research and investigation and get out of the risky child recovery business."

"We've learned our lesson. We're going to be much more careful in the future."

"Yes, please do. I don't want anything happening to my secret weapon. Just keep the cover working. We have more important things to worry about, and you certainly don't need the money. You've got all you need and more in that bank in Switzerland."

They reached the restaurant and were ushered to one of the rear, circular booths by one of the brothers. He promised a short serenade later in the evening. They continued their conversation.

"Well, the boys really came through for you this time," said Maggie.

"They sure did. Now the problem is how to protect them. The recruitment of Pouri Hoseini is a huge deal. We can classify the hell out of it, put it in restricted handling channels and all that. But too many people will still be asking questions about how we obtained the source, not to mention how we rescued Yasmin from Hezbollah. I can only deflect and obfuscate so much. If the director finds out that I'm using outsiders for these kinds of jobs, especially MacMurphy and Santos, shit will definitely hit the fan."

The waiter came and began reciting a list of daily specials, but Rothmann cut him off mid-sentence and ordered a bottle of Chateau Talbot Bordeaux and medium-rare veal chops for their dinners.

Maggie asked, "How did you handle the fallout from the boys' activities in the Golden Triangle? As I recall, there were dead bodies strewn everywhere by the time they finished."

Rothmann laughed. "There certainly were. Mac and Santos forged a wide path through drug land on that gig. Khun Ut is still doing hard time in Bang Kwang prison in Bangkok."

"Well, how did you handle it?"

"Easy, we made it look like rival factions went after Khun Ut. He was the main man up there at the time, so it made sense. Having Charly Blackburn around to corroborate our story made it easier."

"Then why not do the same thing in this case? Make it look like Iran tried to get its hostage back from Hezbollah, but she managed to escape in the process and called me to help get her out of there."

"That could work. After all, we don't have to convince a lot of people. Yes, that's a good cover story. You could have known Yasmin from a while back, perhaps from down on The Farm when she was going through training. When she escaped, she could have immediately called you and you ran to her rescue and spirited her out of the country and back here. That'll work."

"Okay, I'll go over the story with her tonight so she'll be prepared when she arrives in the morning."

He raised his glass and they toasted to their success.

"Damn, this wine is really good," she said.

"Only the best for one of my secret weapons," he replied.

# CHAPTER 60

A bu Salah cursed himself for being so stupid. Nasrallah's last question still rang in his ears. If he could just figure out from whom Walid Nassar was getting his instructions, he might be able to redeem himself. Nasrallah was counting on him to revenge the rescue.

He actually knew very little about Walid. In all the years Walid had been his driver, he had never tried to get to know him. He had never asked about his family or what he did outside of work. Nothing.

Abu Salah still did not believe Walid's story about working for Iran. It was just too implausible. Neither the Ministry of Intelligence nor the Ayatollah gave a damn about Hezbollah. Then again, they would care about the CIA hostage. Would they fully trust Hezbollah with such a prized possession? Maybe not.

His mind returned to Walid. He wracked his brain for anything, any tidbit of information that might lead to a connection to the interlocutor. Then it dawned on him. Walid had an older brother, someone he admired. No, wait, not a brother. Maybe an uncle? Someone who once worked for Hezbollah. Yes, that was it: an uncle who brought him into the organization.

*What was his name?*

He called a few of his contacts within the organization and quickly learned that Walid Nassar's uncle, Nabil Nassar, was on some sort of a disability pension from Hezbollah. The disability resulted from a gunshot wound that left him confined to a wheelchair. He also learned that Nabil lived above the Al Bouchrieh Pharmacy on Massaken Street.

It was a good lead, well worth exploring further.

■  ■  ■

It was dark by the time Abu Salah arrived at Nabil's apartment building. He hit the intercom by the entrance door and Nabil answered. Abu Salah identified himself by name and said he was Walid's colleague.

"Yes, of course, I know who you are. Please come up." Nabil hit the buzzer.

Nabil was sitting in his wheelchair in the doorway when Abu Salah opened the door. They shook hands and Abu Salah followed Nabil into the apartment.

"Will you join me in a cup of tea? The water is hot. I was just fixing some for myself."

"I will join you," said Abu Salah, sitting in a chair. "I am sorry I came so late. I wanted to pay my respects but I did not have your address until now. You have heard, haven't you?"

Nabil raised his eyes toward the sky and brought his hands up to his face. "Praise be to Allah, I received the news yesterday. Only yesterday. His family did not contact me. I am, well...It was in the press, but..."

"I understand. Not everyone believes in what we do. I just wanted to say how very sorry I am. Walid was my driver for many years and..."

"He spoke of you often. Thank you for coming. You are very kind."

Nabil served them tea from a large aluminum pot. Abu Salah looked up from his cup and studied Nabil before speaking. "What were you told about his death?"

Nabil sensed something in Abu Salah's tone. "I was told he died in an automobile accident. Is this not true?"

"Maybe," said Abu Salah. "It is possible, but..."

"Is that why you are here? To tell me Walid's death was not an accident?"

"No, I came to ask if you had any reason to believe it was not an accident, if you knew of anyone who would want him dead..."

Nabil gently put down his teacup on a table in front of them and looked up into Abu Salah's cold eyes. He could see why Walid had hated this man so much. "What are you getting at? Walid had no enemies other than the enemies of Hezbollah."

Abu Salah decided to take a stab. "What about Iran? Would Iran want him dead?"

"Of course not. The Ayatollah...I mean Iran...They..."

"Tell me about Iran. He was talking to them, wasn't he?"

Nabil felt a sense of anguish. Had he been trapped? Did Abu Salah know? He did not know how to respond. Finally, he said, "I know nothing about Iran other than that they are our benefactors and allies in the cause."

Abu Salah's eyes drilled into Nabil's. "Yes, they are, especially in this cause. They own the hostage and we just do their dirty work. Isn't that true?"

"Yes...I mean..."

"So, you know about the hostage. Walid told you, didn't he? What else do you know? What did Walid tell you about the hostage and Iran?"

Nabil hesitated before replying. "He told me you were guarding an American CIA hostage. He said Hezbollah had captured the hostage..."

"For Iran. He told you that, didn't he?"

"Yes, but..."

"So, tell me why Iran would want to kill Walid."

"They wouldn't. Iran..."

"I see. He was talking to Iran. He was talking to Iran behind our backs, wasn't he?"

"No! I don't know..." Suddenly it dawned on him. "It was you, wasn't it? It was Hezbollah. You wanted him killed because you thought he was talking to Iran..."

Abu Salah stood up and walked to the window. He looked out on the street for a moment and then turned back to face Nabil with his .38 revolver in his hand. "He was talking to Iran and you were his link."

Nabil was trembling with rage. "Get out! Get out now. Walid said you were a thug and he was right. Get out of my house right now."

Abu Salah calmly walked over to Nabil and placed the barrel of his gun in the middle of Nabil's forehead. "I have one last question, you traitorous sonofabitch. And if you don't answer truthfully, I'm going to blow your fucking brains out."

Nabil's mind raced. Something was wrong here. Iran was an ally, a friend, a benefactor. Neither he nor Walid would ever betray Hezbollah or Iran. They were Shiite brothers, united in a just cause. And yet, here was this out-of-control man accusing them both of betrayal.

He looked up at Abu Salah and said, "It was you. You killed Walid and pushed his car off the cliff to make it look like an accident."

"Yes, and I'm going to put a bullet in your brain if you don't tell me who you were passing information to."

Nabil decided to make one last attempt to reason with the monster. "We were passing information about the treatment of the hostage to the Ayatollah in Iran. He was concerned that you thugs were mistreating her and that you would try to sell her for ransom. It appears the Ayatollah had every right to be concerned."

"And who was your contact? Who was your intermediary with the Ayatollah?"

"His name is Hadi Kashmiri, an Iranian."

At that moment, Nabil took advantage of Abu Salah's proximity and slapped the gun away from his head. In the same motion, he reached up with a powerful right arm and pulled Abu Salah down toward him. His left hand held Abu Salah's right wrist in an iron grip that twisted Abu Salah's hand until the gun dropped from it. When the gun hit the floor, he released the wrist and slammed his fist into Abu Salah's ear with a vicious left hook.

Abu Salah tried to pull back but succeeded only in pulling Nabil out of his wheelchair and onto the floor on top of him. Nabil took advantage

of his position and landed several blows on Abu Salah's head in a fero-
cious ground-and-pound attack. Abu Salah tried to shield himself, but
the fists and elbows mercilessly rained down on him. He needed to get
free. Nabil's legs might be useless, but his upper body strength was enormous. Abu Salah twisted and bucked until he was finally able to roll free.

Dazed, Abu Salah continued to roll frantically away from Nabil.
Nabil crawled toward him, using his powerful arms and dragging his
legs behind him. But he was too slow. Abu Salah reached the revolver,
rolled again, and exploded into a kneeling crouch with the gun pointing
directly at Nabil.

Nabil made one last desperate attempt to lunge at Abu Salah, but
the gun barked and a devastating hollow-point, Hydra-Shok bullet
smashed into Nabil's left shoulder, expanding and penetrating and
knocking him backwards.

The two men froze. Nabil lay prone on the floor with his good arm
in the push-up position and his head raised. Abu Salah crouched with
his gun hand extended. They stared at each other without speaking for
what seemed like an eternity. And then the gun barked again. The
hollow-tip bullet caught Nabil just under the right eye, and the back of
his head erupted. Blood and brains splattered on the clean wall behind
him and on the white robe of his murderer.

# CHAPTER 61

Abu Salah dropped his gun, charged into Nabil's bedroom, and ripped open his closet. He tore off his ruined *dishdasha* man-dress and used a relatively dry swath near the hem to wipe his face, hair, and hands. Then he quickly folded it in half and used the sleeves to tie it around his waist. It hung in loose folds as he grabbed a low-hanging *dishdasha* from the closet and threw it over himself. He ran to a bathroom he had passed on his way to the bedroom and looked in the mirror.

Faded scarlet streaks marbled and warped his face. He rubbed it clean with wads of toilet paper and flushed them down the toilet. Then he bolted out of the bathroom, snatched his gun from the floor, and bounded down the apartment stairs to the street. He stuffed the .38 snub-nosed revolver into his pocket and took a deep, calming breath and started walking up the street at a leisurely pace. Nabil's *dishdasha* was too loose in the shoulders, but the rest of it had looked convincing enough in the mirror.

He noticed people on the street craning their necks in the direction of Nabil's apartment. In an effort to blend in, he stopped and looked up in that direction as well. Several people glanced at him suspiciously, but he moved on without making eye contact. He hailed a cab a couple of blocks away. Eighteen minutes later, he was home.

The following morning, he called Nasrallah's office to schedule an appointment. When Nasrallah's secretary informed her boss that Abu Salah was on the line, he took the call.

The first words out of Nasrallah's mouth were "Where were you last night?"

Abu Salah did not like the tone in Nasrallah's voice. "I…sir…I would like to report to you. I…you will be pleased, sir."

"Have you seen a newspaper this morning? Was that you?"

"No…I…"

"Then get one, you idiot. The police are looking for a man matching your description who was seen in the vicinity of a murder last night. And judging from the identity of the victim, I'm pretty sure that would be you, Abu Salah."

"But I…I need to talk to you. I have important information for you, sir. The Iranians are behind it. The Nassars were both reporting to Iran. The intermediary is an Iranian named Hadi Kashmiri."

After a long silence, a calmer Nasrallah said, "Iran is not behind it. The American CIA is behind it because they have our hostage. It is a fact. Get that into your head. They may have been using this Hadi Kashmiri as an intermediary, and the Nassars may have believed they were helping Iran, but this is a CIA operation. Kashmiri is quite well known in Beirut and Iran. He is the dog you need to kill. He is working for the CIA. He is the connection."

Abu Salah breathed a sigh of relief. From the tone of Nasrallah's instructions, he could tell he was still in the game. "Where can I find this Hadi Kashmiri, sir?"

"He is an Iranian businessman. He travels frequently between Beirut and Tehran and Europe, but his main residence is in Cyprus. I suspect he is there right now. He will not show up in Beirut or Tehran anytime soon. Not with this mess blowing up in his face."

"Then I will go to Cyprus."

"Yes, the authorities are looking for someone matching your description anyway. It is just a matter of time before they find you. I suspect your fingerprints are all over the crime scene. It is best that you leave here immediately."

Abu Salah gasped. Other than his bloody *dishdasha*, he had taken no precautions to erase evidence from Nabil's apartment. He had to leave the country quickly. "Thank you, sir. I will not let you down this time. I promise..."

# CHAPTER 62

MacMurphy called Kashmiri as soon as he heard the news about the murder of Nabil Nassar. Kashmiri reported that he had tried to call Nabil several times, but his phone went to voicemail each time.

"You didn't leave your name or anything, did you?" asked MacMurphy, readjusting the bandage on his arm.

"Of course not. I left no messages at all."

Satisfied with the gauze's new placement, MacMurphy said, "Good, but the police will still get your number from Nabil's phone. Better toss that phone and get a new throwaway." His wound was healing nicely, but it still smarted occasionally.

"Okay. Then what will out next step be?" Kashmiri sounded worried.

"The bitter truth is this whole thing's unraveling. I'm sorry. They're moving back up the chain and you're next. It looks like Walid led them to Nabil, and we have to assume Nabil has led them to you."

Kashmiri's voice was strained. "Yes, I understand...I..."

"Where are you now?"

"I'm home. In my house on Kanari Street."

"Well, get out of there. Right away. Move in with friends. Anything. Just get out of there and don't check into a hotel in your name. Call me when you have a new phone. Culler and I will get there as soon as we can."

Kashmiri's voice trembled. "Okay...okay, Mac...I'll...okay..."

■ ■ ■

Santos and MacMurphy packed up their gear, vacated the Coral Beach Hotel, and headed for the marina where Fotopolous was waiting on the *Theano* with the engines running. They loaded their gear aboard the yacht, locked the Land Cruiser, stashed the car and hotel keys on top of the left front wheel, and sailed across the calm Mediterranean toward Limassol. The vehicle would be returned and all bills would be paid by Fotopolous's contact. Very neat. No strings left dangling. No connections.

It was late when they arrived at the marina in Limassol, so Santos and MacMurphy remained on board with all their gear and spent the night on the yacht. Early the next morning Kashmiri called to give them the number of his new phone.

"Where are you?" asked MacMurphy.

"I'm staying with friends. I told them my air conditioning went out and they invited me over. It is just across the bridge from my place, still in the Strovolous area on Perikleous Street. But I don't know how long I can stay here."

"Don't worry," said MacMurphy. "You can move back home when we get there. We're in Limassol now. We'll leave after breakfast and get there later this morning."

"Do you want to meet me here?"

"No, meet us in front of the Hilton Hotel. We will follow you back to your place in a rental car. I'll brief you when we get there. Do you have a valid U.S. visa?"

"I...um, yes. Multiple entry. Good for another two or three years. Why do you ask? Am I going to America?"

"Maybe. We'll talk about it later."

As soon as MacMurphy ended the call, ideas and possible courses of action tumbled through his brain. His priority was to protect Kashmiri, but Kashmiri was also his link to the Hezbollah killer. If he wanted to smoke out and neutralize the assassin, he would have to use Kashmiri as bait. On the other hand, he could simply get Kashmiri a new identity and resettle him in the United States.

He discussed these options with Santos, who said, "What are you asking me for? You know my answer and you know what you ought to do. Let's kill the sonofabitch who killed our assets and end this thing right here."

So, it was unanimous. Hadi Kashmiri would have one more mission before heading for resettlement in America under the CIA's political asylum quota system, Public Law 110.

# CHAPTER 63

A few minutes before noon, Santos and MacMurphy drove a nondescript, midnight-blue Lexus sedan rental up to the circular entrance of the Hilton Hotel. They spotted Kashmiri sitting in his gray Toyota sedan under the portico and pulled up beside him. MacMurphy rolled down his window and signaled for Kashmiri to pull out in front so they could follow him to his house.

Upon arrival at Kashmiri's home, MacMurphy parked their car in front of the house and got out to survey the location with Santos. Kanari Street ran through the upscale Strovolous neighborhood, which was a few miles away from the center of Nicosia. The three-bedroom, one-story house sat on a corner lot directly across from the Pedieos River, an ephemeral stream.

"Look at that," said MacMurphy to Santos, indicating the streambed. "That's going to present a problem." It was approximately fifty meters across, heavily foliaged, and hedging in a narrow, sandy creek that ran down its center. The creek was little more than a trickle at this time of year.

Santos replied, "Yeah, plenty of concealment for someone waiting in ambush. It's probably a torrent of water during the rainy season, but you can step across it right now."

MacMurphy crossed the street from the garage and looked down into the dense foliage. "If I were looking to take out Kashmiri, I'd wait in the bushes right over there and nail him as he pulled into his garage. That's the perfect choke point."

"Yep," said Santos, "that's how the Greek '17 November' terrorist organization took out our station chief in Athens a while back. What was his name? Dick Welch, I think."

"Very similar," said MacMurphy. "No matter how many times you change your arrival times and navigation routes and run your surveillance detection routes, you always end up pulling into your driveway at home. And that's where they'll shoot you."

Kashmiri had parked his car in the garage and come out the side door to join Santos and MacMurphy. "Want to see the rest of the house?" he asked.

He led them from the garage and through an adjacent pool area to small set of porch steps. They walked up the stairs and stepped through a sliding glass door into a kitchen-dining area. To their left was a large living room comfortably furnished in dark blue leather with complementary carpeting and drapes. The house's front entrance was at the far end of the room, and, according to Kashmiri, three bedrooms were located further down a hall to their right.

"Very nice," said MacMurphy. "You live here alone?"

Kashmiri blushed. "Most of the time. I've been divorced for several years. I do have a housekeeper who also does some cooking when I need it. She comes in three days a week."

"Can you cancel her services for the next week or two?" asked Mac-Murphy.

"Actually, she is off right now. I just won't tell her I am back in town. She gets paid whether I'm here or not."

Santos asked, "Who else knows your comings and goings? Neighbors?"

Kashmiri laughed. "The entire neighborhood knows everyone's business."

"So, if anyone asked one of your neighbors whether you were here, your neighbor would know and say something, right?" asked Santos.

Kashmiri laughed again. "Well, it would depend on who asked. Most of these people are pretty close-mouthed when it comes to the neighborhood. I suppose if someone had a good reason to ask that question, that person would get a good answer. Otherwise my neighbor would just play dumb and shrug."

MacMurphy thought a moment and said, "Perhaps you should leave your car out in the driveway for the time being. Pretend your garage is full or the door is broken or something like that."

Kashmiri looked quizzically from MacMurphy to Santos and back again. "So, I'm going to be the bait. Is that it?"

MacMurphy glanced over at Santos and then turned back to Kashmiri. "Not if you don't want to be. You could get on a plane to America tonight. We can take care of this job ourselves. In fact, the more I think about it, the more that makes sense."

"No, I'll see this thing through. One way or the other, I am probably done in this part of the world. Hezbollah and Iran will have a price on my head for the rest of my life."

MacMurphy said, "We'll take care of that. We're not going to leave you hanging out there. You'll get a new start—even a new identity if you want one—in America. You stepped up for us and we will step up for you. That's the way it works."

# CHAPTER 64

I t was late in the afternoon when the Iranian in the brown suit abruptly stood up from the chair across the desk from Nasrallah. He looked down angrily at the Hezbollah chief and wagged his index finger directly under Nasrallah's large nose. "Stop! I have heard enough excuses from you. Now you will listen to me, you pompous ass."

Nasrallah was not used to being addressed in this manner. He removed his steel-rimmed glasses with trembling hands and set them down carefully in front of him, trying desperately to compose himself. "Sit back down!" he ordered.

"I prefer to stand," said the Iranian, still peering down at a shocked Nasrallah. "And you are through giving orders. You have thoroughly botched this entire operation. Our hostage is gone and that Neanderthal of yours is leaving trails of bodies behind him like an enraged animal."

"Now just you listen, I..."

"I told you to shut up! We are through dealing with you. You are done. Tehran has decided we will take over from here on out." With that, the Iranian turned and stormed out of the room, slamming the door behind him. He hurried to the street and took a taxi directly to the Beirut ferry pier. There he met a female colleague. They shook hands, exchanged words in Farsi, and walked together to the departure lounge where the 4:00 p.m. ferry to Limassol was already boarding.

The woman looked like she belonged on the streets of Manhattan or Paris. She was attractive and in her mid-thirties, and she wore a dark-blue pantsuit over a white, ruffled blouse with a blue and white *hijab*. She carried a matching dark blue designer bag over one shoulder and pulled a small overnight suitcase behind her.

No one noticed the well-used Glock 17 nine-millimeter pistol concealed in the shoulder holster under her jacket or the small Glock 43 nine-millimeter backup pistol in the ankle holster on the inside of her left leg or the four-inch-long suppressor in the bottom of her handbag.

■ ■ ■

At that precise moment, a few minutes before nine o'clock in the morning in Langley, Virginia, Maggie's throwaway phone rang. She recognized the voice immediately.

"I must make this very brief," said Pouri Hoseini. "First, my congratulations to the guys. Second, give Yasmin a huge hug for me and tell her how happy I am for her. That is all they are talking about over here. They are furious. And they know the name of the person who arranged things—the driver who helped abduct me—and they have sent a team to get him."

"Wait, wait! Slow down. Yes, our driver. What kind of team? Where?"

"A man and a woman, professionals from our office. They know who he is and that he is at his home. They are on their way there now."

"I understand..."

"And that other crazy guy, Abu Salah, is going after him too, apart from our two people."

"I understand. Thank you so much. Are you okay?"

"I'm fine. Tell them good luck for me. I have to go. Bye..."

Maggie hung up the phone and immediately called MacMurphy to relay Pouri's message. Then she dropped the phone into her purse and headed directly up to Rothmann's office on the seventh floor of the headquarters building.

# CHAPTER 65

MacMurphy clicked the phone off and stood there for a moment collecting his thoughts before speaking. Kashmiri and Santos looked up at him from their seats in Kashmiri's living room. They had only heard his side of the conversation, mostly one-syllable, affirmative words and a series of grunts, but they instinctively knew it involved all of them.

He slipped the phone into his pocket and plopped down on a couch across from them. After a moment he said, "Not only are we going to have to deal with that nutcase Hezbollah prick, Abu Salah, we also have to prepare for a team of professional assassins, a man and a woman, that Iran just sent after us."

Unfazed, Santos asked, "Is that all?"

Kashmiri laughed nervously and looked over at MacMurphy for reassurance.

MacMurphy continued, "It's just the three of them that we know of. One from Hezbollah and two from Tehran. Maggie just got a call from Pouri Hoseini, so the information is up to date. I guess Iran doesn't trust Abu Salah to get the job done, so they're sending a couple of their own people."

Santos said, "We know what Abu Salah looks like. But do we have descriptions of the other two?"

"All we know is that they are professional hitters from the Ministry of Intelligence in Iran, they know Hadi by name, they know where he lives, and they are coming here to kill him."

"Do they know about us?" asked Santos.

"I don't know. All we can assume is that they'll be prepared for someone to be here to protect Hadi."

"Yeah," said Santos. "Maybe we need to get Hadi on a plane out of here. We can handle this without him." He looked over at Kashmiri who was looking very distraught.

"I think you're right," said MacMurphy. He looked over at Kashmiri who was shaking his head. "It's too dangerous for you here. If it were just that thug Abu Salah, I'd say you could hang around and watch the fireworks. But the Iranians are good, very good..."

"I'd rather stay and see this through," said Kashmiri.

Santos leaned over and put his hand on Kashmiri's arm. "You're going to have to start thinking long term. Face it, you're on Hezbollah and Iran's hit list and that's pretty much a forever list."

"He's absolutely right," said MacMurphy. "I'm sorry it turned out this way but we've got to deal with reality. You are done with Lebanon and Tehran and maybe Cyprus as well. The bait's essentially the same whether you're in the house with us or not. As long as they think you're here, that's enough. You need to leave now."

Kashmiri needed no further prompting. He packed a suitcase and Santos drove him in his gray Toyota to the airport in Larnaca where they waited together for the next flight out of Cyprus. It was a Cyprus Air flight to Athens. Kashmiri planned to sleep overnight at an airport hotel in Athens and then grab an early morning flight to Paris. He intended to wait there until further notice. He wasn't ready to fly to America. Not just yet, anyway.

Kashmiri left everything behind. He told no one where he was going, but he left a note with MacMurphy to show to any inquisitive neighbors who might question MacMurphy and Santos's presence in the house.

MacMurphy emptied the Lexus rental of all personal items, including the duffel bag full of arms and ammunition, and brought them into Kashmiri's home. Then he changed into jogging clothes and drove the

Lexus to a parking garage near the center of the city. He left the car in the garage and jogged the three-plus miles back to Kashmiri's house.

Santos returned late that night and parked Kashmiri's Toyota back in the driveway for all to see.

Now they needed a plan.

# CHAPTER 66

Santos arose early the next morning and was standing outside the Electronics Unlimited store on Aphrodite Street when it opened at 7:30 a.m. MacMurphy was still in bed, sleeping like a teenager. But by the time Santos returned an hour later, MacMurphy was standing in the kitchen in his boxer shorts with coffee brewing nearby on a counter.

"Where did you go?" MarcMurphy asked.

"I couldn't sleep. I kept thinking, 'Here we are with no surveillance again.' We need cameras around our perimeter to keep track of what's going on around us. After all, we can't just sit in this house and wait for someone to break in and try to kill us, now can we?"

MacMurphy yawned and poured two mugs of coffee. "Guess not. Good idea. I wish we could ask the station for some surveillance help, but I guess that wouldn't sit too well with Rothmann."

"I picked up six miniature low-light cameras with RF transmitters and a monitor/receiver. We can stick one on each corner of the house and maybe one on the garage pointing out over the streambed. Whoever is coming to get Kashmiri will have to do some preliminary casing. Maybe we can catch them in the act and be better prepared when they strike."

"Do you think the gear will actually work?" asked MacMurphy with a grin. They had an ongoing dispute about the advantages and disadvantages of using technical equipment in operations. As a case officer, MacMurphy was skeptical of all technical gear—it worked well on the bench but often failed in the field. Santos, however, was an audio tech by trade and swore by his gadgets.

"Of course it'll work!" he exclaimed.

"Well, you better set it up fast," said MacMurphy. "I don't think they're going to waste any time scoping us out."

"That reminds me. When I left this morning, I passed a blue and yellow taxi heading this way from the other direction. There were two guys in the front seat and the passenger craned his neck at my car as they passed by."

"Could be anything," said MacMurphy.

"Yeah, but then I saw the same taxi with the same passenger coming back toward me when I returned with the gear. I think it could be Abu Salah."

MacMurphy was interested now. "What makes you think it was him?"

"Well, it would make sense that he would want to case the place before making any moves, and the only way he can do that is to make multiple passes by the house. Kind of like the surveillance situation we faced back in Beirut. And he looked like an Arab. You know, beard and one of those beanie hats. And he was in a taxi. Abu Salah doesn't drive, remember?"

MacMurphy stood there, holding his coffee cup, eyes wide. "Of course. Did he get a look at your face?"

"I don't think so. Not a good one anyway. Hadi's windows are tinted, which I noticed is pretty common in Cyprus."

"Well, you've certainly had a good morning. I guess we have a plan now. Let's get those cameras installed *tout de suite* and keep an eye out for that cab. If it's him, I don't want you up on a ladder when he drives by."

They watched and waited for the taxi's next pass. Sure enough, about thirty minutes later, the taxi approached from the north along the streambed, slowed, passed the garage side of the house, turned the corner on Kanari Street, cruised by the front of the house, and continued out of the area.

As soon as it was out of sight, Santos grabbed his box of cameras and a roll of duct tape while MacMurphy pulled a ladder out of the garage. They started sticking cameras under the eaves of the roof on the corners of the house as fast as they could. Santos installed the cameras from the ladder while MacMurphy kept it steady and watched for traffic. They were interrupted by a passing car and had to seek cover only once. The car was not the taxi.

Twelve minutes later, the cameras were in place and Santos was hooking up a split-screen monitor on a coffee table in the living room. Ten minutes after that, they saw the blue and yellow cab make another pass. This time, it came from the west along Kanari Street, passed the front of the house, turned north up along the Pedieos stream, and drove past the garage side of the house.

The cameras worked perfectly.

"See that?" said Santos. "My gear works just fine."

"Unbelievable," said MacMurphy with a shake of his head. "This must be a first."

They took turns watching the split-screen monitor for the rest of the day. Kashmiri's car remained in the driveway and the taxi continued its passes at roughly thirty-minute intervals. There was now no doubt that the taxi was conducting surveillance of the house and little doubt that the surveillant was Abu Salah.

At around six o'clock that evening, after watching the taxi circle around for almost twelve hours, MacMurphy stood up, stretched his back, and said, "I've had enough of this. Let's have a little fun with the bastard."

Santos looked up from the monitor. "What do you have in mind?"

"The next time he makes a pass, I'll jump into Hadi's car, head in the opposite direction and hang out someplace for a couple of hours. Then when you tell me he's just finished a pass, I'll return and park the car back in the driveway."

Santos nodded his big head. "Good idea. At the very least, it'll get him to tighten up his surveillance. It'll also confirm that Hadi's still here and probably unsuspecting."

"Right, it might force his hand. Do you think he'll make his move tonight?" asked MacMurphy.

"Depends on how patient he is. Driving around in circles must be getting pretty old by now."

MacMurphy thought a minute and said, "We can influence his actions. The way I see it, he can only hit his target in one of two ways. He can follow the car and make his hit somewhere out on the street—in the car or on foot coming out of a restaurant or something like that—or he can wait until he knows his target is in the house and make his hit there. Which would you prefer?"

"At the house," replied Santos. "And we'll have more control here."

"I agree."

# CHAPTER 67

The taxi's next pass started from the north. It passed the garage and Kashmiri's car and then took a right on Kanari Street. As soon as it passed the house, MacMurphy hurried out through the sliding glass doors in the kitchen-dining area, bolted to the driveway, and jumped into Kashmiri's car. He drove north toward the center of Nicosia and stopped at a familiar restaurant called Nightbirds.

He chose Nightbirds because it was an out-of-the-way place located directly on the Green Line. It also served the best lamb chops in the country and had a parking lot behind the building.

He spent the next two hours chowing down on lemon-rice soup, lamb chops, and half of a bottle of the local Palomino wine. The lamb chops were wonderful. The wine, not so much. He left with a doggie bag of lamb chops and soup and the rest of the wine for Santos.

Back in the car, he called Santos for a surveillance update. Santos told him the last pass happened about twenty minutes ago, but the passes were occurring at shorter intervals. They agreed that MacMurphy should drive close by but hold off on his final approach until Santos called. A few minutes later, MacMurphy's phone rang. "Step on it, Mac. They just made another pass from the north and are heading west on Kanari Street as we speak."

MacMurphy accelerated and shot into the driveway less than five minutes later. When he re-entered the house, he found Santos with his eyes glued to the monitor.

"Their passes are getting a little frantic but you made it back without being seen. I hope you brought back something to eat. My stomach thinks my throat's cut!"

MacMurphy set the soup, lamb chops, and wine on the coffee table and went into the kitchen for a plate and utensils. "Those lamb chops are out of this world but the wine tastes like horse piss. There's a beer in the fridge if you prefer."

Santos tasted the wine and grimaced. "Did you actually drink half of this bottle?"

MacMurphy nodded. "It wasn't easy. I forgot how bad Cyprus wine is."

"I'll take a beer."

Santos ate while watching the monitor and MacMurphy joined him at the coffee table. MacMurphy noticed it was getting dark and turned on the lights in the house. When he returned, he asked, "Do you think tonight's the night?"

Santos had a mouth full of lamb chops. He nodded and washed them down with a gulp of beer. "He hasn't got many resources, so I think it's going to be a very straightforward attack. He thinks Kashmiri is home alone and unsuspecting. I think he'll come in late tonight and try to kill Kashmiri in his bed."

MacMurphy said, "What about the other two?"

"I haven't given them much thought. Pouri said they were pros, but even pros have to start somewhere. That somewhere is right here."

MacMurphy said, "Yes, they have to come here if they want to find Kashmiri."

"Do you think they're here in Cyprus yet?"

"Don't know, but I guess we have to assume they are. Your cameras are our first line of defense."

Santos smiled. "Now you admit my tech gear is important."

"Reluctantly," said MacMurphy.

# CHAPTER 68

The Iranian and his female partner sat across from one another in the tiny kitchen of an Iranian safe house in downtown Nicosia. Oddly enough, several years ago, Hadi Kashmiri had rented the small, one-bedroom apartment for the Iranian Ministry of Intelligence. At the time, he was an active support asset for the Iranians.

The Iranian, still dressed in his rumpled brown suit, looked over at the woman and said, "I cannot believe we don't know more about this Hadi Kashmiri. Is that really all we have? A description and an address?"

"That is all I was given. Perhaps they think that is all we need to know. After all, the scope of our operation is very narrow: find him and kill him."

"Perhaps. It should not be too difficult. I agree that the best place to hit him is in his driveway while he is getting in or out of his car. You know where to set up. There is plenty of cover across the street in the brush. Anyway, it is getting dark, so we should go. I will drop you off a little north of his house and you can follow the streambed down to a good position, like we discussed when we did our drive-by earlier. Are you ready?"

"I will be in a moment." She got up and went into the bedroom. When she returned a few minutes later, she was dressed all in black—running shoes, slacks, a long untucked shirt—and carried a black ski mask in her hand. "How do I look?" she asked, turning like a model.

"I don't know. I can't see you," he joked.

She worked the slide of her Glock 17, confirmed she had a full magazine and a round in the chamber, screwed the suppressor on the barrel, and tucked the long gun into her shoulder holster. She double-checked her backup Glock 43 in the same manner and slipped it back into her ankle holster.

"Let's go," she said.

# CHAPTER 69

MacMurphy came out of the bedroom wearing his black *dishdasha* robe and *kufi* hat. Underneath the man-dress, he wore a Kevlar vest. A suppressed H&K .45 was holstered at his hip. As he walked, he carried the two POF-416 automatic sub-machine guns, night-vision gear, and communicators.

He handed one of the rifles to Santos and said, "You'd better keep this close while you're watching your favorite movie."

Surprised, Santos looked up from the monitor and said, "You're not going out there, are you?"

"I'm not going to leave you in here unprotected." He handed Santos his communicator. "Stick this in your ear as well. Keep me informed on what's going on and I'll do the same for you. I'll be across the street where I can keep the house in view. We'll have Abu Salah surrounded if he comes back here tonight."

They did a quick commo check before MacMurphy slipped out through the sliding glass doors. As an afterthought, he poked his head back into the house and said, "Better lock this door behind me, Culler. We don't want to make it easy for him."

MacMurphy slipped out of the house again, hurried past the lighted pool deck, and stepped through the gate that led to the driveway and garage. At the end of the driveway, he hesitated for a moment beside Kashmiri's car. Then, confident the coast was clear, he darted across the street in a low crouch and disappeared into the underbrush.

Before he went too far, MacMurphy slipped on night-vision goggles and tested the green line of his POF. Satisfied that everything was working well, he moved quietly through the thick underbrush like a hunter stalking a deer. Several minutes later, he arrived near the side of the road. The position was farther south than his entry point, and it gave him a view of Kashmiri's car as well as the side and front entrances of the house.

He dropped down into the prone position, pushed himself under a bush, and sighted his rifle at the house, testing his field of fire. The green line danced from the Toyota in the driveway, across the sliding glass doors leading to the pool and patio and around the corner of the house to the front door. Confident that he was in a good position, he settled in for the long wait.

Twenty minutes later, Abu Salah stepped out of his taxi on the outskirts of Strovolous—about two miles north of Kashmiri's home. He was dressed in dark, western-style clothing and carried his .38 snub-nosed revolver in his right pants pocket. Night had fallen, but the glow of a half-moon gave him enough light to find his way through the deserted Nicosia streets to his target.

He was a simple man and his plan reflected this mentality. He would find a hiding place near the driveway and wait for Kashmiri to emerge from the house. Then he would empty his .38 into his target and disappear into the brush of the Pedieos streambed. From there he would make his way north back into central Nicosia and the fleabag hotel where he was staying.

As Abu Salah walked through the streets, the Iranian drove his rented dark green Ford Focus along the Pedieos stream for one last pass by Kashmiri's house. He and his passenger noted that the lights were on throughout the house and that Kashmiri's car sat in the driveway.

It was 9:37 p.m.

They turned right onto Kanari Street, drove past the front of the house, and circled back to a spot about one hundred meters north of Kashmiri's house. There he let the woman out on the side of the road. She immediately disappeared into the underbrush of the Pedieos streambed, running low like a ninja. Moments later the Iranian's earbud came alive. "I will let you know when I am in position. You can move out of the area but don't go too far."

"Okay," he replied. "Good hunting…"

■ ■ ■

MacMurphy made a mental note of the green Ford Focus that had passed by twice in the past few minutes. However, he failed to notice that there were two occupants in the car during the first pass and only one during the second pass. He also didn't see the dark figure who had snuck onto Kashmiri's property and crouched in the shadow of the garage, which was two meters away from the right front wheel of the Toyota.

But Santos did.

MacMurphy's earbud came alive. "Did you see that?"

"See what?"

"Someone slipped out of the shadows and huddled at the corner of the garage. Looks like he's settling in. I think it's our guy."

MacMurphy scanned the driveway and garage area with his rifle-scope. "I can't see him."

"Well I can. You've got to admit these cameras of mine work great."

"Another first. What do you want to do?"

"Cover me. I'm going around the back to sneak up behind him. If he squirts out the front, he's yours."

"Roger that. But do me a favor and wear your vest."

"Yeah, yeah…"

Santos grabbed his night-vision goggles and POF before donning his Kevlar vest. He checked the monitor one last time before slipping out the front door. Keeping in the shadows, he moved stealthily down to the corner and around the back of the house. When he got to the far end, he dropped down into the prone position and peered around the corner. The guy was still there at the far end of the house, sitting with his back to the garage, peering around the corner.

He rolled out and sighted the green line of his POF just behind the guy's left ear. He took a breath, let half of it out, and tightened his finger on the trigger. Suddenly he stopped. What if it is not Abu Salah? What if it's just some homeless bum settling in for the night?

Santos studied the figure through his riflescope. He had never actually laid eyes on Abu Salah. But this guy seemed to match the description he had of him, scruffy beard and all. Still, something was off. It looked like the guy was wearing western-style clothes, something Abu Salah was not known to do.

He continued observing the man through the scope. The guy was definitely in the right place at the right time. Still...

The woman noticed movement near the side of the garage. She strained her eyes but could not make out what it was. She had a good vantage point—she was concealed in the brush about twenty meters across the road from the corner of the garage—but it was dark. She wished she had thought to bring binoculars.

She saw the figure stop and look around. It was definitely a person, maybe Kashmiri. But why would Kashmiri be outside of the house at this hour? Doing a reconnaissance? She wondered if the figure was just Kashmiri checking out the area before getting into his car. Perhaps he suspected that someone was coming to get him.

The woman waited and watched. She was on her belly with the long, suppressed Glock held out in front of her. As dark as it was, this would still be an easy shot.

Then the person sat down and leaned back against the garage wall. Odd...

# CHAPTER 70

Santos rolled back around the corner of the house and whispered into his lapel mic, "I don't know whether it's him or not."

MacMurphy replied, "It's probably him."

"But what if it's not?"

"Throw something out there and see what he does. If you see a gun, shoot the sonofabitch."

"Okay."

Santos found a pebble and threw it about ten feet in front of the guy. It landed silently on a grassy area and the guy did not move. He found a larger stone and tried again, aiming higher into the foliage. The guy jumped up and looked in the direction of the noise. A .38 caliber revolver was in his outstretched hand.

Santos rolled out on one knee, placed the green line on center mass and squeezed the trigger. A silent burst of four 5.56mm rounds ripped Abu Salah's side from shoulder to waist, and he went down in a heap with a yelp.

Santos waited for a moment and checked for movement. When there was none, he stood up and approached the body, keeping the green line poised on its still form. As he looked down at the lifeless body with his POF held loosely at his side, he felt two solid punches hitting his chest. The force of the blows cracked something and knocked him down hard on his back. He rolled painfully and came up with the POF aimed in the direction of what he immediately recognized as a silenced double-tap. The green line danced across the bushes on the other side of the road, but he saw nothing.

"Someone's out there, MacMurphy. Just caught two in the chest. Think a rib or two is cracked. Whoever it is can really shoot."

"Are you okay?"

"Yeah, just hurts like hell."

"I'll circle around. Stay down."

MacMurphy slid out from under the bush and took off in a low crouch toward the shooter's position. He knew instinctively where an assassin would set up an attack—in the brush directly across the road from the driveway. This coincided with the direction of the fire that hit Santos.

He planned to circle behind the shooter and take him out from behind. He moved through the underbrush as swiftly and quietly as possible. The terrain in front of him was illuminated in a soft green glow. He thanked God for the night-vision technology and hoped his adversary did not have it.

It was hot and humid. Sweat ran into his eyes and soaked his shirt. He continued moving carefully through the heavy brush. He winced each time a twig snapped or a branch rubbed across his chest. MacMurphy stopped for a moment and whispered into his lapel mic, "See anything?"

"Nothing. I'm set up behind the body by the garage. Good cover. Where are you?"

"Circling around from behind. Don't shoot me."

"I'll try not to..."

"Thanks..."

MacMurphy reached the sandy streambed and turned north. As weak as it was, the stream still cleared foliage as it cut through the brush, which made MacMurphy's movement easier. He quickened his pace. After about one hundred meters, he stopped and focused on the slope leading up to the road. No movement. He proceeded up the slope and through the heavy underbrush toward where he thought the shooter was hiding.

He slowed to quiet his movements and darted his eyes into the thickest bunches of foliage, looking for any sudden shaking or rustling. Seeing nothing, he lunged forward onto a rock that trembled and slipped down the slope. His stomach lurched as the ground suddenly disappeared. He fell hard and stifled a yell as the jagged edge of a rock cut through his robe and carved through his shin. Clenching his fist against the pain, he looked down and saw the sharp, flat rock his foothold had been stacked on top of.

He tensed and listened hard to determine if his fall had alerted the shooter. The night was quiet except for a symphony of croaking frogs and a gentle breeze rustling through the trees. Determined not to be caught compromised, he worked quickly to dress the wound with strips of fabric he tore from the bottom of his robe. Pain and adrenaline made his leg shake, but he gritted his teeth and continued working. As he tied the last strip into place, he briefly considered emailing the robe's manufacturer to laud the nondescript man-dress for its ever-surprising versatility.

Suddenly he heard a thrashing in the underbrush about twenty meters to his right. He steadied his leg, quietly raised himself onto the opposite knee, and sighted his scope on the source of the sound.

*Maybe it's an animal*, he thought.

Sounds are magnified in the woods, especially when all of a hunter's senses are focused on his prey. His earpiece sounded. "Someone's out there, Mac. I just hit him. He went down. I'm crossing the road."

"Don't expose yourself. The shooter is right between us. Wait! I hear something..."

■ ■ ■

The woman felt a sharp blow hit her left bicep. The impact spun her around and knocked her to the ground. She cursed silently and winced from the pain. She lay there in the brush, breathing heavily. Her left arm throbbed and hung uselessly at her side.

*Who is this person?*

She had hit him square in the chest. Twice. She knew she had not missed.

*Shit! He's wearing a vest. He must be. It's not Kashmiri. He must have hired security. Damn.*

She could barely move the fingers on her left hand. She examined her injured arm. It throbbed but, surprisingly, there was not a lot of blood. She used a handkerchief to tie a tourniquet around the wound and then sat there in the bushes, thinking.

*There may be more than one of them. And if they are wearing vests, they may also have night-vision gear. They must be professionals. Damn!*

She whispered into her lapel mic, "I'm hit. He has security here. Need help."

The Iranian was parked several blocks north in a residential area. "I'm on my way. I will approach on your side of the road with the passenger door open. Be ready to jump in."

She began crawling slowly toward the road.

■ ■ ■

Santos had his rifle braced across the lifeless body of Abu Salah. The green line of death stretched out from the muzzle of the POF and into the brush on the other side of the road.

Whoever he shot had gone down. He could see no movement. He waited a few more moments and then decided to take a closer look. He crawled along the grass to the side of the road, stopping every few feet to steel himself against the pain in his chest and to scan the area through his riflescope. Still nothing.

He saw the lights of a car approaching from the north. Its headlights illuminated the road and cast a bright glare into Santos's night-vision goggles. Santos rolled closer to a bush along the property line to avoid being seen. He bit his lip as his chest hit the ground and shut his eyes tightly until the car passed him.

Santos contemplated crossing the road but decided he was better off where he was. Whoever was over there was an excellent shot and the road offered no cover whatsoever. Better to wait and let MacMurphy come up behind the shooter. His earphone sputtered. "What was that?"

"Nothing. Passing car. I'm near the end of the driveway. Decent cover. I'll stay here. Where are you?"

"Coming up. Slow going. But something is moving up there. Keep alert."

"Will do."

Moments later Santos noticed movement in the bushes on the other side of the road. Lying painfully in the prone position, he presented a very small target and had a good view of the brush line bordering the streambed. "Something's moving," he whispered into his mic.

Senses heightened with adrenaline, he moved his scope back and forth along the brush line, the green line seeking out a target. He focused on a spot between two bushes where he thought he saw movement. One of the bushes moved and he let out a breath and tightened his grip on the trigger.

Suddenly he heard the roar of an engine approaching rapidly from the south. He glanced down the road to his right and saw a car approaching fast with its lights out. His pulse quickened and he turned his rifle toward the approaching car, ready to shoot.

The headlights came on in a blast of light that blinded him through his night-vision goggles. He ripped them off and squeezed his eyes shut. When he looked up through squinted eyes, his vision was clouded with bright dancing stars. But he could still make out the outline of a car screeching to a halt directly in front of him. He could barely see the figure on the other side of the car darting out of the brush and running toward the open passenger door.

Santos heard the rapid poof, poof, poof of suppressed fire from the other side of the road and bullets pelting into the car. The car started to take off. Pushing through the searing pain, Santos shoved his rifle to his shoulder and fired off a long burst into the door on the driver's side.

Bullets from both sides of the road struck the car in a cacophony of breaking glass and popping metal. The car slowed almost to a stop and then rolled until it came to rest in the grass.

# CHAPTER 71

Santos and MacMurphy rushed up on either side of the car, rifles at the ready. They peered at each other over the roof of the dark green Ford Focus. "I recognize this car," said MacMurphy. "It passed by earlier. Twice. Must have been the one that dropped off the shooter."

"I'll bet it was in better shape then. Sure is a mess right now," said Santos.

Both front doors were pockmarked with bullet holes and the windows were completely shot out. Glass covered the inside of the car and gathered in menacing piles around its exterior. The engine had stalled out but the lights were still on. Santos reached in, shoved the dead driver aside, and switched them off.

The driver was slumped over the wheel. His brown suit was matted with blood and riddled with body shots. One round had entered behind his left ear and blown a chunk out of his forehead. Blood and brains spattered the windshield.

The passenger hung out of the passenger door, face down in the grass. MacMurphy grimaced as he bent down and pulled off the ski mask. The woman's long, dark hair spilled out. "Guess what?" said MacMurphy. He did not wait for a response. "Our shooter was a woman."

"No shit? We just killed a woman? She was one hell of a shooter..." His hand gingerly covered the two bullet holes in his Kevlar vest. He noticed the torn hem of MacMurphy's robe and saw blood trickling down his trembling ankle. "Fuck, what the hell happened?"

MacMurphy followed Santos's stare and shrugged. "Occupational hazard. I tripped while chasing the shooter. It looks worse than it is. Still, I might've hit the driver on my first round if my leg hadn't been shaking."

Santos said, "You still landed the hit. And it could've cost more than a shaking leg."

MacMurphy shook his head and said, "You're right. They were both good." He looked up and down the street. "Let's clean up this mess before another car passes." It was quiet except for the croaking frogs along the streambed.

"Right," said Santos. "Let's push this thing over there and out of the way so it will look like it's parked alongside the road."

MacMurphy winced as he leaned down to lift the woman into the car and close the door behind her. She was riddled with 5.56 caliber rifle bullets, but her face was untouched. Eyes wide open. Surprised. He noticed how attractive she was even in death. The long Glock was still clutched in her hand.

The two of them pushed the car up a few feet until it was fully parallel to the road. It was harder to do than either one of them expected. Santos had to give his chest frequent breaks from the pressure of pushing, and MacMurphy had to navigate a slight limp.

MacMurphy said, "Make sure we're not seen. We need to clean up and get rid of everything. Go get that other guy and drag him over here behind the car."

Another car approached from the north. They heard it before they saw its headlights. Both of them took cover behind the assassins' car. MacMurphy groaned as his bad shin landed on a fallen branch. The car drove past and disappeared down the road, tires crunching on broken glass.

Santos leaned his rifle against the car and hurried across the street to where Abu Salah lay. The .38 revolver lay in the grass next to Abu Salah's hand. He carefully picked it up and stuffed it in the corpse's pocket. Then he grabbed a handful of shirt behind the neck, braced himself against the pain in his chest, dragged the lifeless body across the street, and dumped it behind the car.

MacMurphy had already pulled the Iranian out from behind the wheel and stuffed him into the back of the car on the floor. "You can put that asshole on top of this one in the back," said MacMurphy. He found the trunk lid button and pressed it. "I'll dump the lady in the trunk."

Moments later, they stood quietly behind the car, sweating from adrenaline and exertion. Santos said, "Stay here. I'll get something to clean off the seats and windshield and a blanket to cover those two guys in the back. Then we need to get this wreck as far away from here as possible."

Santos soon returned with a blanket and a towel from the house. They started cleaning the blood off the front seats and the windshield and covering the bodies in the back. The windshield remained smudged but, fortunately, the worst streaks were on the passenger side. It would not obstruct the driver's vision much.

Another car passed by but did not stop or slow. They ducked out of sight—MacMurphy was more mindful of his leg this time. As soon as it passed, they policed the area of brass bullet casings and kicked glass out of the road. The casings disappeared into the trunk along with the bloody towel.

MacMurphy said, "That's enough. Let's get out of here. We can finish policing up the brass in the morning. You want to drive this or Kashmiri's car?"

Santos said, "You know where you're going. So you take this and I'll follow you."

"Stay close. We'll take the old Larnaca road. It runs parallel to the highway but it's pretty quiet. If I recall correctly, we passed a wooded area near a small village when we drove from the airport to Kashmiri's house. It's about ten miles from here. Just a wide spot in the road. We'll find a place around there where we can pull the car off into the woods. If we're lucky, it'll be days or weeks before anyone finds this mess."

"Sounds like a plan," said Santos.

■ ■ ■

It was early in the morning when they returned to Kashmiri's house. The terrain was not exactly as MacMurphy remembered. They had to search for more than an hour to find a suitable place to cache the demolished Ford Focus. But once the car was pulled out of sight and into the brush and covered with branches, it was almost invisible from the road. The dark green color of the car helped its camouflage considerably.

Back at the house they poured themselves generous portions of cognac, congratulated themselves on a job well done, showered, tended to their injuries and went to bed. The next morning they were anxious to wrap things up and get out of the country. They finished policing the brass and cleaned up Kashmiri's house, leaving no evidence behind.

Late in the afternoon, they drove Kashmiri's car to the parking garage where they had left the Lexus rental and drove back to Kashmiri's house in the two vehicles. They locked Kashmiri's car in the garage and drove the Lexus south to the Limassol Marina. There, they handed the duffle bag full of arms, ammunition, Kevlar vests, clothing, and other suspicious items to Fotopolous on the *Theano*. Fotopolous was instructed to dispose of the items in any way he saw fit.

Their next stop was Larnaca Airport where they returned the Lexus and booked a Lufthansa flight to Frankfurt. The last thing they did before boarding the plane was call Maggie and tell her all was well. Their mission was accomplished and they were heading home.

Rothmann would be very pleased.

# POSTSCRIPT

Yasmin Ghorbani enjoyed a successful career as an operations officer in the CIA. After being brought inside by the DDO, she handled Pouri Hoseini from headquarters for nearly three productive years. Pouri became a prolific and high quality source on Iran's nuclear program, foreign affairs, and intelligence operations.

Yasmin was later assigned overseas to a succession of increasingly important positions in Egypt, Morocco, and Saudi Arabia before returning to headquarters as a promoted member of the Senior Intelligence Service. She was awarded the position of deputy chief of the Near East Division.

Pouri Hoseini worked as a denied area agent for the CIA for several years until her husband was promoted to a political counselor in the Iranian embassy in London. She continued to report clandestinely from London during the three years of his assignment. At the completion of the assignment, when they were due to return to Tehran, she and her entire family defected to the United States. They were resettled with new identities in Houston, Texas.

She and Yasmin were reunited in America and remained friends for the rest of their lives.

Hadi Kashmiri declined the CIA's offer of resettlement in America. Instead, he continued to run his businesses and travel frequently in Europe and the Middle East, although he never again set foot in Iran or

Lebanon. On one of his trips to London, almost two years after Mac-Murphy and Santos left his house in Cyprus, he was shot in the back of the head with a .22 caliber pistol in front of his apartment door.

The assassin was never identified.

Sayyed Hassan Nasrallah continues to run Hezbollah. Although his grasp on the organization was greatly diminished after the escape of the American hostage and the deaths of Abu Salah and the two Iranian operatives, he was eventually able to negotiate a firmer foothold at the expense of war-torn Syria, which resulted in even closer cooperation with and enhanced assistance from Iran.

Hezbollah now employs as many as 65,000 fighters, making it by far the largest guerilla force in the world. It employs an arsenal of more than 130,000 rockets and anti-ship missiles, more than the combined total of all non–United States NATO member states. This arsenal could seriously threaten Israeli and American shipping in the region.

Intelligence estimates indicate Hezbollah may also possess chemical and biological weapons. In 2016, Nasrallah threatened to launch rocket attacks at an ammonia plant north of Haifa. A hit on these tanks could create a nuclear-bomb effect greater than the devastation wrought by the bombs dropped on Hiroshima and Nagasaki during World War II.